D1059843

PREPPER JACK

by DIANE CAPRI

Published by: AugustBooks
http://www.AugustBooks.com

ISBN: 978-1-942633-40-2

Original cover design by: Cory Clubb
Digital formatting by: Author E.M.S.

Prepper Jack is a work of fiction. Names, characters, places, and incidents either are the product of the author's imagination or are used fictitiously, and any resemblance to actual persons, living or dead, business establishments, events, or locales is entirely coincidental.

Published in the United States of America.

Visit the author website:
http://www.DianeCapri.com

ALSO BY DIANE CAPRI

The Hunt for Jack Reacher Series
(in publication order with Lee Child source books in parentheses)

Don't Know Jack (The Killing Floor)

Jack in a Box (*novella*)

Jack and Kill (*novella*)

Get Back Jack (Bad Luck & Trouble)

Jack in the Green (*novella*)

Jack and Joe (The Enemy)

Deep Cover Jack (Persuader)

Jack the Reaper (The Hard Way)

Black Jack (Running Blind/The Visitor)

Ten Two Jack (The Midnight Line)

Jack of Spades (Past Tense)

Prepper Jack (Die Trying)

The Jess Kimball Thrillers Series

Fatal Enemy (*novella*)

Fatal Distraction

Fatal Demand

Fatal Error

Fatal Fall

Fatal Edge (*novella*)

Fatal Game

Fatal Bond

Fatal Past (*novella*)

Fatal Dawn

CAST OF PRIMARY CHARACTERS

Kim L. Otto

Charles Cooper
Lamont Finlay
Carlos Gaspar
John Lawton
Michael Flint
Holly Johnson
Pinto Vigo
Mason O'Hare
Jake Reacher

and

Jack Reacher

Perpetually, for Lee Child, with unrelenting gratitude.

PREPPER JACK

DIE TRYING

by Lee Child

1998

Reacher had no problem with how he had gotten grabbed up in the first place. Just a freak of chance had put him alongside Holly Johnson at the exact time the snatch was going down. He was comfortable with that. He understood freak chances. Life was built out of freak chances, however much people would like to pretend otherwise. And he never wasted time speculating about how things might have been different, if this and if that.

CHAPTER ONE

Monday, April 11
12:30 p.m.
Albuquerque, New Mexico

MASON O'HARE HADN'T seen the threat coming.

He was running late, which was unavoidable during the busy tax return season. His tardiness shouldn't have mattered much. His lunch date would have been comfortably seated in the air conditioning with a cool drink, relaxed and waiting.

Mason had borrowed a sedan and parked in a lot two blocks away. He felt reasonably sure he hadn't been followed, but he was no clandestine operations expert. He worked a regular job. Had a girlfriend with a kid.

He was a regular guy in a tough spot, that's all. No more, no less.

He hurried nervously along the unfamiliar section of San Felipe Street, glancing back over his shoulder and scanning side to side from behind the oversized sunglasses he'd bought at the drugstore that morning.

Mason had never been to The Last Chance Saloon. It was a tourist spot located in an adobe building in the heart of historic Old Town Albuquerque. He'd checked the place out online before he'd chosen it. He'd heard Bruce Ray mention the place a couple of times, but no one Mason knew hung out here. He didn't expect to be recognized.

He looked both ways before he jaywalked quickly across the street to the saloon's entrance. He planned to start working out when tax season ended. He'd made the promise to his girlfriend several times before, but somehow he never found the time to follow through.

All of which meant that he was a little breathless, somewhat paunchy, more than a little out of shape, and plenty nervous. He'd had very little contact with law enforcement in his lifetime and he'd have been very happy to keep it that way.

But the way he looked at it, he'd had no choice but to poke his head out of his hole and report what he'd seen. And now here he was. Nothing he could do to change things at this point. He just had to suck it up and get it over with.

Mason pulled the saloon's heavy wood door open and stepped into a cold cave of darkness, realizing instantly that he'd made another serious mistake. The place was way too busy. There were too many people here.

The noise of a hundred conversations going at once, along with some kind of piped in Mexican music, slammed against his ears.

The air-conditioned dining room was dimly lit, but it was the change from the hot, bright sunshine coupled with his dark sunglasses that blinded him.

Sweat dripped from his armpits and trickled down inside his shirt. What had possessed him to wear a suit and tie today? He never wore suits anymore. Not since he'd moved to Glen Haven. No wonder he was uncomfortably hot and sweaty. Could he possibly get heat stroke so early in the season?

He stood inside the doorway at the end of a long line of patrons waiting for a table. He removed his sunglasses and dropped them into his breast pocket, allowing his eyes to adjust to the darkness. He reached into his pocket for a handkerchief to blot the salty rivulets from his brow.

A casually dressed man approached from the shadows on his left.

This guy wasn't a local. His skin wasn't sun-leathered and he had no crinkles around his eyes from squinting against the relentless sun. He was six feet tall, give or take. Normal looking brown hair. Nicely dressed in what fashionistas called business casual.

"O'Hare?" the man asked.

When Mason nodded and shook his hand, he said, "John Lawton."

Lawton tilted his head to the dining area on his left. "This place is jammed. There's two tour buses in the parking lot out back. They've taken every table in the place and it looks like they just got seated. Probably won't finish up for a while. We won't be able to talk here. Is there another spot nearby?"

Mason considered the question, which made him more nervous. He wasn't familiar with the restaurants in the area. He didn't know another place to suggest.

Lawton tapped him on the shoulder and walked toward the exit because conversation was impossible inside the saloon. Mason unfolded his sunglasses, slipped them onto his face, and followed.

On the sidewalk, Lawton inclined his head toward the

Albuquerque Museum of Art and History and Old Town Plaza. "Let's walk."

"Yeah, sure. We can do that," Mason replied, taking a few steps beside Lawton on the sidewalk, hustling to keep pace. "I'll need to get back to work soon, though. They'll start to wonder where I am. I almost never leave my desk during tax season, you know?"

Mason glanced around, hoping to see the plaza crowded with tourists. But it was one of those almost freakish times when, for no reason at all, the popular destination was practically deserted.

After walking along for a few yards, Mason heard footsteps behind them on the sidewalk, following in the same direction, keeping pace. The footsteps made him uneasy, too, but looking behind seemed foolish, somehow. So he didn't.

At the traffic light on the corner, Lawton paused while two pickup trucks, an SUV, and a couple of sedans sailed through. The light turned yellow.

They waited for a white panel van to pass before they stepped into the crosswalk.

Mason noticed the van's front windows were tinted darker than permitted by law and the back had no windows at all. He figured it had to be a hundred degrees or more inside that steel box.

The van sped up to rush through as the light turned red.

The crosswalk sign flashed "walk."

Mason and Lawton stepped off the curb, which was the last normal thing he remembered.

Everything after that was one big blur.

On the other side of the traffic light, just beyond the range of the cameras mounted on the pole at the corner, the van's driver mashed the brakes.

The wheels locked.

The tires squealed as they skidded leaving black marks on the pavement.

The van jerked to a full stop.

The side door zipped open.

Lawton had been a step ahead. Before he had a chance to react, he was propelled from behind and his feet scrambled to keep him upright. He lurched toward the open maw of the van and tumbled inside.

Within the dim interior of the van, two men grabbed Lawton and shoved him face down onto the floor. One man struck him on the head with the butt of a shotgun. His body went limp.

A split second later, Mason felt a hard shove against his back. He stumbled forward, almost losing his balance.

"What the hell?" Mason swung his arms wide and swiveled his head to see who had pushed him.

He tried to pivot, but there was not enough space between him and the big dude holding the pistol jammed into his back.

All Mason had a chance to see was a beard, a baseball cap, and a pair of sunglasses.

"Get in the van," the man said gruffly. Like he wouldn't take no for an answer.

"What do you want?" Mason said, preparing to stand his ground. He was slightly off-balance, his weight on one leg.

The big man used his left forearm like a crossbar and put his weight behind it as he shoved Mason into the van. Inside, two men knocked him to the hard, steel floor.

The big man jumped inside, slid the door closed, and ordered the driver, "Get us out of here!"

The van lurched forward and kept accelerating, headed north. The big man staggered into the front passenger seat.

The kidnapping was practiced and efficient and completed in less than sixty seconds, from the time the van stopped until it sped away.

Mason was on his knees, dazed, probably in some kind of shock. He'd fallen against Lawton, who was out cold.

A pair of rough hands patted him down, found his wallet, and pulled it from his pocket.

The guy cursed and said, "You're gonna want to see this, Hector."

A solid blow to the back of Mason's head bounced his nose to the floor and smashed it all over his face. He tasted his own blood before he fell into oblivion.

CHAPTER TWO

Monday, April 11
12:10 p.m.
Detroit, Michigan

FBI SPECIAL AGENT KIM Otto's late night at work followed
by an early morning meeting with her team had caused her to
miss her morning run along the streets of Detroit.

She exercised for stress relief as well as exercise and training.
When she missed a day, she felt out of sorts, body and soul.
Which was why she'd completed her run on her lunch hour today.

There were more people on the streets at noon, which was
not great. Navigating around them was a nuisance. She changed
up her route, running along the side streets and through the park
instead of north and south on Woodward Avenue.

But there were compensations to the change of scenery. The
weather was warmer than early morning. There were no icy
patches on the sidewalk to worry about. She pounded the
pavement, basking in the slices of sunshine that fell between the
tall buildings, until she'd completed her miles.

Which left her in front of one of her favorite places on earth. One of Detroit's best coffee shops. She pulled the door open and stepped inside to wait in the line of java addicts, inhaling the best brew in the world.

After she'd left Jake Reacher in San Diego back in February, her life had settled into a predictable pace. She'd picked up a few routine cases in the Detroit Field Office, consisting mostly of paperwork and phone calls and assisting in occasional surveillance instead of dodging bullets. She arrived at work in the mornings and returned home again in the evenings on a more or less steady schedule, like a normal human being with a dependable government job she'd always loved.

It was the same kind of work she'd done before that first four a.m. phone call from the Boss back in November had upended her life and sent her on a breathless chase, hunting Jack Reacher.

She hadn't found Reacher. Not yet.

But she would. Eventually.

Because Mrs. Otto's daughter Kim was no quitter.

Even if hunting Reacher was the scariest assignment she'd ever had.

Not that she'd let anyone know that. Not a chance.

There were downsides to this peaceful break in the assignment and her new work rhythm, though. The search for Reacher had pumped her adrenaline sky high for weeks, making the routine field office work she'd once found fascinating now seem sleepy and dull by comparison.

Which caused her to question her career choices, too. The Boss she'd admired since before she joined the FBI had tested her faith. She was no longer sure she could trust him. The knowledge worried her.

But she didn't have time to think about that today.

The line moved slowly toward the barista taking orders. Kim shuffled along with everyone else in the line until she heard a woman shriek like a frightened three-year-old behind her.

"He stole my purse!" she said, pointing the gloved hand that extended from her mink coat toward the guy dashing out the door.

"Oh, hell," Kim said, pivoting on the balls of her running shoes and heading after the guy. Chasing purse snatchers wasn't her usual line of work. But that looked like a twenty-thousand-dollar Cartier bag. Which made it grand larceny, at the very least.

More importantly, a ring of thieves had been working the neighborhood lately. The locals suspected a counterfeit luxury goods ring. Kim lived here. She didn't like the idea of letting him get away with anything.

The dude wasn't a very good thief and he was a slow runner, too. He might have been a high school footballer, but the weaving between cars parked at the curb like a running back failed. She caught him in the middle of the second block.

She wasn't even slightly breathless. But she was pissed off that she'd missed her coffee.

She grabbed the guy and walked him to the closest precinct. When she handed him off to the desk sergeant, she identified herself and gave him a business card.

"You can find the owner of that bag at Java Joe's on Woodward," she said. "Give me a call if you need me. I gotta get back to work."

She hurried to the lobby of her apartment building, slightly winded but feeling smug about braving the cold instead of running on the treadmill inside as she usually did in the mornings when the temperatures were cold.

Walter Hill, the private security guard manning the front desk, waved her over.

"Hey, Kim. Have a good run?" he asked, friendly as always.

"Yeah. Great." Breathlessly, she swigged water from the bottle she'd attached to her belt.

"You're working pretty hard out there," he said. "But don't forget to have a little fun, too. That John Lawton seems like a nice guy, for a Treasury agent. The good ones won't wait forever, you know."

"You sound like my mother." She grinned to take the sting out of her words and moved along. Her mother was constantly asking about her nonexistent love life. Avoiding the topic had become second nature.

Walter nodded like an indulgent big brother. "I'd be proud to have one of my daughters dating a man like John Lawton. My guess is your parents would, too. Have they met him yet?"

"Not yet," she said, waving her way past the desk as she headed toward the elevator.

She and Lawton had been dating now and then, when they had the time, for a few months. He lived in New York, which made the dating sporadic. She liked him well enough. He was fun and interesting to talk to. Nice-looking, too.

She punched the elevator's call button and waited for the car to arrive. It seemed to stop at every floor on the way down. She stretched her sore muscles so they wouldn't stiffen up.

Maybe Lawton had been coming around a little too often lately, if Walter Hill was already pleading his case.

She'd given little thought to whether there was a chance the relationship could develop into something more. She wasn't looking for that and she assumed Lawton wasn't, either. She'd been married once. Not an experience she wanted to repeat.

The elevator finally reached the first floor. The doors opened and several people she didn't know piled out. She entered the car and selected her floor. She pushed the button to close the doors and held onto her stomach as the elevator shot skyward.

Lawton was working on some big case somewhere out west now. Chasing down a whistleblower who'd called the tip line, he'd said before he left. She hadn't heard from him for a few days and she hadn't noticed whether his absence was making her heart grow fonder. Which she supposed meant he wasn't all that special to her.

Still pondering the question, when the elevator stopped at her floor, she walked down the hall and used her key to enter her apartment. Maybe Lawton would be back in a couple of days. Did that thought make her body hum with anticipation?

She considered the question as she showered and dressed. John Lawton was a good guy, just like Walter said. But no. He wasn't what her younger sister would call "the one."

Which meant he was a great guy to date. Nothing more. And that was fine, too. Left her open to new possibilities.

The digital clock on her bedside table caught her attention. She was late already. Her supervisor was waiting to hear the results of last night's operation in Greektown. A routine arrest after a boring surveillance. Nothing remotely anxiety provoking about it. Which didn't mean she could blow it off, either.

When Lawton came back, she'd know what to do. If nothing else, the Reacher assignment had taught her to trust her gut.

She grabbed her gun and her keys and hustled back to the office.

CHAPTER THREE

Monday, April 11
1:30 p.m.
Albuquerque, New Mexico

FOUR BLOCKS FROM THE Last Chance Saloon, Pinto Vigo waited behind the wheel of a black SUV. The IRS agent had left the restaurant prematurely and Vigo's team had to scramble, but they'd done the job adequately.

Except for the extra hostage, everything was on track.

He tapped his fingers on the steering wheel, marking time until he could safely follow the van to the meeting point. He thought about how to deal with Mason O'Hare. He was both clueless and beloved at Glen Haven. Vigo would need to tread carefully with him.

Kidnapping a member of Glen Haven was just one more piece of bad luck in a string of bad breaks Vigo's cartel had suffered lately. And the timing couldn't have been worse. His big shipment was on its way and expected to arrive Friday. Nothing must interfere. He needed the money.

He wasn't worried about being noticed while he waited for the van. Nothing about the vehicle was the least suspicious.

The SUV was purchased with cash and registered to a man who didn't exist. Which meant its Nevada license plates were legitimate.

Should Vigo be stopped by authorities for any reason, a records search would turn up nothing out of the ordinary.

He possessed a valid Nevada driver's license issued to the same nonexistent man who owned the SUV. The license tracked to the normal batch of identifiers for an American citizen with no criminal history. He had a birth certificate, a passport, a social security number. He had a job and he paid taxes.

He also had a fictitious wife who possessed a similar set of counterfeit credentials.

Her real name was Maria Vigo. She was Pinto's sister, his only surviving family. His father and his brothers had been killed long ago. Only Maria was left to stand back to back with him and she was tough as nails. Like he was. Like their father had been.

Vigo and Maria had many enemies in the US and in Mexico. Which had made him a vigilant and careful man. He was also a vulnerable one. He'd learned the hard way that there truly was no honor among his enemies. They'd kill him and steal his people and his business in a hot second if they had the chance.

Which was why the Last Chance Saloon, a front for Vigo's operations here in Albuquerque, was staffed exclusively with cartel members.

Maria worked as a waitress at the Saloon, where she could keep an eye on his business and his crew could keep a careful watch to be sure she was safe. Maria's bodyguard was Big Sela Juarez, a monstrously huge and violent woman, who protected his sister around the clock.

Vigo pictured Big Sela and grinned. She was a vicious piece of work, to be sure. She was paid well for protecting Maria, but she would have done it anyway. She was a little in love with Maria.

Vigo smirked. He was masterful at finding and exploiting the weak spots in people. It was a skill that had served him well.

In Vigo's experience, love was like electricity. Useful and dangerous at the same time. So he kept an eye on Big Sela, but his gut said Maria would never be harmed by someone else as long as Big Sela was around. A man like Vigo lived and died by instincts.

His cartel had been active in Albuquerque for years. He'd moved central operations here several weeks ago. The system Vigo had in place had worked well until now.

Someone inside the organization could not be trusted. He didn't know the identity of the mole, but he knew it wasn't Mason O'Hare because the nerdy accountant didn't know anything about Vigo's business. He wasn't the one responsible for leaking information that resulted in several recent losses.

He checked the clock on the dashboard. The van had a fifteen-minute head start. Vigo pulled out into the street and drove the speed limit to the spot outside of town where the van would be waiting and he'd get the name of the mole.

CHAPTER FOUR

Monday, April 11
2:30 p.m.
Chihuahuan Desert, New Mexico

MASON REGAINED CONSCIOUSNESS WHEN his body bounced on the hot steel floor as the van traveled over rutted road. He heard the wind rushing past, but no traffic sounds. His wrists were tightly bound behind his back and a rough canvas bag covered his head. He lay on his belly, shoulder to shoulder with another man, probably Lawton.

"Pull off here."

The voice giving orders from the front passenger seat belonged to the big man.

The van's left tires ran off the shoulder of the road and bounced hard through a big hole, slamming Mason and Lawton against the floor. Lawton groaned slightly, letting Mason know he was awake.

The van continued off-road for about fifty feet of rough terrain and then stopped. The engine idled a few seconds before the driver shut it off. Mason heard the van's door hinges scrape open and the two men up front climbed out. Then the side door was shoved back and a rush of welcome fresh air came inside.

"Get up! Now!" A man grabbed Mason and another grabbed Lawton. Mason was muscled outside where he was pushed to the ground. He heard Lawton land just as hard.

Mason felt the heat and the hard dirt, but he saw only the inside of the canvas bag over his head. He assumed Lawton had the same view.

"Get up!" A sharp boot kicked Mason in the side. He cried out in pain and scrambled to his feet. He heard a similar blow land on Lawton, who probably stood, too, but he offered no complaint.

Calmly, Lawton said, "I'm a federal agent."

Two of the men laughed and the big guy, the one Mason assumed was the leader of the pack, said, "You think we care?"

"You should," Lawton replied. "Makes me worth more. My team will do whatever it takes to get me back."

The leader said, "Let's go."

Mason felt a gun jab into his back and a hand shove between his shoulder blades. He stumbled forward but managed to stay upright. His leather-soled shoes slipped on the rocky surface as he shuffled along.

He heard Lawton walking beside him and the four kidnappers walked behind. They advanced twenty feet or so before Lawton stumbled and fell against Mason's right side, knocking him off his feet. Mason landed painfully and let out an involuntary yelp.

A split second after Mason went down, the fight started. He heard a sickening crack, like a tree branch breaking, and one of the kidnappers began to scream. He landed hard on top of

Mason, knocking the wind out of him. From the guy's stench, Mason guessed the guy wasn't Lawton.

Mason scrambled along the ground to get the man's weight off him. With his hands secured behind his back, the struggle seemed impossible.

He heard the unmistakable sounds of flesh hitting flesh and grunts of pain from the men fighting with Lawton.

Another man fell to the ground near Mason's feet. He rolled aside. It seemed safer to stay on the ground.

A moment later, a vehicle with a powerful engine pulled up and stopped. Mason heard a door open and close, followed by the deafening blast of a shotgun. Then, by more screaming from one of the men on the ground.

Mason's terrified heavy panting filled his canvas hood with damp breath. He heard a second blast and another man screamed, but only briefly before the sickening sound of a gun butt slamming into a human body.

A loud grunt followed the blow and a heavy thud shook the ground behind him when Lawton fell.

An eerie silence seemed to fill the air once the fighting stopped.

"Get him back in the van," a new voice ordered roughly.

One of the men jerked Mason roughly to his feet and shoved him into the van's open doorway. He stumbled and fell. He lay still, until he felt a needle puncture his neck.

It was the last thing Mason felt before his whole body seemed to collapse into nothingness.

CHAPTER FIVE

Monday, April 11
2:45 p.m.
Chihuahuan Desert, New Mexico

AFTER MASON WAS STASHED in the van, Vigo tilted his head toward the dead men. "Get that garbage away from the road."

"Of course," Hector replied, without the least whiff of disapproval.

Hector had always been a practical man. No doubt he realized the precariousness of his situation. Vigo had shot and killed two of his own men without warning. He could easily do the same to Hector and Freddie when he was finished with them.

Hector scanned the area until he saw a pile of rocks about a hundred feet away. They could stash the bodies behind the outcropping. The occasional vehicles speeding past on the roadway shouldn't notice. If they covered the bodies with loose dirt, perhaps the vultures wouldn't find them for a few hours.

"Freddie," Hector said, tilting his head toward the first body. "I'll take the head. You grab the feet."

As always, Freddie did as he was told. His unquestioning obedience kept him alive. He approached his dead compatriot and lifted his feet as Hector lifted the head and shoulders. They began to move toward the outcropping.

The relentless sun was hot and the rocky terrain was difficult to walk. They waddled along as swiftly as possible. Hector was sweating profusely before they'd reached the halfway point. Freddie, too. But they kept going.

Vigo nodded his satisfaction. The situation was far from ideal.

Traffic out here was sparse but unpredictable. The longer the project took to complete, the more likely they were to be discovered. Which would mean more bodies to dispose of.

Vigo resisted the urge to curse. One motto he lived by was never let them see you sweat. Never show weakness of any kind. His enemies swarmed like vultures. One whiff of weakness and he'd be the one lying in a shallow grave. Like his father and his brothers.

While Hector and Freddie labored, Vigo turned his attention to the hostage.

Viciously, he jabbed Lawton in the stomach with the shotgun butt. Lawton grunted and bent double. Maybe something ruptured inside his belly. Good. He wouldn't live long enough to die of such injuries.

While his head was lowered, Vigo reached out and grabbed the canvas bag. He yanked roughly to remove the bag from Lawton's head, leaving him to stare at the ground.

"Stand up." He held the shotgun aimed at Lawton's belly.

Lawton struggled to comply. Slowly, he settled his weight over his feet, staggering to balance with his hands secured behind his back.

"Do you know who I am?" Vigo asked.

He squinted against the bright sunlight behind Vigo. He cleared his throat twice before he could speak. "Should I?"

Enraged by the lie, Vigo raised the butt of the shotgun and gut punched Lawton again, harder this time. He groaned in agony and fell to his knees.

Every federal agent in the country knew who Pinto Vigo was. And this particular agent was being fed inside information from a mole within Vigo's cartel.

Vigo needed to know the mole's name. Lawton could reveal the traitor. And he would. His bravado would prove painful as well as futile.

"Get up!" Vigo screamed. Lawton made no effort to stand.

Hector and Freddie had moved the first body and trudged back across the desert for the second one. Vigo used the moment to calm his fury. He waited while they lifted the second body and juggled it toward the rocky resting place.

Vigo stepped closer and repeated the command quietly. "Get. Up."

Lawton said nothing.

Vigo rested the barrel of the shotgun against Lawton's head and pushed. "You're a firearms expert, right? If I shoot you with this shotgun at close range, you already know your head will explode into a million little pieces so small not even the vultures will find them."

He paused for a couple of seconds, holding the barrel in place. "This is your last chance. Get. Up."

Lawton cleared his throat, lifted his head, and looked Vigo directly in the eyes. "We both know you're not going to kill me. Not until you get what you want."

Vigo's nostrils flared and his breathing quickened at the insult. He spoke calmly. "Let us both agree. You know who I am. You know how I deal with my enemies. You, Lawton, are placing yourself in that position. Tell me what I want to know."

Lawton said, "Even if I had whatever information you want, I wouldn't give it to you."

The insolence! Blinding rage coursed through Vigo's body. His finger itched to pull the trigger. Why not? There were other ways to learn what he needed to know. His posture shifted slightly, preparing to shoot.

Which was the opening Lawton had been waiting for. Swiftly, he stepped forward. He used the momentum to turn his body ninety degrees. His right shoulder bumped Vigo's hand holding the shotgun's barrel and knocked him off-balance. The barrel lifted upward.

Vigo pulled the trigger. The blast fanned out, slightly to the right and slightly above where Lawton had been standing a split second before.

Lawton's momentum carried him through. He stumbled against Vigo and knocked him to the ground. Lawton landed on top of Vigo, which left him temporarily winded.

Lawton pushed forward and landed a glancing head butt to Vigo's chin. The thrust pushed Vigo's head into the gritty ground.

Vigo was dazed, but still conscious. He yelled. Hector and Freddie came running toward them.

Before Lawton could do more damage, Hector grabbed the shotgun and slammed it into the back of Lawton's head. Somehow, he managed to stay in place.

Freddie ran up and pushed Lawton off Vigo with a heavy boot.

With his hands still tied behind him, Lawton couldn't adjust or fight back. He rolled off Vigo and kept rolling toward the van, making an effort to get beneath it and out of reach.

While Vigo scrambled to stand, Hector strode toward Lawton and, from a better angle, bashed his head with the shotgun butt again. Lawton immediately stopped moving.

Vigo rushed to Lawton's prone body and kicked him repeatedly, screaming in incoherent rage with every blow. He kicked until he was exhausted, breathing hard, and Lawton was a bloody, pulpy mess.

When he'd finished, he stood back to admire his work while he took a few deep breaths to calm his adrenaline rush.

Once he could speak decisively again, he said, "Get him in the van. Take him to the basement. Come back here and bury the two bodies."

Hector and Freddie lifted their third body, this one not quite dead, and tossed him into the van.

Hector said, "What about the other one? O'Hare?"

"Is he still out?" Vigo dusted the grime off his clothes and slicked his palms over his hair.

"I gave him a big dose. Enough for a few hours." Freddie said as he climbed into the van and checked O'Hare's pulse. "Yeah. He slept through the whole thing. Probably won't remember much of anything when he wakes up. That stuff kills some of the brain cells, you know?"

Damn Lawton.

This should have been easy. Get the name of the mole. Kill Lawton. Bury the body. The end.

Lawton had escalated the situation. Vigo had plans.

Operations were in motion. Inventory was on its way. The mole could screw everything up. Vigo had to find him and kill him and he needed to do it before the inventory arrived.

O'Hare was another problem. If the CPA didn't make it back, Vigo's home base would become another problem to deal with instead of a viable operations center.

Twenty-seven resident preppers at Glen Haven, three of them kids, had been a solid cover for months. They had jobs. They came and went. It had been easy to hide out there without being discovered.

How could he deal with the twenty-seven do-gooders if he killed O'Hare?

Twenty-seven hostages were feasible, but not easy to control. He'd need more manpower. Which meant putting more of his crew at risk of exposure. Given the war he'd been waging with the other cartels, he couldn't replace them with more loyal soldiers rapidly enough to handle the new inventory when it arrived.

Twenty-seven dead bodies would be exponentially more problematic. Their various little jobs and side hustles meant tourists and deliveries and pickup services were constantly in and out of Glen Haven. People would get curious and then insistent. More bodies would inevitably follow.

Vigo kicked the dirt in frustration. Then he shrugged. "Take him farther out into the desert. Leave him there. He'll find his way back. Or they'll find his body. Either way will buy us some time."

"Will do," Hector said as he walked around the front of the van and started up the engine.

Freddie closed the side door and climbed into the passenger seat. They pulled out onto the road, heading away from Glen Haven.

Vigo watched the van until it seemed to disappear off the edge of a flat earth. Then he let out the long stream of profanity he'd been holding back. When he was spent, he walked back to the SUV, fired it up, and drove to the storage facility where he parked it inside, tossed the wallet with the counterfeit ID into the glove box, and closed the garage door.

He walked to the bus stop half a block away. He boarded the bus that dropped him near a parking lot on the outskirts of town where he'd left the old pickup truck and climbed aboard. He started the engine and headed back to Glen Haven, still furious.

CHAPTER SIX

Monday, April 11
6: 30 p.m.
Albuquerque, New Mexico

MASON AWAKENED FACE DOWN on the side of a dusty road, parched and hurting and alone. No white van. No kidnappers. No Lawton.

He'd never felt so relieved in his life. He was still breathing. They hadn't killed him.

His hands were no longer bound behind him and the canvas hood was gone.

He rubbed the deep welts on his wrists to get the circulation going and gave himself a quick pat down. His head pounded like a guy with a hammer had given him a dozen solid whacks. Dried blood crusted on his face from his busted nose. He chewed the cracked mess off his lips and spat the bits on the ground.

He pushed himself up from the gravel and dusted the grime off his ruined business suit. He tested his joints and limbs, which were sore and achy but seemed to be more or less intact and functioning.

He patted his pockets. Whoever had abducted him and dumped him here had left him with his keys and cell phone. His wallet had been returned to the wrong pocket. The credit cards, driver's license, and the little bit of cash he'd stuck in one of the slots in case of emergency was still there, too. His watch wasn't expensive, but it hugged his left wrist, same as always.

Which meant he hadn't been robbed.

Not killed. Not robbed. And left alive.

Why go to all the trouble of abducting him, driving him into the middle of nowhere, and then leaving him here?

But they'd had to know he'd find his way back home eventually. He'd make a report. They'd be found. Arrested. Sent to prison. Or worse, because of Lawton being a federal agent.

The only thing that made sense to Mason's fuzzy thinking between throbs in his head was that they'd wanted him out of the way for a while, but not forever.

Out of the way of what?

For how long?

And why?

He set the questions aside for now.

He couldn't think straight. Not with the pounding in his head.

First things first. Stay alive. Get home.

He turned around slowly, a full three-hundred-sixty degrees, to get his bearings. He saw no signs of human habitation in any direction. Flat land covered with sand and scrub and not much else. The road ran to infinity at either end where the pavement seemed to fall off the edge of the earth.

He felt the hot sunburn on his balding head and tender face from the unrelenting desert sun. But now the big yellow orb was low in the sky. It would set soon enough. Which would give him some relief from the heat but would bring total darkness and nocturnal creatures seeking food.

He wasn't worried about desert predators. Most of them wouldn't attack humans. He'd be more likely to die of dehydration or heat stroke than untamed animals.

Except for snakes. There were deadly poisonous snakes out here. But he brushed that thought aside. He had no weapons. Nothing he could do about snakes except avoid them. Which he could only do as long as he could see them and his vision was a little blurry.

The wind had kicked up while he'd been unconscious. He'd be glad of his suitcoat in a couple of hours when darkness dropped to early spring temperatures.

Mason grimaced. Sandblasting by desert grit in the dark would not be pleasant, with or without the snakes.

Again, he noticed the road. All roads lead somewhere. Until he knew what exactly was going on, his best bet was to get moving. The road was straight and flat. It would be easier to navigate the road in the dark than the uneven terrain off-road.

He began to walk along the pavement while he figured out what to do next.

His thoughts were slow and foggy and disjointed. His head began to pound with each step. The painful rhythm of it kept him alert and moving.

He pulled his cell phone out of his pocket and woke up the screen. No cell service. Which meant he couldn't call for help. Nor could he access maps or a compass or anything else that might help pinpoint his location or help others to find him.

The phone's battery was showing a 56 percent charge. Which was good. At least he could use it for a flashlight when he needed to. Such as to watch for snakes.

He dropped the phone into his pocket and kept moving.

His dress shoes were not made for long distance walking, but they were all he had, so he ignored the heat radiating through the pavement and the blisters forming on his toes.

The sun was on his right and low on the horizon, which meant he was walking south. He began to think about his location. Where was he, exactly?

They had drugged him and dumped him here midafternoon. They couldn't have driven far from Albuquerque, given the timeframe.

The north edges of the Chihuahuan Desert was a likely distance. He'd been there with Cheryl and her son, Micah, several times. Day trips. Out and back in an afternoon.

Yes, they could have easily dumped him there and then taken Lawton wherever they planned to go, all before sundown. That made sense.

If he was anywhere near the Chihuahuan Desert, then Albuquerque would be to the north.

He thought about it a bit longer and then nodded, concluding he'd guessed correctly. He was pleased with his powers of deduction. His head pounded steadily, as the blood throbbed in his temples, but he could still think clearly enough.

Assuming he was correct, he turned around and retraced his steps, soon passing the spot where he'd awakened, and continued walking northward.

He checked his watch and estimated that sunset would happen in about an hour. He'd walk as far as he could. It was better to walk at night while the desert wasn't so hot. Along the way, perhaps he'd see a sign or something to indicate where he was.

His shoulders slumped. Not that it mattered where he was. Unless the sign was beside a gas station or a shop of some sort, it would do nothing but satisfy his curiosity. If he was right about the Chihuahuan, there would be no shops, no signs, and few people.

The times he'd explored the area with Cheryl and Micah, they'd joked about being alone out here and how they'd handle it. He remembered that they'd come up with exactly zero great ideas.

He wanted to get back home. He missed them already, and he'd been gone less than one day.

As he walked, he thought about home. It kept him going.

He lived in Glen Haven, an intentional community. Cheryl and Micah lived there, too. What his parents might have called a commune back in their hippie days. While their roots might have been in the hippie communes of the 1960s and '70s, today's intentional communities were less about free love and drug culture and more about lifestyle choices.

Glen Haven was a social experiment, Mason supposed. Residents shared their lives as well as the costs of running the place.

He'd never trusted the government to take care of him after he ran away from home at nineteen. He'd bounced around, finally graduated from community college, and eventually found Glen Haven. The community suited him. It felt like home and family after all the years alone. He'd been lucky to find it. Lucky they'd wanted him.

All he had to do now was not screw things up and he'd have a home for life. Cheryl and Micah, too.

At Glen Haven, they didn't live off the grid, although they could. They were set up to thrive in case of disaster. Given the state of the world, the founders always said, disaster could come at any time. And probably would.

Mason wasn't sure he agreed that doomsday was upon them, but he liked the option of being independent from government supplied water, electricity, and other so-called services. Those services came with strings and heavy price tags attached. Prices Mason didn't want to pay.

He liked that all Glen Haven residents were trained in basic survival skills, too. Even the children.

And everyone at Glen Haven contributed to the whole. They held jobs off-site, or they worked in the community's herbal goods business or, as Mason did, they worked freelance in various jobs like accounting or graphic design.

Which brought his thoughts back to Cheryl. They'd met shortly after Mason moved onto the compound three years ago. They'd come to love each other and they hoped to marry one day. Micah was a bonus. Such a great kid. Mason hoped to have a couple of kids of his own to add to the family eventually.

He stubbed his toe on a crack in the pavement and fell to his hands and knees. "Ah!" he yelled as he went down. The fall started his head to throbbing again. He was tempted to lie down and take a nap, but he didn't.

He pushed back on his heels, dusted the grit off his palms, and staggered to his feet. He felt blood trickling down his shins from his knees, but he didn't stop to look at his wounds. He had to keep going.

He glanced around. There was still no evidence of civilization as far as he could see in any direction. Which didn't necessarily mean no human lived anywhere near here. Squatters lived in the desert.

"A vehicle could come along. The point of any road is for vehicles to travel, right? Surely this road wouldn't be here if no one ever used it," he said reasonably, as if he was trying to make Micah feel less afraid.

Had he lost his mind? Maybe. But talking aloud made him feel better.

He might get lucky, even though he figured he'd already used up his quota of good luck for the year. He shook his head to banish that kind of thinking.

"You're lucky to be alive. All you need to do is stay that way."

He kept moving north. If no one came along to offer him a ride, he had a long trek ahead and he'd cover as much ground as possible in the dark. "When you get closer to Albuquerque, the cell service will kick in. You can call someone, if you don't find a ride before then. You'll make it back to Glen Haven eventually, one way or another."

He struggled to remain alert to his surroundings, even as his mind wandered. After an hour's walking, he stumbled and fell again.

"Pay attention, Mason! What's wrong with you?" he scolded himself as he pushed himself upright. "Tell me what happened. Talk it through."

He took a few steps first. Then he said, "I'm a little cloudy on the exact facts."

He drew a few deep breaths to settle his heart rate. "I remember leaving the Last Chance Saloon with Lawton. Four men in a van abducted us. I didn't recognize the van or know the men."

He squeezed his eyes shut briefly. When he opened them again, he said, "I can't picture them clearly now."

There were definitely four of them. One was bigger than the others. He seemed to be the leader of the gang. Were they all white? Hispanic? Lots of people around here were of Hispanic origin. So that would be a solid guess.

But the truth was that he didn't know. He'd seen them briefly, inside the van, where they stood in shadows. That's all.

"At some point, someone will ask for a description of the attackers. You might be asked to identify them in a lineup," he said, as if speaking aloud might jog his memory. It didn't.

He'd have to say he had no idea what they looked like. Which bothered him until he realized his inability to identify them might be why they let him live.

Still, why couldn't he remember?

Maybe he had a little bit of brain trauma. He rubbed the lump on the back of his head. A solid blow to his head and then his head hit the floor of the van hard enough to smash his nose. That could explain the near-constant headache and why he couldn't recall those guys at all, couldn't it?

Two miles down the road, he remembered the stop they'd made and the fight that had ended with another stint in the van and the needle in his neck. He rubbed the sore spot where the needle punctured his skin.

"There were four of them and they had guns. Shotguns." He recalled the blasts. Vividly. "Maybe someone was shot."

He wasn't sure. But Lawton had been hurt. The others, too. Mason recalled the sickening snap that had sounded like breaking bones.

He mulled it over. Tried to recall the exact sequence. He'd had the canvas bag over his head, so he couldn't see anything. He'd been disoriented, off balance. His head was pounding, even then.

Lawton told them he was a federal agent. The leader said he didn't care. He didn't seem surprised, either. Like he already knew.

A new thought occurred to Mason.

"Maybe they weren't after me at all. Maybe they didn't follow me to the Last Chance Saloon. Maybe Lawton was the target all along."

Which made a lot more sense, didn't it?

Lawton was a U.S. Treasury agent. He was a logical kidnapping victim, wasn't he? Who knew what he'd done to those guys. Maybe they wanted revenge or something, even.

Mason nodded. "Yeah. They had to have been watching Lawton. They knew he was there and they picked him up. Had nothing to do with me."

He kept walking, one foot in front of the other, testing his new insight.

The sun was almost even with the horizon now and the wind had turned cool. But the exercise was warming him up, so he was as comfortable as it was possible to get, under the circumstances.

He continued puzzling through his situation.

He wasn't a logical choice for a kidnapping. He couldn't even pay a decent ransom. He didn't make a lot of money and what he did earn went to fund Glen Haven.

"I was simply in the wrong place at the wrong time. A random victim," he said, trying out the only answer that made sense, as if he was explaining things to Cheryl.

He nodded, "Yep. I was unlucky. A one-time thing. That's all."

He found that idea oddly comforting. If he wasn't the target, it meant he could simply try to forget this had ever happened. Never tell a soul. Not even tell Cheryl. Do nothing to make those guys nervous about him, to make them come back and finish him off.

"That's a little cowardly, isn't it? What about Lawton?"

Lawton could take care of himself, surely.

But after another hundred steps or so, Mason had to admit, "That won't work."

Cheryl would be worried sick. He'd have to tell her about it when he got home. She loved him. They were planning to get married. Mason was the only real father ten-year-old Micah had ever known. Micah would call him Dad one day.

"You can't lie to them, Mason," he reminded himself. "That wouldn't be right."

The others would want to know, too. Mason was reliable, always around. One of the guys everyone at Glen Haven counted on. He wasn't there right now. He hadn't come back from town today. Hadn't returned the sedan to Gavin Ray, who would need it for work in the morning.

Mason's mere absence, regardless of the reason for it, would be enough to raise suspicions. They'd be curious, at the very least. They'd ask what happened. He'd have to tell them.

Not only that, it was so close to the end of tax return season. He had a dozen returns yet to complete and file. His clients were counting on him. Everyone expected him to stay steady, do his work, carry his share of the load.

Yes, the more he thought about it, the clearer it became that he'd been swept up by mistake. He was sure that no one would want to kidnap him. For what? His life was as exciting as a sloth's.

He grinned. "Maybe even less exciting."

Those men were rough and violent. They had weapons. The attack and abduction was flawlessly accomplished. Like they'd practiced. Like they'd done it before, lots of times. Which he figured they probably had.

"I don't know any men who would do that. Lawton does. He must have been the one they wanted," he said, as if the matter were now clearly established.

"Besides, if they'd meant to kill me, they could have done it and dumped me further off the road for the vulture: never have been found." His voice was a little shaky. "But didn't."

They hadn't killed him when they had the chance.

So they didn't want him dead.

"It had to be Lawton they were after." He said it firmly tl time. Definitely.

No other reasonable conclusion he could come to, actually

He felt better, simply thinking this thing through.

He nodded. The movement jacked up the throbbing in his head, grabbing all of his attention.

Which was when he noticed something rubbing against his side as he walked. It must have become dislodged when he fell back there.

He reached into his front pocket and pulled it out. It was a piece of cardboard. Torn from a cereal box or something. The cardboard had been white on the inside before grimy hands had ripped it from the box.

He stopped and squinted in the dim light to read the ten words aloud. "No Cops. Tell no one. We know where you live."

He read it again. Twice more. At some point, his hands had begun to shake. He stuffed the cardboard back into his pocket and started walking again.

Were the words a threat or a warning?

Hard tremors ran down his spine.

CHAPTER SEVEN

Tuesday, April 12
8:30 a.m.
Detroit, Michigan

KIM RAN HEAD-FIRST INTO the still-biting wind wearing a lined cold weather jogging suit, gloves, and a hat. She jogged a one-mile stretch of the nearly deserted Woodward Avenue sidewalk through downtown Detroit.

The calendar had proclaimed the change of seasons three weeks ago. Old man winter had laughed.

Her wind-chafed nose and cheeks probably resembled those of a Christmas elf, making her seem harmless enough. A few hardy souls hurried along, bundled against the cold blowing off the Detroit River from Canada. The ice had melted, but the water temperature was still frigid.

An erratic spring had finally arrived in the Motor City and a couple of warm days had lured her outside to run while the weather held. Another storm was forecast later in the week, but weathermen were notoriously unreliable here. With luck, they'd continue their losing streak and the warm weather was here to stay. She'd experienced enough cold the past few months to last a good long while.

At the foot of Woodward, she turned around and retraced her route, heading north for the last lap before she jogged home, showered, and went to work.

Inside her building, Walter Hill was standing guard with a ready smile for her, as always. "You certainly do run a lot. Something chasing you?"

"Still pretty cold out there," she replied with a smile, pulling her gloves and hat off and stuffing them into her pockets.

"Yeah, if you don't like the weather in Michigan, just wait a minute, and it'll change," he joked. He reached for a manila padded envelope from beneath the counter and handed it to her. "This came for you by courier about half an hour ago."

Her pulse was a little rapid, but maybe that was left over from her run instead of quickened by the sight of the envelope. No reason to feel apprehensive about it. She knew what was inside. She'd received several others exactly like it since November.

She took the envelope from him and tucked it under her arm. "Thanks, Walter. Gotta get off to the salt mines."

"At least it's warmer down there." He grinned and gave her a mock salute.

"Right." There were actually salt mines eleven hundred feet under the streets of Detroit. But she worked above ground in the Patrick C. McNamara Federal Building on Michigan Avenue, just a few blocks from her apartment.

She tossed the envelope on the kitchen table, pushed the button to brew the coffee she'd set up before she left, and headed toward the bathroom.

When she'd showered, pulled her long, dark hair back into a low ponytail, slapped on a little makeup, and dressed in her usual black pantsuit, she came back to the kitchen for the coffee. While she sipped the hot, black nectar, she stared at the envelope on the table.

It was the usual size and shape. Same color. Same kind of padding. She held it in her palm to judge its heft. Satisfied she'd guessed correctly, she pulled the zip strip open and poured the contents onto the table.

The only item in the envelope was a single use burner cell phone, *almost* exactly as she'd expected.

"Huh." She'd only been half right. She'd expected a new cell phone.

But this one was not the same as all the others.

Which meant the Boss hadn't sent it.

He acquired his burners from a single trusted source who sold to no one else. He trusted only one brand because the encryption was exceptionally secure. This one was not the Boss's usual brand. Which meant someone else sent the phone.

She picked up the empty envelope and examined it. Unlike the cell phone, this envelope was exactly the same as all the others she'd received. Common. Indistinguishable. It could have been purchased in bulk by the federal government from the manufacturer. Consumers could have bought the same envelopes by the dozen in any local Walmart or grocery store.

In other words, the envelope was nothing special. Its very ubiquity was the sender's intent.

Whoever sent this envelope knew what kind she'd be expecting.

The sender had taken care to duplicate the delivery and the envelope to make her think the Boss had sent the burner.

Probably to entice her to open the envelope. Which she might not have done if she'd suspected an unknown sender.

Basic security protocol kicked in. She didn't fire up the burner.

Turning the phone on inside her home or near her existing cell phone would defeat the purpose of receiving a burner cell from an anonymous source, because her personal phone would automatically connect to it and allow the burner to be tracked.

The whole point of any burner was to defeat any sort of trace.

She pondered the point for a moment. The Boss listened to and often watched her every move. She was his canary in whatever coal mine he thought Reacher was inhabiting. He wanted to know where she was and why, every minute of every day.

Whoever sent this burner might not have known about her Reacher assignment. But then she'd have to believe sending the envelope, delivering it to her home, and including a burner cell phone, all of which mimicked the Boss's style, was all just a lucky guess.

She didn't believe in that kind of luck.

More likely, the sender knew all of that and expected her to understand he wanted to avoid the Boss. Otherwise, he'd simply have called her normal phone.

Which meant this guy knew more about her than her home address and the type of envelopes the Boss used. He also knew that she was under constant surveillance, which he apparently wanted to avoid.

Only two people knew the Boss was always watching her and why and how to mimic his systems. Even more to the point, how to avoid him.

One was her former partner, Carlos Gaspar.

The other was Lamont Finlay, PhD, Special Assistant to the President for Strategy. A man with a lot of important responsibilities and a terrifying amount of power.

Gaspar had the means and knew the methods to send her the burner. But why would he? He had retired and left the FBI for a cushy private sector job a few weeks back. She actually talked to him all the time. Mostly about his family and her nonexistent social life, but still. Communication between them was normal.

She shook her head. If Gaspar had wanted to have a confidential conversation for some reason, he'd have done something simpler. They had developed several techniques for avoiding the Boss when they'd worked together. He could easily have used any one of those, and likely would have.

She sighed. Having eliminated the obvious, she was left with only one likely answer that made sense.

Lamont Finlay had probably sent the burner. But why?

Their prior dealings had been limited and always initiated by her. He'd never attempted to establish contact with her before. Why was he doing so now?

She cocked her head and stared at the burner, as if it might give up its secrets by telepathy or something.

Didn't happen.

"Okay, then." She drained the last of the coffee, rinsed the cup, and turned it upside down on the drainboard. She mumbled one of her mother's bromides. "When you only have one choice, it's the right choice."

The only way to find out what Finlay wanted was to talk to him.

Kim dropped her personal phone onto the table and slipped the burner into her pocket.

She trusted Finlay, to a point. But not far enough to be alone with him with no method of contacting another human. So she grabbed a fresh burner from her desk drawer and checked her gun. She never left home without it.

She donned her coat and gloves and left the building, walking briskly toward a location she knew offered a slender gap in the Boss's satellite coverage.

Six blocks away, she fired up Finlay's burner and stopped walking. An initiation text message flashed on the screen. It said simply, "Press 1."

She pressed 1. The phone rang three times before he picked up.

"Can I offer you a ride?" The deep, resonant voice was unmistakable. She recognized it immediately. Just as she'd expected. "The limo is parked across the street."

She scanned the area for the vehicle and spied it idling at the curb in front of Comerica Park. In a couple of weeks, this area would be teeming with people. But it was too early in the season for baseball. Tigers' opening day wasn't scheduled until next week and the sidewalks around the stadium were all but deserted now.

Kim hustled over to the armored Lincoln. Finlay's Secret Service right-hand man, stepped out to open the door for her. "Good morning, Agent Otto," he said.

"Agent Russell," she replied as she slid inside. He closed the door and returned to the front passenger seat. The driver pulled away from the curb, headed north on Woodward Avenue away from the city.

Russell lowered the glass wall behind the front seat and turned to face her. "We have about thirty minutes to drive. Make yourself comfortable. There's coffee in that insulated cup for you."

He raised the privacy divider and she settled into the plush interior with the hot coffee and enjoyed the ride as she considered all the reasons Finlay might have for summoning her.

Everything that came to mind was about Jack Reacher.

They had absolutely nothing else to discuss.

CHAPTER EIGHT

Tuesday, April 12
10:30 a.m.
Bloomfield Hills, Michigan

WHEN THE LIMO REACHED Bloomfield Hills, they passed the location where Jimmy Hoffa had been abducted in broad daylight all those years ago. A different restaurant operated there now, but unlike the restaurant, the case had not been closed.

The FBI had worked the disappearance for decades, but Hoffa's body had never been found.

An involuntary shiver ran all the way up her spine.

Making a person disappear wasn't as easy as old movies made it seem, but it wasn't impossible, either. Not that she was worried. She reached into her pocket for an antacid and chewed it to calm her stomach.

A few miles farther north, Finlay's driver turned the limo onto a private road lined with tall hedges on either side. Every hundred yards or so, Kim noticed a wide driveway and a single mailbox set into a stone enclosure.

Bloomfield Hills was the richest zip code in the state of
Michigan, and among the wealthiest in the country. Even the
mailboxes occupied their own homes.

She wasn't really surprised. Finlay had shown a penchant for
luxury every time she'd met with him.

In theory, Finlay was a government servant, just as she was.
But somehow, his salary seemed to come with way more perks.
Which was one of the reasons Gaspar didn't trust him. Ethical
cops didn't live as large as Finlay, Gaspar often said. He didn't
approve of Finlay anyway, but the lavish lifestyle made him
more suspect in her ex-partner's mind.

Half a mile farther, the driver turned right and continued past
the tall hedges. They traveled along a well-maintained, winding
driveway through rolling lawns that must have required an entire
crew. Spring flower gardens surrounded the residence ahead.
Maybe the gardening crew lived on the premises. There was
certainly enough housing to accommodate a full staff.

The house was a brown Tudor revival style mansion
complete with finials, scalloping, and lancet windows. Kim
counted twenty chimneys before the limo moved too close to
count the rest.

The driver curved right into a circular driveway and pulled
up in front of a private building larger than a boutique hotel. The
place might have been somewhat smaller than Meadowbrook
Hall, a public museum nearby where Kim had attended a few
weddings over the years.

Kim recalled that Meadowbrook Hall had been a private
home built by the auto heiress Matilda Dodge Wilson in the late
1920s. A private home with 88,000 square feet and 110 guest
rooms wasn't considered obscene at the time, apparently. Car
companies were thick on the ground in this area back then and

their owners amassed the kind of wealth Kim could only imagine. They had to have something to spend it on, she supposed.

Still, she wondered who built this estate. and who owned it now. Probably one of those early auto magnates.

Not that it mattered who built the place. But learning who owned the house now and how he was connected to Finlay could be relevant.

She shrugged. Gaspar's useful all-purpose gesture. She'd find out, all in good time.

Russell opened the door and Kim climbed out of the limo.

"Welcome to the slums, Agent Otto," he teased with a grin. She'd always liked Russell.

"Lead the way," she replied, wondering again why Finlay had summoned her here.

She'd have asked Russell, but from experience she knew he wouldn't tell her. His discretion was admirable. Not all Secret Service agents were so reticent. She figured his loyalty meant she respected and approved of Finlay. Which told her something about both men, but nothing about why she was here.

The driver pulled away and Kim walked beside Russell to the front entrance. He pushed the heavy door inward and they stepped across the threshold and back in time at least a hundred years.

The cavernous entrance hall was significantly larger than Kim's entire apartment and much more ornate. Everything was meticulously preserved, restored to its original glory. She stared at the elaborately carved wood and stone elements, and the soaring plaster ceiling, feeling like a very tiny smudge of humanity by comparison.

"How much do you think it costs every day to run this place,

Russell?" she asked, craning her neck to look at the huge antique Tiffany lamps hanging from the elaborate ceiling.

"Way more than I make, that's for sure. Ten grand a day? More?" Russell replied as they walked along toward the elevator under the stairs, which was concealed by a wood panel identical to those that lined the rest of the hallway.

The place was like a museum. Everywhere she turned, she noticed the meticulous craftsmanship. She identified paintings by Gainsborough and Rivera, but she wasn't familiar with the other artists whose work adorned the walls.

Russell pushed a corner of the wood panel and it slid aside. She entered the elevator and he joined her inside the car. Russell pulled an old-fashioned accordion gate across the entrance and manually closed the ornate brass interior door. He pushed the lever on the wall to raise the elevator slowly to the third floor.

He adjusted the lever and the elevator car bounced to a stop. He pushed the door open, then the gate.

"Watch your step," he said, pointing to the two-inch difference between the elevator car and the floor. He waved her out into another well-preserved hallway furnished with the glamour of the early twentieth century.

"This way," Russell said as he pointed to the left with his palm.

They walked further into the depths of the house, footsteps echoing on the polished wood floors, about halfway down the corridor where they reached solid double doors on the right.

Russell knocked and then turned the brass knob and pushed the heavy door inward.

This suite of rooms seemed lighter and more welcoming. Finlay was seated behind a desk in front of a window. He looked up from a note he was writing and said, "Good to see you, Agent

Otto. Thank you for coming. Coffee and pastries on the table over there. Help yourself. I'm almost done here."

Russell backed out and closed the heavy door behind him. Kim guessed he wouldn't stray from his post until this meeting was over, when he'd escort her back to the city.

Feeling uneasy, she filled her coffee cup, returned to a chair near Finlay's desk, and waited until he explained himself.

It was an odd dynamic. He'd never summoned her before. Nor had she fully appreciated how much he actually knew about the Boss's methods. In the past, she'd been the one who'd come looking for him, hat figuratively in hand, and always for a specific purpose.

The shift in their relationship was subtle and disconcerting, in some subliminal way she couldn't put her finger on.

He looked as confident and classy as ever. He'd removed his suit jacket to reveal a crisp white dress shirt. The cuffs were fastened with gleaming gold square cuff links. The collar sported a smartly knotted yellow bow tie that matched the socks showing between sharply pressed trousers and highly polished bespoke cap-toed shoes.

He looked like a wealthy Wall Street hedge fund manager, which was fitting for a man who wielded such power. If he had actually held any control over her life whatsoever, he'd have been as intimidating as hell. As it was, she felt only mild disquiet. Again, she wondered, what did he want?

A few moments later, he laid the expensive fountain pen on the desk, folded the creamy white stationery in half, stuffed it into a preaddressed envelope, and sealed it firmly with a hot wax circle and placed it on a small silver plate. He pressed a button.

Russell entered almost instantly to collect the envelope and then left again.

When they were alone once more, Finlay folded his hands across his flat stomach and said, "You look well rested, Otto. No Reacher hunting lately?"

Kim shrugged. Whether she'd been actively investigating Reacher or not when he'd summoned her was none of his business. And he probably already knew the answers anyway.

Her Reacher assignment was not even sanctioned black ops, but was deep under the radar. Which meant that only three people in the world should have had knowledge of the job. Finlay was not one of the three.

Yet, somehow, he knew more about the situation than she was comfortable with, and he knew she knew it. Finlay had been keeping an eye on her since the Boss first tasked her with completing Reacher's background check, ostensibly because he was being considered for a classified assignment. She'd trusted the Boss back then. Now, not so much.

But even if there was a classified assignment waiting for Reacher, she had no idea what it was because her clearance wasn't high enough. Finlay's clearance was well above hers. If he didn't know the nature of the assignment, he could easily have found out.

Whatever he knew, he didn't share with her. Why should she share with him?

He smiled. "Relax. I brought you out here because I'm doing you a favor."

"How's that?" she sipped the coffee as if nothing he might possibly say could change her life, even though they both knew otherwise.

He inclined his head toward a closed door to his left. "A witness is waiting to tell you everything she knows about Reacher."

She felt her stomach do a couple of flips and reached into

her pocket for another of the antacids she kept there. Finlay made her beyond nervous. No way she could hide the fact.

She raised her eyebrows. "Why?"

"Because I asked her to." He smiled again, which set off her internal alarms in an even bigger way.

Her internal threat level moved all the way to red and held the needle there.

She'd come out here with no backup. Not even Gaspar knew where she was. Any tracking devices the Boss might have accessed were back in her apartment. Finlay could make her disappear in an instant with nothing more than the snap of his fingers. No one would ever know.

But why would he do that? He'd helped her before. Gaspar didn't like it, but more than once, she'd relied on Finlay instead of the Boss.

Still, Gaspar was wary of Finlay and she trusted his instincts almost as well as her own. She didn't have a clue what this was all about, but whatever Finlay was doing here would be more for his benefit than hers. She was sure of that.

"If your witness is willing to talk about Reacher, why hasn't Cooper mentioned her before?"

Finlay shrugged. "Your boss is a strange man. His reasons are his own. I can't speak for him."

"And you wouldn't tell me even if you knew," Kim replied. He didn't argue. Did the Boss know about Finlay's witness? What would he say to her in the moment?

Kim felt ambivalent and conflicted. This whole setup felt like a trap. Yet Finlay hadn't tried to hurt her in the past. Quite the opposite. He'd helped her out more than once.

"Do you want to talk to Holly Johnson or not?" He asked. "I've got other things to do."

What's the worst that could happen? There were too many pitfalls to consider thoroughly. She was already here. Hard to see a way that simply talking to the woman could cause any kind of problem. Kim took a deep breath to calm herself. "Yeah, sure. Why not?"

"I promise she won't shoot you. Not unless you do something to provoke her, anyway." Finlay laughed.

It was the kind of laugh that made some women swoon, she was sure. But the laugh simply made Kim more nervous.

He stood and walked toward the doorway on his left. He turned the knob and inclined his head. "Come with me."

CHAPTER NINE

Tuesday, April 12
12:05 p.m.
Bloomfield Hills, Michigan

FINLAY HAD MADE THE introductions and left them alone. Kim assumed the place was under constant surveillance. He didn't need to join them. He'd be recording everything, anyway.

She was perched on a loveseat across from FBI Special Agent Holly Johnson, who sat poised and relaxed on an identical loveseat opposite. A low coffee table rested between them.

Johnson was probably in her early forties, Kim guessed. Dark hair. Very light makeup. Professionally attired. Slender, fit, and well groomed. A plain gold wedding band adorned her left ring finger.

Given her age, Kim figured Johnson had been in the FBI for a long time. Which meant she had moved up the ladder from where Kim was positioned. Might as well get that out of the way first.

"I work as a field agent out of the Detroit Office," Kim said, giving her a chance to reciprocate.

Johnson nodded. "I know."

"How about you?"

Johnson shook her head. "That's classified, I'm afraid. And I don't have a lot of time to talk today. Let's get to your questions on Jack Reacher."

Figures. None of these witnesses ever wanted to divulge their secrets. "What did Finlay tell you already? No need to cover old ground."

"He says you're completing a background check on Reacher, who is being considered for a classified assignment above your clearance level," Johnson replied easily. "Of course, we all know that's a load of crap."

Kim concealed her surprise and cocked her head. "Why's that?"

"Because your orders come straight from Charles Cooper. He's pretty far up the FBI food chain, but that guy's so crooked they'll need to bury him with a corkscrew," Johnson grinned.

"So what do you think is going on?" Kim asked, genuinely interested.

Johnson shook her head. "Damned if I know. It's not my assignment, so I don't have to know. What I'm concerned about is Cooper's intention here. Reacher doesn't deserve to be targeted for any of Cooper's black ops nonsense. If I can stop it here and now, so much the better."

"He's my boss. Yours, too, for that matter. Neither one of us needs to get crossways with him," Kim said.

"Okay. Fair enough. You're in a tough spot," Johnson nodded. She softened her tone. "I'm not worried about Cooper. But you're right that you should be. He can ruin your career in a hot New York minute. End your life, too, if he feels like it. Don't you forget that."

"Seems like he could do the same to you," Kim replied evenly.

Johnson said nothing for a couple of moments. She glanced at her watch and then seemed to choose her words carefully. "As I mentioned, my time is limited. We can get into my situation another day. For now, let me tell you about Reacher and then you can ask me specific questions, okay?"

Kim had no choice, so she simply nodded.

Johnson said, "I haven't seen Reacher in more than fifteen years. Back then, he was fresh out of the army and he was a helluva soldier. Young. Fit. Capable. Smart. One of our finest, to be sure."

"Were you in Margrave, Georgia, with him and Finlay, then?" Kim asked, because Margrave was the first place Reacher surfaced after his military discharge fifteen years ago.

Margrave was where Joe Reacher had died, too. It was where the girl who might be Reacher's daughter lived now. And it was where Reacher had met Finlay.

Whatever the glue that held Reacher and Finlay together now, it started fifteen years ago in Margrave. Maybe Holly Johnson could shed some light on that, too.

"No. Totally different situation." Johnson shook her head, dashing Kim's hopes. "Reacher and I were kidnapped together. By some crazy paramilitary group. They took us out west and planned to kill us both. But for Reacher, they probably would have succeeded."

"What did Reacher do?"

Johnson's gaze was as steely as her tone. "Exactly what he was trained to do. He kept us alive. And before you ask, yes, a lot of what he did back then would have been enough to get him arrested. A military tribunal would have convicted him and sent him to prison. Hell, a civil jury probably would have, too."

Despite her words, Johnson didn't sound the least bit concerned about Reacher's lawbreaking. Which was a pattern Kim had come across before. "But?"

"For my money, everything he did and everything I did, was justified. We were at war with those nuts. It was kill or be killed. We were fighting for our lives. We had an undercover FBI agent embedded with them and they killed him. In the most horrific way. I'll never forget what they did." Johnson shivered involuntarily. She took a deep breath. "Anyway, there's no doubt in my mind that I'd be dead now if it wasn't for Reacher. I'm never going to forget that. And Cooper would be wise to keep his distance from me if he has anything detrimental to Reacher in mind. When you talk to him, you can tell him I said so."

Kim nodded, trying to make sense of what she was hearing. "Why would Cooper care what you think?"

"Listen to me." Johnson leaned forward and clasped her hands between her knees. "Cooper can't be trusted. Whatever he wants you to do, whatever he's been saying, you can be sure you're not getting the whole story. Be wary of him, Otto. You're a solid agent. I checked you out. Don't let him lead you into the kind of trouble you don't need or want and can't get out of. Stay alert. For your own sake as well as Reacher's."

Kim nodded slowly. "So this group. The ones that kidnapped you. Why did they choose you?"

"That's a long story. It was a nutty plan. The guy who thought it up was as crazy as they come." She paused. "But he was a heartless stone-cold killer, too. Very dangerous combination. Several times, I didn't think we'd make it out. I thought we'd die trying. Because of Reacher, we survived."

"*Was*? You said the guy *was* crazy. So he's dead now?"

Johnson stared and said nothing, which was all the answer

Kim needed. She'd been hunting Reacher for a while and she'd run into too many similar situations. She knew what had happened without being told.

The guy was dead.

Reacher had killed him.

And Johnson was okay with that.

Hell, she sounded like she'd probably give Reacher a medal for it, even if neither the military nor civilian justice system would agree.

"Was everyone in the paramilitary group crazy? Or just the leader?" Kim asked.

"You mean were they likely to blow themselves up so they could get virgins in the after-life or drink poisoned Kool-Aid or something?" Johnson's grim smile slashed to one side of her face. "Nothing that blatant. The leader didn't want his own people dead. Some of them were prisoners themselves. Some just wanted to be left alone. Others were disenchanted with our government, looking for a better way."

Kim nodded. "There's a lot of that going around these days, too."

"Yeah, and it's scary. Even though I understand how they feel. The government's been letting us down for a long time," Johnson agreed. "There was one guy Reacher talked to back there. James Ray. He was a soldier once. Married. Two sons. They all lived out there on the compound. He seemed decent enough, even though his reasoning was sideways, like he'd been brainwashed or something."

"What happened to him?"

Johnson leaned back slightly and seemed to relax a bit. "You know, I never followed up on that. Once we got clear of that place, Reacher and I went our separate ways. The people from the group were processed appropriately, I guess. Some of them were probably tried and convicted. I don't know what happened to the others. Never asked. Didn't care."

"And you didn't know Reacher at all before this happened?" Kim cocked her head, processing what she'd learned. "Just some kind of crazy coincidence that the two of you were kidnapped together?"

"It's crazy the way things happen sometimes. They wanted me. Reacher was just unlucky. Wrong place at the wrong time." Johnson offered a genuine smile. "I was picking up my weekly dry cleaning on my lunch hour. It was heavy. Nine suits on hangers weigh a lot, you know. And I'd had a sports injury, so I was struggling with the hangers one-handed. He was passing by and offered to help. Next thing we know, we're both grabbed off the sidewalk and tossed into the back of a van at gunpoint."

"Sounds like some serious bad luck and trouble, doesn't it?" Kim arched her eyebrows.

Johnson shook her head. "Having him along was the luckiest thing that ever happened to me, but I felt sorry for him."

"Yeah, I can see that. A guy trying to do a good deed gets kidnapped and almost killed. You'd feel guilty about it. Anybody would," Kim replied. "You've never had any contact with Reacher since then?"

"Nope. So when you find him, tell him to give me a call, will you? I'd like to buy him a drink and show him pictures of my kids," Johnson said, pulling a business card out of her wallet and handing it over.

Kim took the card. "You have kids?"

"Two. Boy and a girl. Twins. Finlay says your man's a Treasury agent. You got any kids?"

Kim shook her head. "My relationship with Lawton isn't at that level."

"Well, mine are ten years old now. Some of the hardest work of my life, raising kids. Some of the most rewarding, too," Johnson replied with a genuine smile. She stood up and fastened her jacket. She pulled a small flash drive out of her pocket. "This contains the reports of what happened back then. Look them over. You'll find it helpful. I've got to get going. But call me anytime if you think of anything I can help you with. It might take me a while to return the call. But I'll get back to you when I can."

They shook hands. Kim asked, "One last thing. If you wanted to find Reacher now, how would you do it?"

Johnson leveled her gaze and without a blink, she said, "I'd ask Finlay."

"He says he doesn't know where Reacher is or how to contact him," Kim replied.

Johnson smiled as she headed for the door. "And you believed that?"

"Why would he lie?" Kim asked, more curious than surprised.

Johnson turned to answer. "Everybody lies, Otto. The usual reason is self-interest. I've got nothing to hide where Reacher is concerned. I laid it all out years ago when we were first rescued. It's doubtful everyone you run across can honestly say the same."

"You believe Finlay falls into that camp," Kim replied flatly, because that's what she believed, too.

"It's a safe bet. You should ask him," Johnson replied. It was the last thing she said before she left and closed the door behind her.

CHAPTER TEN

Tuesday, April 12
12:45 p.m.
Bloomfield Hills, Michigan

KIM SPIED A LAPTOP on the desk across the room. She
figured Finlay had left it there for her to find. She started it up,
inserted the flash drive Holly Johnson had given her, and waited
for the contents list to open.

The laptop was fast and the files were well organized. In a
couple of minutes, Kim was reading the summary of events
outlined in Agent Johnson's final reports of the Montana incident.

The kidnapping and everything that followed came after
Reacher left Margrave. After whatever Finlay and Reacher did
together there, too. It made sense that Finlay would have kept
tabs on Reacher after that.

Kim's eyes widened as she skimmed the data. The first
surprise was Agent Johnson's pedigree. That explained a few
things. Like why Cooper couldn't touch her and why she
wouldn't be worried about him making the effort.

She was the daughter of a powerful army general and the goddaughter of a former United States president. No wonder she'd been the target of a kidnapping. She should have had Secret Service protection but didn't. Kim grinned when she read the reason. Johnson had refused. She could take care of herself, she'd said.

Because Johnson was the author of the reports, Kim figured the accounts were somewhat sanitized. She spent no time on interpretation. That could come later. For now, she simply read the words on the page and digested them.

Johnson and Reacher had been held as prisoners at the Montana compound. Separately and together, they had engaged the enemy and emerged victorious. She reported several fatalities as "death of enemy combatant."

Reading between the lines, Johnson seemed emotionally affected by two of the men involved. One was the embedded FBI agent she'd mentioned. Kim winced when she read of his death at the enemy's hands. She figured Johnson had included the gruesome details partially as a means of justification for the carnage she and Reacher inflicted.

The other man Johnson highlighted in the reports was her boss, FBI Special Agent McGrath. Reading between the lines and relying on instinct, Kim guessed McGrath might be the man she'd married and the father of Johnson's twins. She seemed overly concerned with supporting and almost glorifying his actions in the reports.

Mentions of Reacher bordered on clinical precision. Johnson reported each conflict, his combat skills deployed, and the predictable results.

She'd included the body count, which was staggering.

Kim skimmed the reports again to be certain she hadn't missed it, but she found no mention of Finlay at all.

After she finished her second pass, Kim ejected the flash
drive, slipped it into her pocket, and stood to stretch her aching
shoulders. She had several unanswered questions, but the
answers weren't included in the flash drive's contents.

A moment later, she heard a brief rap on the door. Without
invitation, the door opened and Finlay walked in. Which
confirmed Kim's suspicions about Finlay's surveillance of
activities in the room.

"You read Johnson's reports?" he asked as he took a seat and
gestured for Kim to do the same.

"Why didn't the government go in and get her out of
there?" Kim asked. The question had been bugging her. It made
no sense that they'd have left Johnson and Reacher to fend
for themselves. "Johnson was a VIP. About as close to royalty
as it gets in this country. Goddaughter to a sitting president.
Daughter of one of the Joint Chiefs of Staff. Romantically
involved with a high-level FBI official. If there was ever
a time for a well-planned extraction, surely that was one such
time."

"They were worried." Finlay shrugged. "They'd tried armed
intervention in a few other touchy situations and all they got was
a big black eye. People died. They looked like bullies and
incompetent fools to boot."

"You mean like Ruby Ridge, Waco, and the Elián González
fiascos?" She cocked her head. She could almost see it
unfolding. The panic in the White House leading to impotence
in the face of terrorists who would not hesitate to kill.

Finlay nodded. "Those are three that come to mind, yes.
There were others."

"So they were trying to figure out what to do and, by the
time they had a workable plan, Johnson and Reacher had already

solved their own problems," Kim said flatly. Made sense. She didn't like it, but she understood it.

"That's pretty close to the truth," Finlay replied.

Kim nodded. Second worst thing in the world for a powerful politician at the top of the food chain was to appear incompetent. The worst thing was when his exposed incompetence was not only true, but also fatal to innocents. Talk about a career killer.

She changed the subject slightly. "Johnson's obviously a Reacher fan. That why you wanted me to talk to her?"

"Partly," he nodded. "Until now, you've been spoon-fed selected information about Reacher. Cooper's been careful about telling you only what he wants you to know and the witnesses you've encountered have been reticent, to say the least. Initially, I thought your situation was curious, but not too dangerous for you to handle on your own."

"And now?" Kim cocked her head. Finlay was an enigma, to be sure. Instinctively, she trusted him. But Gaspar said she was a fool to do so, and he could be right.

"When you started out you were only doing a background check, which seemed harmless enough." Finlay crossed his ankles, probably to avoid mussing the perfect crease in his trousers. "Now that your assignment has changed and you're actively hunting Reacher, you need to know what you're in for."

"Meaning what?"

Finlay took a deep breath and a frown creased his forehead. "Reacher's a complicated guy, Otto. He says he only wants to be left alone to wander the country because he never saw much of it when he was in the army."

"Sounds reasonable enough, doesn't it?" Kim replied.

"It might. For another guy." Finlay shook his head. "Reacher fancies himself as some sort of knight errant. He takes it upon himself to get involved in dangerous situations he should stay out of. Sometimes the situation ends up okay and sometimes it doesn't. Either way, Reacher's the last man standing and there's unacceptable levels of collateral damage."

"You're speaking as the voice of experience, I gather." For the first time, he'd admitted he knew more about Reacher's activities than he'd been telling. Kim narrowed her gaze in an attempt to see through him to his motivation. She failed.

"Some." He smiled, as he often did when he knew she was on the wrong track and he might not want to steer her to the right one. "A long time ago, I arrested Reacher in Margrave, Georgia. I was the chief of police. Two strangers come into a small town and one ends up dead. At the time, I thought he'd killed the other man. The easy answer is usually the right one. We all know now that he wasn't guilty of that particular crime."

"You thought he'd killed his own brother," Kim said flatly. "Tells me something about how Reacher comes across to trained law enforcement personnel."

"In my defense, I didn't know the victim was Reacher's brother when I had him arrested. He didn't know it, either." Finlay's smile vanished and he frowned, to show his seriousness, she supposed. "Like Holly Johnson, we found ourselves in a war not of our own choosing and Reacher fought with us. We're alive now because of Reacher. But yes, his methods were brutal and unorthodox. And highly effective."

Kim nodded. "By which you mean Reacher broke about a thousand laws and killed some bad guys—and you were glad he did. Maybe you even helped him do it. So you let him go instead of arresting him again."

Finlay waited for her to sort things out.

Reacher had walked away from Margrave a free man. Finlay

had, too. Only one way that could have happened. Finlay didn't do his job. Simple as that.

Gaspar was right. Finlay had been a corrupt cop. In Kim's experience, corruption was a character flaw, not a one-off.

Someday, Reacher would pay for what he'd done in Margrave and other places, too. He and Finlay might be allowed to share a cell. They could discuss the meaning of life.

Finlay wasn't the only one covering up for Reacher out of self-interest, either. She figured the Boss fell into that camp, too.

Trust no one.

A long silence filled the room. Finally, he offered the same smile as before. "You're a suspicious person, Agent Otto."

Which only served to confirm her guess. Finlay's involvement with Reacher went way deeper than what she'd learned about Margrave. Way deeper than the hard data reported at the time.

She'd pored over those reports a while back. Nothing suggested Finlay's activities were suspect. Not even remotely. He'd done a good whitewashing job.

So most of what Finlay had testified to in the aftermath of Margrave was fabricated. Perjury to cover up capital offenses. The coverup was often worse than the crime.

Did she want to know more?

If she asked for further evidence and he told her, she'd become the keeper of those secrets. Knowing would require action. The plausible deniability she'd struggled to maintain would fly right out the window.

The Boss already knew everything, and Finlay was still who he was.

The Boss would find out she'd been here and interviewed Johnson, even if he hadn't been listening. And maybe he had. Maybe he was listening still.

Sooner or later, the Boss would ask her what Finlay had confessed.

When he asked, she'd be forced to tell him, or to lie about it.

Either course was a career killer, for sure. Could be a lot worse, depending on who else asked the questions. Some lies carried heavier consequences than others.

It took her less than a moment to decide to apply the sleeping dogs doctrine, as Gaspar called it. Or to leave well enough alone, as her mother would say.

Someday, she fully expected to be forced to testify about the hunt for Reacher. When that happened, the less she knew, the better.

Besides, she could guess that Finlay's involvement with Reacher back in Margrave wasn't as clearly a combat situation as Holly Johnson's harrowing experience in Montana had been.

Finlay wanted to liken his situation to Johnson's. He wanted to believe he'd had no choice. That was pure fiction.

Finlay had been the chief of police. He was the epitome of power and authority in Margrave. He had a department and training and weapons at his disposal. He'd had other legal options, too, and had chosen not to use them for his own reasons.

Kim took a deep breath and exhaled slowly.

For now, all she needed to know was that Finlay's relationship with Reacher was no cleaner than the Boss's. Both knew a thousand times more than what they'd shared with her so far. Just like Gaspar said, they were both using her. But for what?

She'd become a pawn in whatever game these power brokers were playing.

Pawns, as every casual chess player knew, were utterly disposable. Nothing but cannon fodder.

"So why am I here?" she asked.

Finlay nodded, as if she were a particularly dim pupil. Perhaps she was. "You've proven more resourceful than I expected. I'm not a fan of Charles Cooper, but he did well when he chose you."

She said nothing.

"I have a proposition for you to consider," Finlay said.

"What kind of proposition?"

"As you know, I have resources and access that can help you. I'm offering it to you, more than I have in the past."

She frowned. "In exchange for what?"

"Keep me posted. Let me know when Cooper sends you out and where and why. When you find Reacher, advise me before you turn him over to Cooper."

Her breath caught with surprise. "You believe I will find him, then?"

"Eventually. Mainly because you're a tenacious agent. But it will take you a while. Reacher's playing cat and mouse with Cooper now." Finlay paused and she waited until he continued, "But when Reacher's ready, he'll allow you to find him."

"And when that happens, if I tell you first, what do you plan to do?"

Finlay smiled, but he didn't reply.

She didn't press him.

His plans were another thing she didn't need or want to know.

She made him no promises, either.

The conversation was over. They'd reached the point of mutually assured destruction.

CHAPTER ELEVEN

Thursday, April 14
12:25 a.m.
Glen Haven, New Mexico

THREE HOURS BEFORE HE was abducted the second time, Mason O'Hare's focused concentration was interrupted by a phone call from Cheryl. She rarely called him at night, which heightened the tension that was his constant companion since he'd been kidnapped.

"Hey, you," he said easily when he picked up the call. "What's up?"

"I love you," she replied.

He smiled. She told him that often, but he never tired of hearing it. "I love you, too. But it's late. Can't you sleep?"

"I'm already in bed. I wanted to hear your voice before I drifted off." She sounded sleepy. She got up early most mornings for the dawn balloon rides and then her days were full of kids and a thousand other chores she handled around Glen Haven.

"Have a good sleep. I'll see you tomorrow," he said gently.

He waited a few moments until she said, "Good night."

"Good night, honey," he replied softly. She disconnected and he ended the call, too. He didn't want to risk leaving the connection open. Not tonight.

He returned his attention to his spreadsheets. Ten minutes later, he heard a quiet knock on the door.

"Come in," he said, glancing up from the accounting program on his laptop screen. The door opened slowly.

Gavin Ray crossed the threshold holding two ceramic mugs. He pushed the door closed softly behind him. Gavin was easily distinguished from his younger brother, Bruce, who had a port wine birthmark on his face.

"Good to see you sitting there, same as always. Your eyes are looking a little worse tonight. How's the nose? You feeling okay?" Gavin asked. He was one of the founders of Glen Haven and because of that, he seemed to take a fatherly interest in everyone. His heart was as good as gold. The Rays were the glue that held Glen Haven together.

"I'm doing better, thanks. The doc said it's just a matter of my nose healing now. The black eyes will fade. My headache has subsided. I can concentrate better," Mason replied.

The answer was true, as far as it went. Mason didn't mention the constant terror he couldn't shake. If Gavin knew Mason might attract those dangerous thugs anywhere near Glen Haven, Mason would be out on his ear without so much as a twenty-four-hour warning. He couldn't risk it. Even if telling Gavin might otherwise be a good idea. Which Mason didn't believe for a second, anyway.

"That's good. I'm glad to hear it. Brought you some hot chocolate," Gavin offered him one of the mugs and sat in a chair near the desk.

Mason accepted and sniffed the aroma appreciatively. The hot chocolate was one of the products produced and sold by the Glen Haven community. They bought the cacao seeds from another intentional community in Mexico and processed and mixed the cacao with other things, like cinnamon and pepper. The exact recipe was a secret, but whatever the elixir contained, it was welcome on a cool and windy April evening like this one.

"Thanks, Gavin. Again, I'm sorry about keeping your car so long. When I borrowed it, I expected to be back here in a couple of hours," Mason let his voice trail off.

Concern clouded Gavin's features. "I'm not upset about the car. We're worried about you. I thought the best thing to do was to wait for you to explain what happened. But it's been a few days now and you haven't told us anything."

Mason felt his face flush. He couldn't meet Gavin's patient gaze. He knew he owed them all the whole truth, but instinct held him back. His memory still had gaps and he hadn't been able to explain things to himself yet. He had no answers for everyone else.

"I wish I could tell you exactly what happened, Gavin, I really do. It's like I was drugged or something." Mason drank a sip of the chocolate. "Like I said, I left here headed to lunch and several hours later, I woke up about ten miles north of here in the Chihuahuan desert, with a pounding headache and my nose was a mess. I don't know if I fell on it or what. I walked back toward town and when I reached the first place where I could get a cell signal, I called a taxi. He took me to your car and I drove home."

Gavin frowned. "How did you get all the way out there?"

Mason shook his head and lied. "Dunno. Wish I did."

"Do you think you walked?"

Mason pretended to think about it a second or so before he

shook his head again. "My clothes weren't too dusty or wrinkled. My feet didn't hurt. I'm pretty sure they would have if I'd walked all that way in those shoes. They sure did hurt when I walked back. I've still got blisters."

Gavin thought about that for a bit and then nodded. "What's the last thing you do remember?"

Mason cocked his head, as if he was considering the question.

This was where things could get tricky. Because Mason wasn't ready to tell anyone about his kidnapping. Partly because of the threat. *No cops. We know where you live.*

Partly because he'd persuaded himself that Lawton was the kidnappers' target. He wasn't at any further risk if he just kept quiet.

He must have been caught up in something that had nothing to do with him. He felt lucky to be alive. But he didn't want to involve all of Glen Haven in whatever was going on with Lawton. The good people here deserved to live in peace.

Nor did he want to tell Gavin why he'd gone to lunch at the Last Chance Saloon in the first place.

In the days since he'd returned, Mason had slowly spliced together a few more bits of memory, like working a jigsaw puzzle with a thousand black pieces.

Starting from an arbitrary point two weeks ago, he remembered his phone call to the whistleblower's hot line. He recalled the actions that followed, right up until he was tossed into the back of that van the second time, wearing the canvas hood. His memories picked up again from the point where he woke up in the desert alone.

He'd found Lawton's business card in his suit coat pocket and researched public records. He'd confirmed that Lawton was a Treasury agent based in New York.

Which made sense. Lawton was a Treasury agent. Income tax evasion was the exclusive purview of IRS enforcement. The IRS was part of the Treasury Department, so Lawton was IRS. Mason had contacted IRS in the first place. And he should have remembered that, too.

When he'd mustered the courage, Mason had called the number on Lawton's card. It was a cell phone. After several rings, Lawton's voice had invited him to leave a message.

He'd hung up quickly, but now he was worried that the call could be traced. The last thing he wanted to do was to bring trouble to Glen Haven, to Cheryl and Micah. The very last thing on earth. His call to the whistleblower tip line was meant to get rid of those renters. That's all.

Mason didn't want to explain any of that to Gavin, either. Not yet. Not until he had a chance to fix everything himself.

"You know all about how we founded Glen Haven, don't you, Mason?" Gavin said in his soothing voice.

"I, uh, think so. Yeah," Mason replied, wondering where he was going with this.

Gavin kept talking as if Mason had said nothing. "My brother, Bruce, and I grew up in Montana. We lived in a small community with our parents, very much like Glen Haven. We were peaceful people. We lived off the grid and we were happy."

"Sounds great," Mason said sincerely, because it did. Sounded exactly like the life Mason desperately wanted.

"It *was* great," Gavin replied. "Everything was fine until another guy came along with a militia group who wanted to join up with us."

Mason had heard these stories before. As long as Gavin was talking about the past, he wouldn't be asking questions that

Mason didn't want to answer. So he nodded and sipped the chocolate, encouraging Gavin to continue.

"The guy's militia group planned to start a whole new country on US soil. How crazy is that? Before they knew it, our parents were forced to live deeply embedded in that paramilitary group with nowhere else to go." Gavin paused for a sip of hot chocolate.

"Sounds like a terrible situation for all of you," Mason said, truthfully. He hated conflict of all kinds. He liked accounting. He liked putting the right numbers in the right boxes and adding them up to make sense of the world. None of what had happened to him made any sense at all.

"It was terrible. Eventually, the government swooped in and destroyed our home. The people who had been like family to us were scattered." Gavin nodded, a faraway look on his face, as if he were reliving the bad times again. He shivered, almost involuntarily. "Anyway, it took a while to extricate ourselves from everything. Our parents died and left us with some life insurance money. Eventually, Bruce and I came here with a small group of the survivors. This place was a vacant farm. We were able to buy it and start Glen Haven."

"We're all grateful for that, too, Gavin. Glen Haven is special. We feel lucky to live here," Mason replied, because it was true. He was lucky and he knew it. Which was why he wanted to protect Glen Haven as much as Gavin did.

"We did things right this time. No fighting. No weapons. No bosses or titles or unnecessary rules. We're law abiding citizens," Gavin continued. "We want to live in peace. We want a place of safety for our families. To be self-reliant and happy and not be bothered by anyone or anything. That's all. That's not too much to ask."

"I know," Mason said, nodding, eyes downcast lest he give himself away. He might have brought disaster to them all when he made that whistleblower call. He knew that now. All he wanted was a chance to fix it before things got out of hand. But while Gavin was talking, Mason's thoughts had returned to the reason he'd made the call in the first place. He'd had a simple plan. Somehow, the simple plan had gone horribly wrong. An overwhelming sense of dread consumed him. He lowered his gaze. He could no longer look Gavin in the eye.

"You're one of us, Mason. We're your family now. We'll take care of you. No matter what. Never forget that. When you feel like talking about what happened to you, you know where I am," Gavin said kindly. He rested a reassuring hand on Mason's shoulder as he finished the chocolate and left.

His footsteps echoed on the floors down the hallway until the sound faded to nothing, leaving Mason more miserable than before. He knew what he had to do. He only regretted bringing all of this misery home.

First, he'd collect hard evidence. Then, he'd tell Gavin everything. Gavin would know what to do.

Mason waited more than an hour, to be sure Gavin had retired for the night along with everyone else. Then he quickly changed into black jeans and a black long-sleeved T-shirt. He slipped his hands into black leather gloves and pulled a black ski mask over his head.

He rummaged through his closet until he found the night vision headset he'd ordered online. He turned off the lights in his room, quietly slid the patio door open, and carried the headset into the cool night wind.

CHAPTER TWELVE

Thursday, April 14
1:45 a.m.
Glen Haven, New Mexico

MASON STOOD ON THE darkened patio outside his room for a few moments to allow his eyes to adjust to the near total darkness. His goal was to be as invisible as possible. He had no idea whether he achieved it.

His experience with clandestine operations was acquired by watching movies with Micah. He had no desire to be a spy or a SEAL or whatever. He simply wanted to observe without being seen. And take a few photos for evidence.

It was long past bedtime for Glen Haven residents. The buildings were shrouded in darkness, with only a few weak night lights visible through the windows and security lights outside. Even the moon was dark.

He slipped on his night vision, which amplified the available light and gave things an eerie green glow. Once he'd tried the night vision and realized its limitations, his online research had led him to the conclusion that thermal imaging would have served his needs better. He'd ordered a camera, but it hadn't arrived yet. For now, the night vision and his phone camera was all he had.

He scanned the area to be sure no one else was wandering the grounds. Everyone should have been in bed long ago. But he didn't want to explain himself or run into something worse than a curious insomniac.

Glen Haven compound consisted of eight buildings arranged in a horse-shoe shape around a common lawn. The buildings abutted the herb farm. From the street, the illusion was open spaces beyond individual homes.

Most of the Glen Haven residents lived together in the main house which was at the bottom of the horse-shoe, directly opposite the farmland. Two smaller houses flanked either side of the main house.

Mason glanced back. As he'd expected, the three homes were quiet this time of night.

The remaining buildings were used for the herbal products business. Five structures, all pole barns of various sizes.

The largest one held the Glen Haven Herbs manufacturing operation where the herbs were compounded and packaged. Supplies like gardening equipment, fertilizers and such were received and stored in another large building. Shipping the finished product was handled from the third large pole barn.

The last two, smaller pole barns were Mason's focus tonight. Both were barracks used to house migrant workers who helped with the harvest and processing the fresh herbs. Inside each were bunks, a small eat-in kitchen, and two bathrooms on the ground floor. Both had full basements with more bunks and bathrooms below.

Both barracks buildings were usually vacant until harvest time. Glen Haven residents could handle the planting and the tending. It was harvest work that overwhelmed the farm's small staff and required additional help.

Three months ago, Bruce Ray, Gavin's brother, had leased the two residential buildings to generate a bit of additional income before the harvest season. The tenants were another intentional community, fewer than a dozen people, looking for a temporary home. Two of them had lived in the Rays' Montana community back in the day and Bruce wanted to help them out, he'd said at the time.

The renters had moved in and kept to themselves. They had jobs and they came and went at irregular intervals, he'd noticed. They'd chosen not to mingle with the Glen Haven community and everything seemed to be okay at first.

Until Mason had seen one of the renters in the parking area climbing out of his truck while carrying a gun, which caused all kinds of alarm bells to go off in his head.

Guns were forbidden at Glen Haven. Gavin and Bruce had had enough of guns when their Montana home was destroyed years ago. They were adamant. No firearms of any kind were allowed on the premises, period. Not for any reason.

He'd reported the guy to Bruce immediately.

Bruce's response was not what Mason had expected. He'd told Mason not to worry. He'd said the tenants were only temporary. They planned to go soon. Bruce said he'd take care of it, tell them they couldn't carry guns here. Mason had wanted to believe him.

And then he and Lawton were abducted.

Mason had persuaded himself that John Lawton had been the target. But was that true?

He worried that reporting the guy with the gun had put a target on his own back and put Glen Haven at risk, too. He didn't get a good look at the kidnappers. He couldn't say for sure whether they were part of the group living in the bunkhouses. But he worried about it.

He had a bad feeling about them. They were not the kind of people who belonged at Glen Haven. Cheryl and Micah weren't safe here with strangers carrying guns around the premises.

Mason wanted those renters gone. He didn't think Gavin could do the job.

Which was why he'd made the call. He wanted the feds to get rid of those people. He wasn't sure how they could do it. But he believed it was possible.

Problem was, owning guns was not a crime. Nor was carrying them around the grounds or even in their vehicles, necessarily. He needed more.

Which was why he'd started watching them as surreptitiously as possible a couple of weeks ago. And he'd finally found something he could blow the whistle on them for. Something that had worked to get the IRS involved.

Which could have been what got him snatched up with Lawton.

As stealthily as possible, Mason made his way from the main house to the outbuildings. The two barracks shared a parking area off to the side. He counted eight vehicles parked there, two more than the last time he'd looked. Six trucks and two SUVs.

He crept along the back of the vehicles. He pulled off his night vision and used his cell phone to take quick snapshots of the dusty license plates, while shielding the flashes as well as possible with his body.

The vehicles were registered in Arizona and Texas. He figured they could have been stolen.

Quickly, he emailed the images to himself just in case something happened to his phone, and then he dropped the phone into his pocket.

He repositioned his night vision and crept toward the back of the farthest barracks building. A thin stream of smoke wafted from the chimney on the north end. Dim lighting from the appliances in the small kitchen emitted through the window and was amplified by his headset.

He flattened his back against the exterior siding and leaned forward to peer into the building's open floor plan. A small fire was burning in the fireplace. A man sat in a rocking chair with a shotgun across his lap, chin on his chest, as if he'd been staring into the fire and fell asleep.

The shotgun started Mason's pulse hammering hard in his ears. Why would they need a night watchman with a gun?

With his night vision in place, the fire's glow illuminated the whole room. It was a mess. The dining table was strewn with unwashed plates and flatware. A few empty beer bottles clustered at one end. Dirty pots and pans were stacked on the stove.

Mason quickly counted the plates. Twelve. Which probably meant at least a dozen people were sleeping in the bunks down below or in the second barracks building. He might have been able to confirm his suspicions if he'd had the infrared camera. He could have counted the heat signatures from their bodies.

He fumbled to retrieve his phone and snapped a few photos through the window without the flash. The snaps probably wouldn't reveal very much, but he had to try to document what he'd seen. As he had with the license plates, he quickly sent the photos to himself.

A door opened on the opposite end of the room. A man approached the coffee maker and poured a cup of coffee that had probably been made with the evening meal hours ago.

He carried the cup over to the sleeping sentry and touched him on the shoulder. The first man startled awake, handed the shotgun to the new guy, and headed off to bed. Mason snapped a couple more photos, attempting to capture their faces in the dim firelight.

If either man said anything, Mason didn't hear the exchange. Nor could he see the two men clearly enough to identify them. They could have been part of the team that attacked him. But he couldn't say for sure.

Mason ducked and sent the photos into cyberspace. And then he crept toward the second barracks building. The interior lighting was somewhat stronger in the second building. When he looked through the window, he saw a similar scene. Messy kitchen, dinnerware strewn about, and a man sitting in front of the fireplace with a shotgun across his lap.

But he was not alone.

Two men were sitting at the long kitchen table. Handguns rested beside them. A clear plastic bag filled with flat, white pills was in the center of the table.

The men watched as two scrawny young women counted the pills and dropped them into small plastic bags. They closed each bag carefully and dropped it into another box.

Mason flipped his phone to record video of the scene and let the video run for a couple of minutes. Then he took a few still photos. The images were likely to be dark and out of focus, but they'd be better than nothing.

Again, he sent the photos and the video to himself. Just in case.

He backed away from the barracks and carefully made his way home. His heart was heavy with the knowledge that his worst fears had been confirmed.

Not only were the tenants carrying guns, they were drug dealers. And those scrawny women couldn't have been more than teenagers. No way were they old enough to make their own decisions, even if they'd joined the others voluntarily, which Mason doubted.

He hadn't seen Lawton in either barracks. Had these men taken him? Or was the kidnapping a separate incident all together?

Mason shook his head. Not likely to have been separate, was it?

When he'd first called in the anonymous tip, he'd only been worried about the guns. Now, he had hard evidence of worse criminal activities. Mason thought the feds would be more inclined to do something about these people now. If they had kidnapped Lawton, then both the FBI and the IRS would come down on them like a ton of bricks, surely.

The problem now was how to stay anonymous and how to keep Glen Haven from being destroyed in the process. Would anyone believe that Glen Haven wasn't neck deep in the crimes? Not likely. He needed a better plan.

Mason made it safely back, pulled off his night vision, slid inside, and locked the door behind him. He glanced at the digital clock beside his bed. It was after three in the morning. He couldn't call anyone at this hour and it was too dangerous to make the call from Glen Haven, anyway.

He peeled his ski mask off and closed the heavy drapes before he flipped the light on.

"You're one stupid gringo, O'Hare," the big man said from

the chair across the room, shaking his head sorrowfully. "We gave you a second chance. All you had to do was keep your nose out of our business."

Mason remembered the voice. The leader of the kidnappers. The one they called Hector. No doubt at all.

Mason's mouth dried up as he stared at the shotgun pointed directly at him.

CHAPTER THIRTEEN

Thursday, April 14
2:50 a.m.
Detroit, Michigan

KIM'S PERSONAL CELL PHONE pinged on her bedside table, signaling a new text message. She rolled over in a sleepy fog, lifted the phone, and squinted against the bright light to read the curious words on the screen.

"Can't make dinner tonight. Still in Albuquerque with Ross. Join me here? xoxo JT"

She frowned. The text was bizarre on several levels. Which meant simply ignoring it and going back to sleep was not an option.

She tossed the covers aside and headed to the kitchen, carrying the phone. She started the coffee maker and read the words again. They were even more curious the fourth time through.

While the coffee brewed, she hurried to get dressed and collect a fresh disposable phone from her bedside table.

As she showered, she analyzed the message again. Everything about it was wrong.

For starters, the text message itself was total fiction.

She and Lawton didn't have a dinner date tonight. She had no idea who Ross was. There was no way Lawton would have invited her to Albuquerque for dinner, expecting her to drop everything and fly out there. Nor had he ever have signed any message with "xoxo JT."

All of which meant the text message was meant to be something else entirely.

Leading to a host of disturbing issues.

The text appeared to have been sent from John Lawton's phone. Which probably meant his phone had been stolen, cloned, or the number was spoofed.

Only low-level expertise would have been required. A savvy teenage hacker could have done it.

More concerning was that the sender knew Lawton had traveled to Albuquerque on business a week ago. Was he still there? She had no idea.

Lawton worked on matters that he couldn't share with her. To be fair, she didn't share much about her work, either.

They'd been dating off and on, when they had the time, for a couple of months. Sometimes weeks passed when they didn't connect at all.

The reality was that their relationship was casual. Their lives were not so intertwined. She had no intimate knowledge of his exact whereabouts.

So Lawson's absence wasn't noteworthy and Kim's ignorance of his activities wasn't atypical, either. He could have traveled around the world since she'd seen him last, and she might have, too.

She pulled her still-damp black hair into a low chignon on the back of her neck and headed toward the kitchen.

She poured coffee into a to-go cup, grabbed her coat and her gun. She left her personal cell phone on the table, added the new burner to the other essentials in her pockets, and headed toward the elevator.

From the first floor, she pushed through the lobby doors to the dark, windy street. She was reminded again that Detroit was not the city that never sleeps. In the wee small hours of the morning, many streets were deserted.

She glanced around, looking for a ride, but taxis were scarcer than innocent felons at this hour. She hustled a couple of blocks to a taxi stand outside a hot sheets hotel where she'd helped to shut down a human trafficking ring a couple of months ago. She settled into the back seat of a dirty cab waiting at the end of the line.

"Greektown Casino, please," she said to the driver, naming a place that would provide decent cover and operated twenty-four-seven.

The driver rolled out and pushed the button on the meter, all without speaking. He was no doubt used to customers who didn't want to be traced. He could probably be trusted to keep his mouth shut for the right price. She had a fifty-dollar bill in her pocket, which she'd give him at the end of the short ride, intended to buy his silence should anyone ask about her.

From the back seat of the cab, she fired up the new burner and dialed Gaspar. She let the phone ring twice and hung up, which was their signal. She knew he'd be awake. He slept whenever he could, but never well or long. He'd soon call her back on a new phone from a secure location.

The taxi driver dropped her off at the casino. She gave him the fifty and watched him drive away. Then she made her way inside. The place was busy enough. The more activity, the less likely she'd be noticed, and the harder it would be to isolate her activities from all the others.

She found a relatively quiet corner where four slot machines were arranged facing each other. None of the four were occupied and she wanted to keep it that way.

She pulled four twenties out of her pocket and slipped one bill into each of the four slots. She set each machine for one credit per play, twenty-five cents each, attempting to stretch her eighty bucks as far as possible. Slowly, she pushed the buttons, one at a time. Won nothing. Waited a bit. Repeated the process.

She burned through almost fifty dollars and about twenty minutes time before Gaspar rang back on the new disposable phone. She picked up the call.

"Good morning, Suzie Wong," Gaspar said before she had a chance to answer, a weariness in his tone that confirmed he'd never slept tonight at all.

"Sorry to bother you so late," she replied. Since he had retired from the FBI, he'd taken a new job with Scarlett Investigations, a private investigative firm based in Houston. He was also a father of five and no longer her partner. No longer on call twenty-four-seven, either. All of which meant he owed her nothing and he had plenty to do.

She'd tried to respect his boundaries. But he'd offered to help and he remained the only one she trusted implicitly when it came to hunting Reacher. She kept him in the loop and talked to him regularly, precisely so she could call on him for help when she needed it.

She'd also developed a sort of sixth sense where Reacher was concerned. Maybe she was stretching things here, but somehow, her gut said, the puzzling text message involved Reacher. Gaspar could help her sort things out.

"What do you need?" Gaspar said.

She kept it short. "Seems like John Lawton might be in trouble."

He must have heard the background noises, the unmistakable pings and jingles of dozens of slot machines, blaring televisions, conversations and more, because he replied, "You called me from a casino at three-thirty in the morning to talk about your love life?"

She ignored the quip and punched another credit into each of the four slots. "Somehow, Reacher's involved."

He sighed. "And you know this how?"

"I had a meeting with Finlay. His request." She paused to feel his disapproval across the miles and let him get it out of his system. "He introduced me to Holly Johnson, an FBI agent with an old connection to Reacher. Fifteen years ago, after Margrave, the two of them survived a kidnapping and a firefight with some wacko militia group gone rogue. She said she hasn't seen Reacher since, but she's still a fan. One hundred percent."

"No accounting for taste, I guess," Gaspar said sourly.

He understood Reacher thoroughly. They came from similar backgrounds and had similar experiences. But that's where the common threads ended.

Gaspar was as straight as they come. He was steady, reliable, dependable in every way.

But after an unconventional army career as a military cop, Reacher had become a vagrant and a vigilante. He was a hero to some and a criminal to others. And he was one of the least dependable men on the planet.

Gaspar didn't approve of Reacher and didn't trust him. Not at all. He made no secret of the fact.

Kim said, "Finlay had told Johnson that I was dating Lawton before I arrived. How did he know that? And more importantly, why mention it to Johnson?"

"Go on," Gaspar's ears had perked up like a dog hearing a whistle.

His reaction confirmed her instincts. He'd always thought she should be just as wary around Finlay as she was around Reacher and the Boss. All with good reason.

"An hour ago, I got a fake text, claiming to be from Lawton inviting me to Albuquerque for dinner tonight. On the surface, it seems okay, if you know nothing about me or Lawton. Mentions someone named Ross." She took a deep breath. "The message signed off with x-o-x-o and his initials."

"I take it none of this is normal."

"Not even remotely."

"And you think Finlay sent the text," Gaspar said, as if her conclusion was rock solid when it was anything but. "Let's be logical. Why would Finlay want you to go to Albuquerque? And if he did want you there, why not simply tell you himself? It's not like he's ever failed to make his wishes plain before."

"If I knew all the answers, Chico, why would I be talking to you?" She teased, although she was uneasy. "I didn't try calling Lawton. Whoever sent the text is probably monitoring his phone and mine, too. I didn't forward the text anywhere. The Boss is likely to get a copy of it soon enough without me putting a red flag on it by sending it around."

After a moment, Gaspar asked, "All right. Let's parse this thing. Is Lawton in Albuquerque?"

"Possibly. He said he was headed out there last week to meet with a whistleblower. Somebody looking for a big reward for tattling on friends and colleagues who are allegedly cheating on their taxes. He does a lot of that sort of investigation and we didn't talk about it much." She ran a hand over her hair. "Haven't heard from Lawton since he left. He could be in Albuquerque or on the moon at the moment as far as I know."

She waited while Gaspar considered the intel.

"Just to be clear," Gaspar said after a bit, "you're thinking what, exactly?"

She took a deep breath, fully aware that her suspicions might sound a little paranoid to a normal person. Fortunately, she didn't think like a normal person anymore and neither did he.

She walked him through it, one point at a time.

"Everything about hunting Reacher is hinky and off the books," she said.

The assignment was ongoing. It came directly from the Boss. Only Kim and Gaspar knew the specifics and they'd been told to keep it that way.

"Right."

"The operation is so dark that only the three of us should have known about it."

"Until Finlay got involved, and then four people knew," Gaspar replied. "Which was problematic enough. Now there are five."

"Yes." She knew he meant Reacher had to know. There was no other way to explain his actions in the past few weeks.

Gaspar continued, "Which means one of the five is our suspect for the fake text. Neither of us sent it. So which one of the other three did?"

"The Boss has more direct ways of communicating with me. Reacher would have sent a less cryptic message." She paused for a quick breath. "Which leaves Finlay."

"He gave you a direct number a while back. Why didn't you call him instead of me?" Gaspar said.

"If we're right, the text was a clear signal not to contact Finlay using the usual method." Which was odd, too. The whole point of the private number he'd given her early on was to provide a direct line between them.

"I'll do some digging. When are you going to Albuquerque?" Gaspar asked, just when one of her plays happened to hit a noisy jackpot and the machine went a little crazy with the bells and whistles.

"Today. I don't know what's going on, but it involves Reacher," she replied. "Finlay would have no reason to prod me to action otherwise."

"You think it's wise to go after Reacher alone?" Gaspar said, making it plain that he didn't think so. Not at all. But it was an argument he'd never win, and when she didn't respond, he let it go.

Gaspar sighed. "What about the Boss? Cooper will be suspicious when he can't find you. How are you going to do all of this and stay under his radar?"

"I'll be forced to call Finlay. Let him run interference, if I need it. There's no way around it." She paused. "Unless you have a better idea."

He didn't approve of Finlay. But he had no brilliant alternatives to offer, either. He said nothing.

"Just as I thought. When there's only one choice, it's the right choice," she said flatly.

"So why are you talking to me?" Gaspar said sourly.

"Looking for something I've missed, I guess." She noticed another woman hanging around like maybe one of these four was her lucky slot machine.

Kim glared at the woman, turned her back, and fed more rounds into the one-armed bandits. The woman hovered a bit and then left. There was a whole casino full of machines.

"I'll run interference with Cooper for you. He'll call me. When he does, I'll keep him out of your way as long as I can. That's the best I can do," Gaspar finally replied.

"Thanks," Kim said.

"Should I say you've eloped with your lover?" Gaspar teased. "Tell him you're on a secluded island without access to electronics?"

"Yeah. That's just perfect." Kim curled her upper lip. "You doing stand-up comedy in your spare time now, Chico?"

He laughed and briefly it seemed like they were on the same team again. Too bad they weren't. She preferred working with a partner. Call it training or common sense. Either way, two guns were better than one. She popped another antacid into her mouth.

"Keep me in the loop. I'll try to track this burner. But when you ditch it, I won't have any way to find you," Gaspar said.

She took a deep, shaky breath, and popped another antacid into her mouth. "Okay, so when we hang up here, I'm calling Finlay. Find out what he knows. Then I'm off to Albuquerque. Too risky to call Lawton, so I'll just have to hope he's still there. Or that I can find Ross, whoever he is, and learn what's going on. I'll touch base with you as often as I can."

"Meanwhile, send me the reports you got from Holly Johnson."

"Already done."

"Good. I can follow up on those while you're in the air. I'll see if I can learn anything about Lawton's activities. And I'll find out who 'Ross' is, assuming he exists. Let me know if there's anything else you need. I'll be here." He paused briefly, as if he wanted to be sure she heard his next words. "Watch out for yourself, Suzie Wong. Finlay's agenda, whatever it is, can bite you in the ass."

"Thanks, Chico. Give my love to Marie and the kids. We'll talk again soon," she promised and hung up.

She looked at the burner a couple of seconds. She'd hold onto it for now. But Gaspar was right. If she held the phone too long, the Boss would find her. She'd need to destroy it. Soon.

Then she pulled Finlay's burner out of her other pocket and pressed redial. He picked up instantly, which was a little unnerving.

"Took you long enough," he said. "Russell's out front with your ride. We'll be wheels up in ninety minutes."

Without comment, she disconnected, dropped Finlay's phone into her pocket along with Gaspar's, and considered his use of the word "we" as she walked swiftly toward the exit.

CHAPTER FOURTEEN

Thursday, April 14
6:07 a.m.
En route to Albuquerque, New Mexico

KIM WAS BELTED FIRMLY into her seat in Finlay's spacious and luxuriously appointed private jet. Weather was calm and clear all the way to Albuquerque, the pilot had said before takeoff. Nonstop flight-time was projected at three hours and forty minutes.

They'd had breakfast and coffee and exchanged very few words so far. Finlay had called this meeting and Kim waited for him to explain himself. So far, he hadn't.

She unbuckled her seatbelt and stood to stretch. She had come aboard with nothing but the clothes she was wearing when she left her apartment and the contents of her pockets. Wallet, badge, gun, and three burner phones. One of which was still fresh. She planned to remain off the grid as long as possible, but if the Boss had reason to look, he'd find her before the jet landed. He was that well connected.

"You don't have a spare toothbrush aboard, do you?" she asked.

Finlay grinned. "You'll find everything you need in the bathroom. When you finish, we'll talk."

She nodded and made her way past the bunks toward the tail section of the plane. Like everything else aboard, the bathroom was spacious and nicely appointed. She opened the medicine cabinet and found a fresh folding toothbrush and a sample-sized tube of toothpaste. She used them both and dropped the folding toothbrush into her pocket. It was compact and convenient to carry. The next place she stayed might not be as well stocked.

She splashed water on her face and dried with a freshly laundered towel. A few strands of black hair had worked away from the knot at the nape of her neck, so she tucked them into place. Nothing she could do about the dark circles under her eyes until she got some sleep.

She returned to her seat across from Finlay in the main cabin, buckled her seatbelt and waited, ready to hear whatever he had to say.

He pushed a button to lower a flat screen television across the cabin. He pressed a button to begin a slide show presentation. The first slide was a typical FBI head shot photo of a clean-cut guy, south of forty, close-cropped sandy hair, weary brown eyes.

"This is FBI Special Agent Peter Ross. Albuquerque Field Office. Temporarily assisting the Gang and Criminal Organization Task Force," Finlay said. "He may be John Lawton's contact in Albuquerque."

"Lawton is Treasury. IRS enforcement." Kim raised her eyebrows. "Albuquerque has a gang Ross wants to take down for tax evasion? Seems a little tame compared to the more violent crimes gangs do."

"The situation is complicated. More on that in a minute," Finlay said, moving to the next slide. "Mason O'Hare, CPA."

This one was another formal head shot, probably from a state business license photo. A plain vanilla guy, mid-thirties, brown hair, brown eyes. Maybe a little heavier and softer than Ross, but just as bland and boring.

Nothing at all remarkable about O'Hare that would turn heads on the street. The name meant nothing to her.

"Pinto Vigo," Finlay said to identify the man in the next photo.

An involuntary shudder ran through her. She'd seen this exact photo before and recognized the man instantly. He was unmistakable.

Pinto Vigo's was the kind of face that small children conjured in their nightmares. Pockmarked cheeks, deeply scarred. Hard eyes stared from beneath heavy brows drawn together, frowning over the sneer on his full lips. In other photos, she'd seen his teeth. Two were gold crowns, one top and one bottom, left and right of center. What dentists would call numbers nine and twenty-six.

Having seen Pinto Vigo once, you'd steer clear if you had any sense at all.

Finlay said, "Pinto Vigo is one of Mexico's most notorious drug lords and leader of an extremely violent criminal cartel. He learned his trade at his father's knee. Machado Vigo was one of the FBI's most wanted fugitives for two decades."

Kim nodded. If Vigo was involved, the situation just became a thousand times worse. The shudder coursed through her body now in a continuous loop, like a taser charge to the belly.

"After an extensive manhunt, Machado Vigo was charged and convicted of killing two DEA agents. He died in a federal prison two years later at the hands of a rival gang." Finlay sounded like he was briefing a task force. "His son, Pinto Vigo, was twenty-seven when he took over the family business."

Vigo's cartel had infiltrated large swaths of the country, usually settling in small rural communities that attracted migrant workers. Once they'd settled in, they trafficked drugs and laundered money. In some of the larger areas, the cartel trafficked guns and humans, too.

Vigo's cartel hadn't reached Detroit yet, but the field office there was vigilant. They expected him to make the effort. And when he did, he was likely to succeed. The demand for drugs seemed insatiable. It was basic Business 101, supply and demand. Vigo had the supply and he'd go where demand already existed.

"All of these elements tied together somehow?" Kim asked when Finlay finished reciting facts she already knew about Vigo.

Finlay nodded. "And a few more. Bear with me."

The next slide was an aerial photo of what could only be described as a compound of some sort.

"This is Glen Haven," Finlay said. "It's what's called an intentional community these days. Sort of like a self-sufficient commune. It sits north of Albuquerque."

She counted eight large buildings arranged in a horseshoe shape. The three at the toe of the shoe looked like McMansions, with the one in the center about twice the size of the two that flanked it. The other five were outbuildings of some sort. Three smaller ones on one branch of the shoe and two on the other branch. The U shape opened onto a field planted with crops she couldn't identify from the bird's-eye view.

"At last count, there were twenty-seven full-time Glen Haven residents, including Mason O'Hare. There are three kids, all about the same age. The rest are adults. Residents live in the three mansions. All of the buildings have full basements. The two bunkhouses are for migrant workers who help with the harvest of plants used in the manufacturing of herbal supplements," Finlay explained. "The other outbuildings are used for the herbal business and to store hot air balloon equipment."

Finlay put up another slide. Two photos side by side. Both men. Obviously brothers. Dark hair, dark eyes. Both late thirties, Kim guessed. Only the port wine stain birthmark on the younger brother's forehead easily distinguished them.

"Gavin and Bruce Ray are the co-founders of Glen Haven. Their father was James Ray. Called himself Gavin," Finlay said. "You read about Gavin Ray in the reports Holly Johnson gave you. Gavin Ray saved Reacher's life back then and paid the price. He almost died trying. Holly thinks Reacher would take a dim view of threats to Gavin Ray's sons. She thinks Reacher might show up to help them out of a jam like this."

"And Pinto Vigo is threatening the sons?" Kim asked, frowning.

"We're not sure what's going on, exactly." Finlay shut down the slideshow and turned to face her. "Ten days ago, Mason O'Hare called in an anonymous whistleblower complaint on the tip line. He reported suspected tax evasion by renters out at Glen Haven."

"Renters?"

"Apparently, Bruce Ray, the younger brother, rented the two bunk houses to some group of transients that seems to be evading taxes, according to O'Hare."

Kim nodded. "How would O'Hare know they were evading taxes?"

"O'Hare's a CPA. He does freelance accounting for a few clients."

"Including Pinto Vigo's cartel and Glen Haven and the Ray brothers?"

"We don't know what connection O'Hare has to Vigo and the cartel. But yes, O'Hare keeps the books for Glen Haven and the Ray brothers," Finlay said, "All three are in full compliance with the tax code as far as we know."

"So who is O'Hare blowing the whistle on for tax evasion? And please don't tell me Pinto Vigo," Kim replied. "Saying drug cartels violate the tax code is like saying ice cream is cold."

Finlay grinned. "Just because it's obvious doesn't make it any less true."

Kim scowled toward him. "And let me guess. Lawton called FBI Special Agent Ross for intel because he's local."

"Probably that, and they're buddies. Known each other awhile and worked together before. We don't know exactly because they never got a chance to discuss any of this," Finlay explained, waving his hand toward the big screen.

Kim frowned. "Why not?"

"Lawton called Ross at home. Presumably because he didn't want the FBI Albuquerque field office knowing his business. He didn't tell Ross why he was in town, but he planned to meet Ross later."

"Makes sense."

"It does. But it didn't work out that way."

"Again, why not?"

"Because Lawton connected with O'Hare at a place called

the Last Chance Saloon. That was Monday, early afternoon."
Finlay paused. "Lawton hasn't been seen since."

Kim felt a hard gnawing in her belly. Should she have
known something had happened to Lawton? Sensed it
somehow? "Has Ross tried to follow up?"

"He's called Lawton a couple of times. Left messages."

She didn't ask how Finlay knew about Lawton's phone
activity. No reason to ask. Every single phone call that
happened inside the US was recorded somewhere these days.
Finlay's resources were vast. He'd have located and heard the
actual conversations and the voice mails, too.

He was worried. Which meant Lawton had something to be
worried about, too.

"What does O'Hare know about the Vigo cartel operating
at Glen Haven?"

"That's one of the things you'll need to find out. And it
won't be easy."

She shrugged. "Seems simple enough to me. Just ask
O'Hare. If he's willing to blow the whistle on some things, he
probably knows a lot more."

"Possibly. But O'Hare disappeared a few hours ago,"
Finlay replied gravely.

Every piece of intel Finlay shared made the situation worse.
How the hell was she supposed to deal with this alone?

"Why aren't the FBI and IRS looking for Lawton? He's a
federal agent. They can't just hang him out to dry." Kim was
angry and made no effort to conceal it.

"Assuming they've figured out that Lawton's been
abducted, which we're not clear on just yet. Then the answer is
the same reason they didn't go after Holly Johnson when she
was abducted with Reacher fifteen years ago. Too risky."

Finlay shook his head. "SWAT teams armed to the teeth storming a peaceful commune doesn't make good television. One screw-up and things can get really ugly, very fast. That's where political and agency careers go to die. We've all seen it happen before. Nobody's willing to take that bet. Not without better intel than we have now, anyway."

He was right. What he said made no sense to a reasonable person, but she understood it. She knew how politicians think. Agency heads, too, for that matter. Nobody wants to risk doing the right thing if it means their own heads on a platter unless they're damn sure first. Especially when civilians are involved.

Kim waited a moment to let everything he'd said sink in. She glanced at the clock. The flight would land in Albuquerque in about an hour, give or take. Not much time to get herself fully up to speed.

"So you think all of this is somehow connected to Reacher and that's why you pulled me in?" Kim cocked her head.

Finlay shrugged. "We never know for sure where Reacher's going to turn up. Most of the time, I doubt that he knows before he gets there. Usually he just steps off the bus or out of a ride he's hitched along the back roads and walks into trouble. Tough to track a guy like Reacher, as you well know."

Kim narrowed her gaze to study his micro expressions. In half a second, she'd reached her conclusion.

He *knew* Reacher would come. Might even be there already.

Otherwise, Finlay wouldn't have spent five minutes thinking about O'Hare or Ross or the commune or even Pinto Vigo. Fighting drug cartels across America was a constant game of whack-a-mole. Finlay wouldn't be on the ground in that effort. That's what federal agencies were for. He certainly wouldn't have bothered to scoop her up and personally bring her out here. No doubt in her mind.

He wanted Reacher.

Like Gaspar said, Finlay was using her to get Reacher. Which meant he couldn't get to Reacher on his own.

Same as the Boss. They wanted her to lure Reacher into the open.

And then what?

Didn't matter just yet. For once, she was hoping they were both right.

Because she couldn't leave Lawton to die at the hands of Vigo's cartel. No matter what their relationship was or wasn't, she would not abandon him.

Nor could she do this alone. Vigo's cartel was one of the most ruthless gangs on this or any other continent. They'd killed two mothers and four children in cold blood simply for driving where they didn't belong in Mexico. They'd done worse to countless others.

She wouldn't abandon anyone to that fate. And certainly not Lawton.

Once she retrieved him, she could think about their relationship going forward. Or not.

She'd need help finding Lawton and getting him out of whatever he'd gotten himself into.

And Reacher just might be the right man for the job.

First things first.

She said, "Start over. Tell me everything you know. Don't leave anything out this time."

CHAPTER FIFTEEN

Thursday, April 14
6:30 a.m.
Glen Haven, New Mexico

THE KIDNAPPER HAD MARCHED Mason across the compound, into the first barracks, and shoved him down the steps into the dark basement. He tumbled awkwardly to the concrete floor and landed hard on one shoulder. The pain forced a yelp from his lips before he could squelch it.

He looked around wildly but saw nothing in the all-consuming blackness. Even his night vision would have been useless here because there was zero ambient light to be amplified.

He lay on the cold floor, rubbing his sore shoulder, hoping it wasn't broken, listening for sounds he could name. He heard nothing recognizable in his dank prison.

From time to time, heavy footfalls crossed the floor above, and a toilet flushed. Aside from the cold seeping through the concrete, he suffered total sensory deprivation until his eyelids grew heavy and he dozed off.

A quick, hard push from a boot to his belly awakened him. Mason's eyes popped open. At first it seemed the basement was flooded with light. He blinked a few times and shielded his eyes from the glare with his forearm.

"Get up, O'Hare," came a rough command as the man moved away.

Mason almost recognized the voice. He'd heard it before, but where? He moved his forearm slowly, allowing his pupils to adjust in short bursts until he could peer into the semi-darkness.

He was lying in a cone of light but the edges of the room were shadowed. He crabbed slowly to his feet, kneading his sore shoulder, checking his joints for dislocations and the like.

"How long have I been out?" he asked, peering into the shadows.

"About four hours, give or take," the harsh voice replied.

Which was when Mason remembered. Lawton. The Treasury agent he'd met for lunch at the Last Chance Saloon. He relaxed slightly. A government agent wasn't likely to kill him in cold blood, he figured.

His brain started to work again. Mason had been in the basements of both barracks buildings before. He squinted and tried to recall the layout.

Migrant workers showered and slept here and relaxed for a bit before bed. Nothing fancy was required or provided. Bunk beds lined the walls. The left side of the room was furnished as a small sitting room. A television was mounted on the wall. There were two bathrooms with showers on the opposite side.

Lawton's voice had come from the direction of the sitting area.

Mason cleared his throat and asked, "You've been watching me all this time?"

"Not necessary. You aren't capable of killing me in my sleep, even if you had the guts to try. Which we both know from our experiences in the desert that you don't have," Lawton replied harshly.

Mason shot back, "What did you want me to do? You're the one with the training. You couldn't get us out of there. What could possibly give you the idea that I might have done something more effective?"

He hobbled over and plopped down on a chair close enough to see and be seen, but out of reach. Just in case. He glanced across the gloom. Even in the dim light, it was obvious that Lawton looked much worse than when they'd been pushed into that van six days ago.

He was still wearing the same clothes, but the suit was filthy and his jacket was ripped. His face looked like he'd gone a few rounds with a competent heavyweight, but his hands weren't scraped up. So he'd probably been restrained while they pummeled him.

Mason shuddered when he realized his situation could have been so much worse.

Lawton had to be hurting and he wasn't wasting any energy. He was relaxed and staying ready. But ready for what?

Mason took a breath, felt the soreness in his shoulder and the rumbling in his gut. He wasn't wearing a watch and there were no basement windows to given him a glimpse into the normal world.

How long had he been asleep? Was it daylight yet?

When would someone notice he was missing again and come looking for him?

Lawton might have been happy to sit quietly for a time, but Mason wasn't. He asked, "Who kidnapped you?"

"What makes you think I was the target?" Lawton replied.

Mason's breath caught. He raised his eyebrows. "I'm a CPA. Nobody would want to kidnap me. You were the target and I got scooped up by mistake. Nothing else makes sense."

"How so?"

"Nobody knew I was going to be there. Can you say the same thing?" Mason said testily, because he felt a little panicked at the very thought that he might be kidnapped and killed and no one would know.

Lawton didn't respond.

Mason insisted. "You didn't call somebody? Mention where we were having lunch?"

"I might have. Casually. Nothing more. But the chances of anyone I know working with a criminal cartel to kidnap me are exactly zero," Lawton growled. "Can you say the same thing?"

"They must be listening to your phone calls. Not that hard to do these days, is it?" Mason wasn't a clandestine operative, but he did like to watch movies. He knew what was going on in the crime world. Sort of.

Lawton shrugged.

"Any federal agent makes enemies," Mason said, continuing with his logic. "It was a well-planned operation. Must have taken some time to set it up. Probably based on surveillance, right? They knew where you were going. They followed you. Prepared to snatch you up. Which they did. I was just unlucky. Wrong place, wrong time. That's all."

Lawton narrowed his gaze but said nothing.

Mason's panic kicked up a notch. "I mean, they let me go. They kept you. You're the intended hostage."

"If you say so," Lawton replied with a shrug.

Mason nodded definitively, as if he'd made up his mind.

"If they'd wanted me, why leave me alive out there in the desert, huh? Why wasn't it me here in the dark waiting for you to wake up instead of the other way around?"

Lawton remained quiet for a few long minutes, until his silence began to get on Mason's nerves. It was one thing to sit in solitude. Quite another to sit in the dark with Lawton and have no communication at all.

"How are we going to get out of here?" Mason finally asked.

"Wish I could say I had a plan," Lawton replied. "I don't even know where we are. The only place I've seen since I got here is this room."

"We're at Glen Haven. This is a basement. We're underneath one of the barracks buildings we use for migrant workers when we need them for the harvest," Mason said.

Lawton nodded. "And you know this because?"

"Because I live here. Well, not here in this building. But here at Glen Haven. In the main residence."

"Still think this has nothing to do with you?"

Mason widened his eyes. His mouth rounded and his breath poofed out. "What do you mean?"

"You called the whistleblower hot line. You said there were men with illegal guns who were living at Glen Haven. You said they were engaged in criminal activities. You said they were evading taxes. That's how you got me out here."

Mason nodded. "Yeah, but they don't know that."

Lawton cocked his head. "No? Evidence suggests the odds are against you on that one, pal. Spill it. See if we can turn this thing around."

Mason took a deep breath and told what he knew, starting with his recon efforts last night and ending with the guns, drugs, and women in the other barracks building.

Lawton narrowed his eyes and kept his comments to himself. He asked no questions until Mason finished his story. He spent a nanosecond analyzing the intel.

Flatly, Lawton said, "So Gavin Ray came to your room for a late night chat. An hour later, you were marched over here at gunpoint and tossed down the stairs."

Mason's heart stopped. His breath stopped, too.

Lawton nodded. "Still think this whole thing isn't about you?"

He knew what Lawton was saying. Gavin Ray had betrayed him. He accepted the truth, but he couldn't speak at all.

Mason shook his head miserably as he struggled to fill his lungs.

Lawton's tone was hard-edged now. "Start by explaining exactly what Glen Haven is. Are you a crazy militia? Survivalist nuts? What?"

Mason gasped. "No. Not survivalists. Certainly not militia. Not nuts, either. We're preppers."

"Yeah? And in your mind, what's the difference?"

"We're not here to hurt anybody. We stockpile the basics like water and food. We've got generators. Some gasoline. Propane. Stuff like that." Mason shrugged. "In case of a disaster, you know? To get us through it until it's over. We're prepared. That's all."

"Prepared? You mean like for a hurricane or an earthquake? Or do you take it further?" Lawton asked. "Tell me you have weapons stored that we can use to get the hell out of here."

Mason shook his head. "We have weapons. Locked up. In the main house. Just for emergencies. Nothing out here, except what they've got with them upstairs."

"Which means they're armed and we're not. How well prepared is that?" Lawton said.

Mason perked up, as if he'd just remembered something important.

"What?" Lawton asked.

"I'm supposed to work the ground crew for a ride at dusk."

"What kind of ride?" Lawton asked.

"We offer hot air balloon rides to tourists."

"What?"

"You know, for extra cash. Best times to fly are dawn and dusk. My girlfriend, Cheryl, is one of our pilots. We've got rides scheduled today."

Lawton stared at him as if he'd lost his mind. "And that's a good thing?"

"Yes. Because Cheryl will come looking for me." Mason paused, worried again now. "You don't think they'll hurt her, do you?"

CHAPTER SIXTEEN

Thursday, April 14
8:30 a.m.
Albuquerque, New Mexico

KIM EXHALED WHEN FINLAY'S jet successfully touched
down at the private airport. Air travel was a necessity she
grudgingly accepted only because she had no choice. Luxury
travel was better than the usual disasters of commercial flight,
but she preferred to have her feet firmly planted on the ground.

She had used the flight time wisely. Finlay's dossiers on the
people involved with Lawton's disappearance were thorough and
as complete as possible. The files on O'Hare and the Ray
brothers were thin, but plausible. All three men had been living
off the grid for a long time. It made sense that there would be
little data accumulated in the public records.

She'd sent the names to Gaspar. He'd dig deeper and get
back to her when he had a chance. Finlay probably had the same
kind of access to intel that Gaspar had, but she trusted Gaspar
more. Simple as that.

She'd brought nothing with her except the contents of her pockets, which now included the folding toothbrush she'd picked up in Finlay's jet. She normally traveled with a suitcase, a laptop, a partner, and constant surveillance from the Boss. She felt strangely unencumbered and unprotected at the same time.

When the jet taxied to a stop, she stood to stretch and buttoned her jacket. Agent Russell came forward into the main cabin from the rear of the plane. He opened the bulkhead door and waited for the stairs to be rolled up.

Russell looked outside, waved, nodded, turned back to her and said, "Your ride is here."

Kim glanced toward Finlay, "You're not coming along?"

He shook his head. "You're meeting Agent Ross. He got word through channels to pick you up. It's better if I'm not in the mix as far as he's concerned."

She raised her eyebrows, the queasy feeling returning to her gut. "And why is that?"

"Because right now this whole Lawton missing thing hasn't even happened as far as FBI and Treasury are officially concerned. But if I get visibly involved, things will get escalated. Ross will run it up the chain of command. Cooper will definitely hear about it," Finlay paused. "None of that will be helpful to you or me, or to Lawton."

She considered his point. Not that she agreed with his reasoning. But the truth was that she wasn't all that comfortable having him around. She'd have more room to improvise if he wasn't standing next to her every second. She nodded.

"What about Reacher?" she asked. "You send him out here, too?"

Finlay grinned. "You've learned nothing about Reacher if you think anybody can send him anywhere for any reason. He does what he wants. You'd be smart to keep that in mind."

Kim didn't comprehend the nature of the bromance between Finlay and Reacher. But for some reason, Finlay had kept track of Reacher all these years. She'd assumed Finlay operated on self-preservation instincts, like most bureaucrats. Which meant on some level that Finlay viewed Reacher as an uneasy ally.

She cocked her head and looked him in the eye. "What did you say to make Reacher *want* to help these guys?"

"When you see Reacher, you have my number," Finlay said dismissing her question and terminating the conversation.

She made her way to the jet stairs and descended onto the pavement.

She saw the familiar FBI standard black SUV parked on the tarmac and walked over. Ross was behind the wheel. She recognized him from his headshots. She pulled the door open and slipped inside.

"Peter Ross," he said, extending his hand.

"Kim Otto," she replied, offering a firm shake.

"Where's your bags?"

"I'm traveling light at the moment."

He gave her a quizzical glance as he slid the transmission into drive and rolled away from the jet. "That makes things easy. You've read the file?"

"Such as it is."

"Right. Well, I'm not sure what we're dealing with here, exactly. Lawton called me at home a few days ago. Said he was in town to meet with a witness. The two of them had lunch. After that, Lawton's gone. No clue where he went. Haven't heard from him again."

"Isn't that a bit odd?"

Ross shrugged. "Not really. Agents get called to new

assignments all the time. I figured he'd left town on other business."

"But you didn't check to be sure?"

He glanced sideways and frowned. "Why would I?"

Kim nodded, but she didn't buy into his methods. "Did he tell you the witness's name?"

"No."

She nodded again. After months of dealing with the Boss and Finlay and their secrets, if Ross didn't know the name, she wouldn't volunteer it. She said, "Apparently he lives in some nutty commune full of preppers on the outskirts of town. Glen Haven. You know it?"

"Yeah. I know it." Ross raised his eyebrows and turned toward downtown Albuquerque. "Maybe that's why Lawton called me. To get intel on Glen Haven. I've been working on an organized crime investigation. That place has recently popped up on our radar."

She cocked her head. "What kind of crime?"

"The whole menu. Guns, drugs, money laundering, sex trafficking. Maybe more," Ross said as he slowed for a red light. "You know who Pinto Vigo is?"

"Is there a federal agent who doesn't?"

"Right." He nodded. "The Vigo cartel has been active in Albuquerque for a while, but his control had always been long distance. We've had a little bit of success picking off a few low level crimes he's been running, but nothing major. Selling pills to junkies, pimping out a couple of prostitutes. Things like that. You know how it is."

"I do," she said. The constant churn of personnel by the drug cartels was a fact of life. No one had been able to stop the flow of willing recruits on the supply side. Just as no one seemed to stem the tide of users on the demand side. Drug cartels seemed to have found the perfect business model.

Ross took a deep breath, as if he was about to reveal a secret. "Lately, we've had unconfirmed reports of Pinto Vigo sightings inside our jurisdiction. We've rousted all the usual suspects and nobody's talking."

"Of course." Kim nodded slowly. "Vigo's famously hot-headed. Not many people point fingers at Pinto Vigo and live to tell about it."

"Exactly. Anyway, I've been working the tips for six weeks or so. Based on what we've found, we believe he's probably operating here in person now. If he is, then something bigger than what we've found so far is probably in the works. But we can't prove any of it. Not yet," Ross said, as the light turned green. He rolled through the intersection to make a left turn.

"Something's changed?" Kim asked. This area of Albuquerque seemed almost deserted at the moment. It was early. Businesses were still closed. She guessed activity would pick up as the day advanced.

He nodded. "A few days ago, a woman walks into my office and tells me about some dudes leasing a couple of Glen Haven commune's outbuildings. From her description, we think one of the guys could be Vigo himself. He's got the kind of face not even a mother could love, you know?"

Kim arched her eyebrows. "That would be quite a takedown for the good guys. Pinto Vigo's been on the FBI's most wanted list since before his old man was murdered. He's only become more violent, like all the cartels since they began active hostilities against each other. His organization has grown fast. Every agency out there has a BOLO out on him."

Ross pulled into the parking lot of a place called the Last Chance Saloon and slipped the transmission into park. "We need to tread carefully here. We don't want to pull the trigger too soon and give him a chance to bolt. We need him to feel nice and comfy and secure until we've got enough evidence to make the charges stick."

"Isn't that why Lawton is here?"

"I hope not. We don't want Vigo for tax evasion. We want to get him for bigger crimes. Make him pay and send a message to the other cartels." He paused. "We're fighting a war here, Otto. We've got to be strategic about this. You know that as well as I do."

"How about we get him for kidnapping a federal agent? Make that one stick and he's going away for the rest of his miserable life," Kim said, even as the idea of using Lawton for bait rankled all the way to her soul.

"Yeah, well, maybe we can do that. One thing at a time," Ross replied, running a hand through his hair.

She neither agreed nor disagreed with him. Instead, she nodded toward the Last Chance Saloon. "What do you hope to find here?"

"This is the place Lawton was meeting his witness. We've looked at the CCTV. He and another guy left here together and since then we can't locate him. It's like he vanished into thin air."

"Who was the other guy?"

Ross replied, "Most likely the witness Lawton came here to interview. But we don't know for sure. We've reached out to Treasury for the name, but they're being cagey about it so far. They say they're not allowed to reveal the name, even to us, without approval from higher up the food chain. We're working on that."

Otto shrugged. Sounded like the usual bureaucratic bullshit to her. Turf protecting. Vigo was a big fish. The team that took him off the player board would get the kind of applause that makes an agency's year. Nobody wanted a misstep that might lead to failure. Nor did they want to share the glory.

Kim's motivations were different. She ran on her standard triple A's. Ambition, adrenaline, and anxiety. Taking down a cartel leader like Vigo wouldn't hurt her career, for sure. But it would publicize the fact that she was here. Which she couldn't justify. Not even a little bit. She needed to stay focused.

Ross continued talking. "We can't identify Lawton's witness from this footage. We did some digging. Found out this place is one of Vigo's hangouts. Rumor is that Vigo's crew has been conducting business in the back room of the saloon."

"Makes sense. Businesses like this are good for money laundering activities. Lotta people, mostly tourists, lotta cash and credit cards changing hands," Kim nodded approvingly. "Not enough evidence to get a search warrant?"

"Maybe. From a friendly judge. But that would tip our hand, too. Our intel says it's likely Vigo has people on his payroll in the courthouse. So we don't want to do it just yet," he said, giving her a side eye to be sure she was keeping up.

She nodded. "I get it. The saloon is a public place, which means we don't need a warrant to go inside and look around."

"Right. Now that we know where Lawton disappeared from, we can ask a few questions about him, take a look around, maybe find out where he is. Could be it has nothing to do with Vigo."

"How likely is that?" She asked.

"Not very."

Kim said nothing. Investigating organized crime was her job

in Detroit. Her experience was that cartel members were vicious, not chatty. When they were threatened, they behaved like cornered predators. They were a thousand times more likely to strike first and justify later.

"Yeah, well, we'll know more than we know now. Just assume that everyone in here is on Vigo's payroll or worried what he'll do to them if they talk to us." Ross stepped out of the Escalade and closed the door.

Kim did the same, buttoning her jacket against the chill wind. "That's a solid plan. What exactly are *you* worried about?"

"Same thing you're worried about," Ross said. "Luring Lawton out here could have been a set up. His witness might be involved with Vigo. Gang members might be inside."

"Sounds like we need backup."

"They're standing by. It's just a guess right now. When Pinto Vigo's old man was running the cartel, he killed a federal agent," Ross replied. "That's what got him sent to prison. Where he was murdered by a rival gang, as you probably know."

Kim raised her eyebrows. "Lawton didn't have anything to do with that, did he?"

Ross shrugged. "Not that I know of. Lawton is a Treasury agent. IRS. Different agency than the one responsible for sending Vigo senior to prison. But close enough."

She knew what he meant. Pinto Vigo wouldn't be the first guy to hold a grudge against the government and lash out sideways.

The familiar shudder traveled along Kim's spinal column and radiated out to all four limbs. Finlay hadn't said, flat out, that Lawton had been kidnapped by the Vigo cartel. He must have known, though. Which was the kind of thing that would drive Gaspar nuts.

He must also believe Bruce and Gavin Ray and even Mason O'Hare were in over their heads. Pinto Vigo would kill them without a moment's hesitation if it suited him. Perhaps he already had.

Would Reacher care enough about an old debt to Gavin Ray to attempt a rescue of the man's sons? Kim never figured Reacher was the sentimental type. He lived in the moment. Did what he wanted to do, when he wanted to do it.

But for some reason, Finlay thought Reacher would care what happened to these two guys, and Finlay knew Reacher way better than Kim did. If Finlay was right, Kim didn't know all of the facts. Simple as that.

Ross said, "You're armed?"

"Yeah." She patted her gun for reassurance and hustled along toward the entrance.

CHAPTER SEVENTEEN

Thursday, April 14
10:30 a.m.
Albuquerque, New Mexico

KIM FOLLOWED BEHIND ROSS along the sidewalk to the entrance of the saloon. While the temperature was warmer than Detroit, a morning chill was in the air. She buttoned her jacket and picked up her pace against the wind.

The saloon's hours were posted on a sign next to the door. Lunch service began on Thursdays at 11:30 a.m. They were early. Ross tried the door anyway. It was unlocked and they went inside.

The exterior door opened into a small entryway. They walked through a second set of double doors into the main body of the saloon, which looked more like a modern Spanish-style restaurant than an Old West movie set.

The walls and the floor were wood paneled. There was a long bar off to one side, the usual display of liquor bottles and beer paraphernalia behind it. The main dining room was an open floor plan filled with heavy wood tables and red vinyl padded chairs. A big stone fireplace filled ten feet of space along one end of the room. Feeble illumination was provided by covered wall sconces, casting an old-fashioned soft glow.

The host's station was unmanned while employees were busy preparing for the lunch service. Kim counted three staff members setting tables with flatware and drinking glasses in the main dining room. A man and two women were bent to their tasks. All three were dressed in black trousers, a white shirt with a bolo tie, and black patent leather shoes.

Additional staff were working in the kitchen, as evidenced by banging cookware and shouted banter behind the swinging doors. Staff members were coming in and out through the doors. Kim noticed two petite women and a lanky young man setting up the buffet in the far corner.

One of the three table setters in the front dining room looked up and caught Kim's eye. He stifled annoyance, slapped a smile on his face, and headed toward them.

When he was close enough to converse at reasonable volume, he said, "I'm sorry. We don't open for another hour."

"We're with the FBI, Martin," Ross said, reading the name tag on the man's shirt and offering his badge wallet briefly. "We're looking for one of our agents. He was here for lunch a few days ago."

He pulled a photo of Lawton from his jacket pocket and showed it. "Have you seen this man?"

Martin accepted the photo and seemed to study it briefly before he returned it, shaking his head. "We serve more than three hundred people a day. I see a lot of businessmen. Tourists, too."

Ross nodded. He leaned one elbow onto the host's stand and lowered his voice, as if he was sharing a secret. "See, Martin, this guy is a good friend of mine. And I'm worried about him, you know?"

"Of course," Martin replied, nodding, giving up nothing.

"So you wouldn't mind if I ask the staff about him, would you?" Ross asked reasonably, as if it mattered what Martin wanted.

While they were busy being chums, Kim studied the two women who were setting tables. Like the other workers scurrying to prepare the buffet table, both were dark-haired Latinas. One of the women was average-sized, mid-twenties probably. Bent to her tasks and working quickly, attention focused.

The other woman was astonishingly huge. The long-sleeved shirt and trousers covered her limbs, but her hands were wide and strong and the size of pumpkins. She was square from shoulders to knees and looked like 100 percent solid muscle.

She could have played for the NFL or won a few trophies on WWF.

Kim clenched her jaw to avoid gaping at her. She was a remarkable specimen of female evolution.

Kim was acutely aware of her own diminutive stature and made every effort to compensate for it. She trained daily to maximize her strength and speed. She'd practiced her marksmanship until she became second to none. Along with her well-documented hyper-intelligence, which far exceeded all norms, she'd found these skills sufficient to give her the advantage 99 percent of the time.

The bigger they are, the harder they fall. Her brothers had taught her that much. And most of the big people she'd come across couldn't outrun her or outshoot her or outthink her.

Most of them.

For the rest, she avoided situations that involved outsized opponents.

But there was no way to avoid the mammoth-sized female. She had to hope the woman was a gentle giant. Or at least, a civilized one who respected the law.

As Kim watched, the big woman glanced toward her and then ducked her gaze swiftly toward the tabletop, like she had something to feel guilty about, which Kim's gut said she probably did.

Kim left Ross and approached the two women.

She had no chance to identify herself or ask any questions before the younger woman bolted toward the exit at the back of the building.

"Ross!" Kim called out before she turned to dash after the fleeing woman. She ran down the aisle in hot pursuit, toward the rear exit.

Which was when the Falstaffian female blindsided Kim with her nemesis, brute force.

She'd taken only two steps when the hulking giant tackled her from behind, knocked her to the floor, and landed on top of her like an anvil crushing a kitten.

Kim had no warning. No chance to sidestep or evade the assault.

She was slammed to the ground and pinned by the woman's massive torso.

Kim's forehead mashed against the floor and her breath whooshed from her mouth as her lungs were pressed against the solid boards. She couldn't speak.

She squirmed and kicked beneath the impenetrable mass that smothered her, trying to break free. No such luck.

Kim was an excellent swimmer. She could hold her breath

under water for two minutes. Maybe longer. But she had no breath to hold.

This was not the way she'd expected to die.

She knew the statistics for suffocation. One minute to avoid all brain damage from oxygen deprivation. At three minutes with no oxygen, significant and lasting brain damage was likely. After ten minutes of asphyxiation, she'd be as good as dead.

She fought to get free enough of the crushing weight to breathe.

She tried jabbing her elbows and kicking her boots. She landed a few solid hits, but the woman barely flinched.

Kim felt lightheaded. She struggled to inhale but the woman's weight was too heavy on her back, pressing her chest against the floor.

A loud roaring in her ears drowned out all other sounds. She couldn't speak. Her field of vision was limited to the hardwood in front of her face.

From a muffled distance, she heard footfalls and Ross yelled, "Let her go! Now!"

The smothering heavyweight didn't move.

Ross's voice was still muffled, but closer. Like he'd crouched to the floor near the woman's huge head.

He shouted, "Let her go or I'll shoot you through the head and shove your dead carcass aside myself."

In response, the woman's heavy arm swept swiftly forward along the floor and knocked Ross off his feet. He yelled in pain before he landed with a heavy thud and scrambled to fight back.

She had raised her shoulder enough to give Kim a chance to suck air into her aching lungs before the giant lay flat on top of her again.

Darkness encroached from every direction. Moments seemed like hours. Kim's consciousness began to fade.

"You cut me, you bitch! I'm warning you! Let her go or I'll shoot!" Ross shouted from the floor out of the woman's reach. "Let her go! I swear I'll shoot you! One! Two!"

The whale made no effort to comply.

"Last chance. Let her go! Three!" Ross yelled. Then a brief pause before he made good on his promise.

Through the dead weight holding her hostage, Kim heard the muffled roar of gunshots. A double tap. If he'd shot her through the head like he'd promised, the big woman could not have survived.

Whatever muscle tension the woman had held in her body relaxed and she flattened out, seeming heavier, as if she'd been holding some of her weight off Kim before.

Kim felt increasingly faint. In small bursts, she jerked little gasps into her lungs, attempting to oxygenate, consciousness fraying more at the edges.

Ross pushed against the woman's dead weight. She must have outweighed him by a hundred pounds or more. She didn't budge. He called out, "Martin! Get over here! Help me move this body! My partner dies, it's on you!"

Kim gasped again and again, small sips, searching for air, but there was little to be had. She squirmed and tried to speak, to let Ross know she was still alive, but no sound came out. She worried that Ross would need a crane to get the dead woman off her, which would take way too long.

Nonsensically, she thought what she needed was a big man. Like Reacher. Either one. Jack Reacher or his nephew, Jake. Ross was reasonably sized and fit, but he wasn't getting the job done.

Reacher could have lifted the dead weight that Ross couldn't budge.

Kim heard Martin's muffled steps approach. Felt the heavy weight of the woman's body begin to move. As Ross and Martin shoved to roll the dead woman aside, Kim pushed with her last bit of strength to crab toward free air.

She drew her first unobstructed breath. Then another. Until she felt strong enough to help. After a solid five minutes of struggling with the body, the three of them were able to free her.

She scrambled clear of the oppressive weight, rolled onto her back, and sucked breath into her lungs, gaping like a fish.

"Are you okay?" Ross asked as he used his cell to call for paramedics and backup.

She nodded and lifted her hand weakly to signal that she was still alive.

CHAPTER EIGHTEEN

Thursday, April 14
11:15 a.m.
Chihuahuan Desert, New Mexico

VIGO AND HIS SISTER, Maria, were suspicious by nature and cautious by necessity. Several cartels were engaged in open warfare against Vigo now. Cartel members were killed at an alarming rate, sometimes five or more died every day.

Which meant Vigo and Maria took extra precautions.

Each morning, they opened new burner cell phones before she left Glen Haven for the Last Chance Saloon. They used the burners exclusively to communicate with each other, and only when necessary. At the end of each day, they destroyed the phones.

It was a crude security system, but it worked well enough.

When the daily burner phone rang twice at eleven-fifteen a.m., followed by a coded text message from Maria, Vigo knew instantly they'd suffered another disaster. He stomped around the barracks and swore out his rage while Hector and Freddie wisely kept their heads down until he controlled himself. For now.

The mole inside his organization had struck again. This time, Maria's message made clear, was worse than all the others.

The text was a single digit. The number 4, meaning death of an important member of the cartel.

Vigo texted back a single character, a question mark.

Maria replied with an X. She wanted to meet. She was at the safehouse.

"I have to go out. You stay here," Vigo ordered Hector and Freddie on his way out the door. "If those two in the basement give you any trouble, shoot them in the knees. Don't kill them. Not yet. I'll take care of them myself. Understood?"

Both men nodded.

"What happened, boss?" Hector asked with a quick glance toward Freddie. They were nervous. Vigo wasn't long on patience or forgiveness, and they'd seen the results too many times.

"That mole dies today," Vigo said and slammed the door behind him. He stomped toward his truck, jumped behind the wheel, and headed down the long driveway to the two-track and then onto the highway, cursing all the way.

The shipment was due to arrive tomorrow. All he had to do was hold his crew together until they distributed the inventory. By Sunday, he'd be happy to burn the whole of Glen Haven to the ground along with everyone in it. Then, he could move on. The very thought cheered him considerably.

Vigo drove to the parking lot, left the truck, and took the bus. An hour had passed before he reached the safe house. He'd passed the time controlling his hot temper and stoking the cold anger that would fuel him now.

Maria's gray Toyota sedan was parked in the driveway, he noted.

He climbed four steps to the front stoop of the bungalow. At the reinforced steel door, he knocked twice, paused briefly, and knocked twice more. The heavy deadbolt slid back on the other side. He turned the knob, crossed the threshold, and closed the door.

Inside, Maria waited. She was still dressed in the garb she wore at the Last Chance Saloon. She'd been pacing the floor, a bottle of water in one hand. Strands of dark hair had escaped the low ponytail at her neck and curled loosely around her face. She'd chewed her lipstick off.

"You find the mole?" she demanded.

"Not yet. I'm working on it," he replied.

"Yeah, well, you'd better work a hell of a lot faster," she snapped like a rabid vixen.

His sister was no emotional female. They were spawn of the same cold-blooded father. Ice ran in her veins.

She was rattled. Which meant her news was exceptionally bad.

"What happened?" Vigo asked as he sat with a resigned sigh.

"FBI, that's what," Maria barked like she was the one in charge here.

"FBI?"

"That damn Agent Peter Ross. Walked into the saloon with another agent. Tiny Asian bitch."

"She's not literally Asian. FBI agents are required to be US Citizens."

"Yeah, whatever. She looks as Asian as Lana Condor."

"Who?" Vigo was truly baffled. What the hell was she talking about?

"Just take my word for it, Pinto. Don't be so literal. The problem is not what she looks like," Maria fumed. "They were asking questions about your Treasury agent."

"Lawton? What kind of questions."

"Whaddaya think?" Maria spat, palpable rage fairly rising off her. "Had we seen him. Did we know where he was. Crap like that."

"Martin is good with such situations. That's why we chose him to interface with the public. He handles law enforcement well enough." Vigo nodded. "Martin told Ross nothing, I assume."

"Less than nothing."

"So what's the problem?"

"The Asian is the problem. She left Ross at the front with Martin and came at me."

Vigo frowned and cocked his head, trying to grasp the facts. "Okay. Then what?"

"Like I'm gonna stand there and let her arrest me?" Maria shook her head. "So I ran out the back and left Big Sela to take care of her."

Vigo suppressed a groan. "Sounds like that should have been simple enough."

Maria replied. "Should have been. It wasn't."

"So what happened?" Vigo asked again, staring at her with amazed horror. Big Sela had never failed to protect Maria. Never. "Did the FBI arrest Sela? We need to send her a lawyer?"

Maria leaned one shoulder against the wall and hung her head. "She caught Sela by surprise. Got past her. Big Sela tackled the bitch. Crushed her, you know, like she does. Would've killed the bitch, too, because she's so damn small."

Vigo nodded. He knew. Sela had crushed her enemies before. It was an unusual but effective method of murder.

"But Sela didn't kill her. Tell me she didn't. The last thing we need is a dead FBI agent at the saloon, Maria." Vigo's temper was rising again, too.

He was already working through the problems in his head. He had contingency plans. Exit strategies. Extraction protocols. Getting his assets out of Glen Haven on a moment's notice. Leaving his business in Albuquerque. Running out of the country ahead of the feds. None of that would be simple. Or easy. Collateral damage was inevitable.

Maria's nostrils flared and her eyes flashed. Deadly calm, she said, "No, Pinto. Sela didn't kill her. Know why? Because the other guy, Ross. He killed Sela first."

Vigo frowned. He blinked. Had he heard correctly? "Big Sela's dead?"

"Yeah. She's dead. He shot her. In cold blood. Right through the head," Maria pointed her finger gun at her head and pressed her thumb down to demonstrate.

Vigo was shocked into silence. Big Sela had never failed. She was as loyal as any dog. And twice as effective.

"And the feds are all over the saloon now. They've got everybody lined up for questioning. They're inspecting the scene with tweezers and who knows what all," Maria said, still angry. "I was lucky to get out when I did. Otherwise, I'd be sitting in a cell now."

"You left our people there?" Vigo couldn't quite process the magnitude of this disaster. He tried to wrap his mind around it. "Our product? Our cash?"

"That's what you're worried about? Your damn business?" She glared at him while she gulped air to retain control. When she spoke again, her tone was soft and quiet. "Big Sela was my closest friend in the world, Pinto. I grew up with her since I was a baby. She's like my shadow. I've never been without her. And now she's dead. And that little bitch will pay. Ross, too."

Vigo clasped his hands between his knees and stared ahead to think. "Where is she now?"

"The Asian? Still breathing, unfortunately. They took her to the hospital in an ambulance." Maria's lip curled and her eyes narrowed. "If she's very lucky, maybe she'll die there before I have a chance to finish what Sela started."

The embers of Vigo's anger became a hot flame in his belly. Maria wasn't the only one who wanted revenge. Starting with the mole. He was the one responsible. He would pay first. Everyone else would follow. Vigo had applied scorched earth plans before. He wouldn't hesitate to use them again.

His nostrils flared as his breath came in staccato bursts on his way to the door. "We can't stay here any longer. I have loose ends to tie up. I'll let you know when it's time. Follow the plan. Be ready to go."

"I'll be ready," Maria promised, her voice as hard as steel.

CHAPTER NINETEEN

Thursday, April 14
2:00 p.m.
Glen Haven, New Mexico

THE DOOR AT THE top of the stairs opened and two men descended wearing heavy work boots. Both men were armed.

The big bearded guy who had abducted Mason came first, carrying a shotgun. He looked like he hadn't slept at all, which wasn't improving his mood.

Mason had never seen the shorter, slighter man before. He'd have remembered the face. His pockmarked cheeks were deeply scarred. Hard eyes stared from beneath heavy brows drawn together, frowning above his full lips. He held a pistol casually in his right hand at his side.

The bearded man stood to one side, facing Lawton, shotgun loosely ready, like he was prepared to deal with whatever trouble came along. Shooting live rounds inside the basement would cause a lot of problems, but the shotgun could be used effectively as a club.

Before anyone had a chance to say anything, the pockmarked man strode across the floor, lifted the pistol, and smashed it across Mason's cheek and recently broken nose. Mason cried out. The blow knocked him to the floor. The sharp, throbbing pain in his face made his eyes water. He began to cry.

"Stop sniveling!" the pockmarked man commanded as he gave Mason a swift kick.

Lawton bolted upright and took a step forward. The bearded guy pointed the shotgun and growled, "Keep coming, lawman. Nothing would make me happier."

Lawton stopped. "You're not going to shoot me, genius. The ricochet would blowback on you. And the blast would be heard all over this place. You don't want that. You're hiding out here because it's quiet and you want to keep it that way."

"Yeah, well, you don't want to push me too far, Lawton," the pockmarked man said quietly. He turned and delivered another fast, hard kick to Mason's soft gut.

Mason cried out. Tears streamed down his face. He whimpered and groaned, crabbed on the floor grabbing his stomach, and pressed his lips firmly closed, afraid he might vomit.

The pockmarked man kicked him again and again, until Mason lost all control of bodily fluids. Vomit and urine splashed on his attacker's shoes.

The pockmarked man jumped back and cursed.

Lawton made good use of the distraction.

He lunged toward the bearded man.

He grabbed the shotgun and deflected it to one side and moved in fast. He hit the bearded man with a solid blow directly to the skinny triangle between his pecs and abs. A huge blow filled with momentum and rage and payback straight into the solar plexus.

The bearded guy's face showed all kinds of distress as he bent low and howled in pain. Lawton waited until he was low enough for a finishing kick to his face. Lawton delivered it swift and hard and precisely on target. Blood spattered everywhere. The bearded guy went down.

Lawton turned to the pockmarked man, who stood pointing the pistol directly at him. "One more move and you'll never walk again, Vigo," Lawton said.

Vigo's stare was meaner as he took a step forward, brandishing the pistol. His lips opened in a terrifying grin. Light glinted from his gold capped teeth.

"You following in your old man's footsteps? That what this is? Gonna kill a federal agent like he did? Show your enemies how tough you are?" Lawton narrowed his eyes and cocked his head. "Give it a try. My team will hound you for the rest of your days. You'll be *lucky* if they let you die in prison like your old man."

Vigo's head might literally have exploded if he hadn't found a way to release the pressure. His face crumpled into a deep scowl. His breathing came hard and fast. He wanted not merely to hurt Lawton but to pulverize him into a sniveling, snotty mess, like he'd done to Mason.

"Get over there," Vigo said, waving the gun toward the far corner.

Lawton backed toward it, never taking his eyes off Vigo.

Mason struggled to rise to all fours and staggered to his feet, intending to follow Lawton.

The bearded man was groaning, coming around to consciousness.

"Not you, O'Hare." Vigo walked toward the big man, bent down, and picked up the shotgun. "You help Hector get up the stairs."

Mason nodded miserably. He wouldn't be much help to Hector or anyone else. He could barely move. He felt like he'd vomit and piss himself again if he tried.

Hector pushed Mason away and managed to stand on his own. He swiped his bloody face clean on his sleeve and moved toward the staircase.

Mason followed behind, moving as well as he could. The two climbed the steps, slowly and laboriously. Mason kept one arm around his belly. The sharp pain he felt every time he tried to breathe probably meant he had a cracked rib or two.

When Mason was halfway up, he looked back over his shoulder. Vigo had walked toward Lawton.

"Turn around. Face the wall," Vigo ordered.

Lawton said nothing. Nor did he move.

Vigo shot the pistol into one of the top bunk bed mattresses, mere inches from Lawton's head. The monstrously loud noise was contained and maybe it had been quiet enough. Maybe it didn't wake the entire Glen Haven compound. But the boldness of the shot pushed Mason up the stairs faster than before.

"If I wanted you dead, you'd be dead already, Lawton. Your time is coming. Think about that," Vigo said, as he backed slowly away from Lawton and up the stairs behind Mason.

At the top of the stairs, a deadbolt slid open and a third man with a gun waved them into the main bunkhouse. When all three were out of the basement, he closed and bolted the door.

"What the hell happened down there, Hector?" he said.

"Don't ask." Hector shook his head. He made his way toward the kitchen for a cold towel and an ice pack for his battered face.

"I'll let you know when it's time to panic, okay?

Everything's fine. Better than we planned." Vigo growled and shoved Mason forward. "Freddie, put this moron in one of the beds. And check him over. Make sure nothing's busted."

Freddie scowled and said, "He stinks. Can I hose him down, boss?"

"Yeah. Do us all a favor," Vigo replied.

"This way," Freddie said.

Mason followed slowly behind him to the other end of the bunk house, through the door to the bedroom. Freddie shoved him into the shower. The water pelted his skin like icy crystals. Mason shivered with pain and cold and horror as he watched his blood run onto the tile and down the drain.

When he decided Mason was done, Freddie turned the water off and tossed him a towel. Then he pushed Mason into the bedroom. All of the bunks were empty.

He gave Mason another shove. Mason stumbled and flopped down onto a lower bunk. Freddie left the room and came back a while later with a pair of jeans and a shirt. He tossed the clean, dry clothes to Mason.

"Get dressed, man. Straighten yourself up. You don't want Vigo thinking you're worthless, do you? Because if that happens, he'll have no further use for you. You don't want that, man. Trust me," Freddie said.

Mason stood and peeled off his wet clothes. He pulled on the jeans and shirt, which he recognized had come from his own closet back in his room.

Freddie nodded. "That's better. Compose yourself. Vigo will be in to see you."

The words alone were enough to chill Mason's whole body more than the cold shower. If he never saw Vigo again, it would be too soon. But he sensed Vigo and his crew were way too comfortable here. They didn't seem to be preparing to move on. Not even a little bit.

"What does he want from me?" Mason asked.

"He'll tell you himself. And take my advice. Whatever it is, you want to live another day, you give it to him." Freddie replied before he left the room and bolted the door behind him.

CHAPTER TWENTY

Thursday, April 14
3:00 p.m.
Albuquerque, New Mexico

MASON HAD LAIN AWAKE worrying for a while. He'd run several scenarios through his head and each one was more terrifying than the last. He worried about Cheryl and Micah. He worried about Glen Haven and the family he had found there.

Vigo was destroying everything that meant anything to Mason and there wasn't a damn thing he could figure out to fix things.

Multiple places on his body complained every time he moved. His ribcage hurt with every breath. His eye had swollen shut. When Vigo hit him with the pistol, his nose had gone all mushy again. Nothing he could do about any of it, but he certainly didn't want Cheryl to see him like this.

Finally, exhaustion and tension overcame him. He'd dozed off.

A sharp poke in the ribs with a shotgun stock jerked him awake. The hard bed had stiffened his muscles. He opened his one functioning eyelid. Vigo stood holding the shotgun, too close to miss his target if he chose to pull the trigger.

"Get up," Vigo ordered, punctuated by another sharp thrust with the shotgun butt.

Mason moaned and grabbed his sore torso as he struggled to a sitting position.

Vigo pulled up a chair and jabbed Mason again before he straddled the chair. Mason had pressed his lips together, but another groan escaped anyway.

"You are going to help me with a problem."

"Okay. Sure." Mason nodded quickly, like a puppy eager to please. He had no idea how he could possibly help Vigo, but he was ready to do it if it meant Vigo would stop beating him.

Vigo's lips lifted slightly at the corner. "Sure you don't need further persuading?"

"Absolutely not. How can I help?" Mason shook his head rapidly from side to side and then stopped immediately because of the sharp nausea the shaking produced.

"Someone at your little commune has been talking to the feds about my business."

Mason started to shake his head again but stopped. "Not me. Definitely not me."

Vigo shot a steely gaze straight through to Mason's guilty conscience. "No. If I thought you were an informant you'd be dead already."

Mason's body began to shake uncontrollably. He clamped his arms around his tender belly protectively and nodded again.

Vigo continued, "The mole I'm looking for has passed on information you wouldn't know. I also don't believe anyone in my organization would trust you with information that could get you both killed. Do you disagree?"

"Not at all. You are 100 percent correct. No one I know has talked to me about you. I d-didn't— I d-don't even know who you are," he stammered. "I th-thought you were just here temporarily. Passing through, you know? Like Bruce said."

Vigo said, "Our plans have changed. We like it here."

Mason gulped. "Sure. It's a nice place."

"We plan to stay awhile. Until our business is completed. We need to find the mole and shut him up. Then we'll finish our business," Vigo said. Almost as an afterthought, he added, "Then we'll go."

Mason said nothing. It seemed safer.

"Agent Lawton knows the identity of this informant. We have tried to persuade him to tell us, but he is…reluctant." Vigo cocked his head. "Perhaps he will tell you."

Mason's eyes widened with astonishment and his mouth formed a little circle. "Me? I don't even know the guy. I met him once. Briefly. We've exchanged only a few words. Why would he tell me anything like that?"

"You should employ some positive thinking, amigo. You'll persuade him to tell you because if he doesn't, you'll no longer be of use to me." Vigo's chilling smile and piercing gaze left no doubt of the consequences of failure.

Mason was too miserable to reply.

"We're sending you back to the basement. You'll find out who our mole is. And then we'll let you go. Otherwise…" Vigo let his voice trail off and he shrugged.

"But how will I do that? He's not simply going to volunteer the guy's name."

"That's your problem, isn't it?" Vigo said. He continued to stare at Mason. "Perhaps you need an incentive."

The words sent another chill straight to Mason's heart. He

shook his head. "No. No, that won't be necessary. I'll do it. I'll figure out how to make him tell me."

"Good. Because the ones you care about most will pay the price if you fail. While you watch." Vigo paused. "And then I'll move on to the others. One at a time. Until you're the only one left."

"What?" Mason could feel his eyes bugging out of his head. He couldn't mean what Mason thought he was saying. "You wouldn't h-hurt them. They don't know anything about this."

Vigo cocked his head and grinned like the devil himself. "You don't know anything about this, either, and look what's happened to you."

Mason's teeth began to chatter and he shivered all over. Surely, these were empty threats. Cheryl and Micah were innocents. They'd never seen or done anything to harm Vigo and his crew. Nor would they. Vigo was a monster. A very dangerous monster.

"You know nothing about me. Ask Lawton. He'll tell you. I am fully capable of keeping my promises." Vigo stood and pushed the chair aside. He walked to the door and gave it a couple of solid whacks with the butt of the shotgun. "Let's go. You've got work to do."

The door opened and Freddie came in. Vigo said, "Take him back to the basement."

Freddie strode over, grabbed Mason's arm and pulled him to his feet.

For a brief, stupid moment, Mason considered fighting back. But how could he? He had no weapons, he couldn't see out of one eye, and his fighting skills were nonexistent.

Miserably, he lowered his head and followed Freddie to the basement door. Freddie pulled the deadbolt back and opened it.

He shoved Mason through to the landing and closed the door firmly behind him, leaving Mason standing there in the dark.

He felt along the wall until he located a light switch. The last thing he needed was to fall headlong down to the concrete floor.

Lawton waited at the bottom and Mason had no idea what to do. But he'd figure it out. He had to. For Cheryl and Micah. And the others.

He flipped the lights on and descended the stairs. "Lawton, we need to talk."

CHAPTER TWENTY-ONE

Thursday, April 14
4:30 p.m.
Albuquerque, New Mexico

KIM WALKED STIFFLY OUT of the hospital hours later with orders from the half-dozen doctors who'd checked her over and wanted her to stay a couple of days for observation. After all their tests, they'd diagnosed bruised muscles, but no fractures or tears anywhere. They told her to take it easy for a couple of weeks to allow her battered body time to recover and see her doctor when she returned to Detroit.

Like any of that was going to happen.

Agent Ross had insisted she follow those orders and he'd threatened to call her boss if she refused. He meant the man she officially reported to back in the Detroit field office. Since her boss had no idea where she was, or why, and she was under orders not to tell him about the hunt for Reacher, it was the one threat Ross had made that actually impacted her decisions.

So she'd said, "Okay, Ross. No problem. Let me know what

you find out when you finish processing at the saloon. I want to know who those two women are. The one that ran. And the one who tried to kill me."

"You got it," he'd replied.

She figured his promise was about as good as hers. Meaning neither one was worth the breath it took to utter the words.

But she'd learned something. Several things, actually.

The most important lesson was that she needed a more reliable partner in this.

Ross wasn't the man for the job. He'd killed to save her from certain death, which was good. But he thought he had the right to tell her what to do, which wasn't okay. Not even a little bit.

And he was FBI.

Which meant he'd have processes and procedures and rules to follow. That definitely wasn't something she could be limited by now.

She also needed her own transportation. Ross had left another agent at the hospital to take her to a local hotel for that rest she was supposed to get. He'd promised to debrief her once matters at the Last Chance Saloon were completed. She wasn't holding her breath until that happened, even if her sore chest might have allowed her to try.

The second agent dropped her off at the local chain hotel. She checked in and went to her room. She flopped onto her back on the bed. Even after her bruises healed, she might never lie on her stomach again.

As it was, when she closed her eyes she felt the big woman's heavy weight pressing her like a panini sandwich again. Her lids snapped open, sweat dotted her brow, and she gasped for air half a dozen times before her brain objectively registered the panic response and she could consciously control her breathing.

She called room service for two large pots of coffee and a hamburger and practiced closing her eyes while she waited. Each time, the panic closed in again, but she forced herself to endure it for a few seconds longer.

By the time the food arrived thirty minutes later, she was able to close her eyes for a full sixty-seven seconds without screaming. Progress.

She drank the coffee and wolfed down the burger. She practiced closing her eyes between bites while she sat on the bed.

Changing her position made the panic marginally better. She felt the perspiration on her brow and the increase in her respiratory rate each time, but she could function. Could she sleep in a sitting position for the rest of her life?

When she'd finished the burger, she called Gaspar on a new burner phone. "Chico," she said when he picked up.

"That's a common name, you know. One of these days, you'll get the wrong person on the other end of the line," he teased.

"But not today," she replied.

"No. Not today." He laughed and then became serious. "Where've you been? I don't have eyes on you out there. And neither does anyone else."

"Point taken." She nodded. He meant that the Boss wasn't watching her every move, there to clean up the mess or send in the cavalry or deliver whatever she needed to get the job done. Neither was Finlay, it seemed.

She'd been operating with a safety net up until now. She was nervous without it. Not that how she felt about it mattered in the least.

Gaspar said, "What do you need?"

"Only two things at the moment. First, a vehicle," she said.

She tried closing her eyes as they talked. Focusing on the conversation helped.

"I can have it delivered within an hour. Give me your address."

"Something I can drive. Not one of those monstrous sedans you like. I need to be able to see over the steering wheel." She found a card on the little desk by the phone with the hotel's address and gave it to him. She could hear the keyboard keys clacking as he set the order in motion.

Her chest hurt like she'd been battered by a charging elephant. Which she had. She ignored the pain, took a deep breath and held it in her lungs, simply because she could.

She'd never again take the simple act of breathing for granted. She did it again, feeling the agony, getting used to the pain so she could deal with it.

"Okay," he said. "What's the second thing?"

"I need a new partner," she said, continuing to breathe as normally as possible, while keeping her eyes closed and focusing on the conversation. The panic had subsided. Her heartbeat slowed to something closer to normal.

"You must be delusional. You think I've got pull with the FBI's HR department? Ask your boss. He's the one who got you into this Reacher gig. He can get you out of it," Gaspar said, huffily.

"That's another whole issue, and you know it. I'm not ready for that yet. Besides, when did you become such a big fan of the Boss?" She kept up the breathing and the pain was becoming tolerable, just as she'd expected it would. The more she directed her focus to other things, the less panicked she felt with her eyes closed. Which was okay, too.

He said, "I'm not a fan. And yes he considers you

expendable. But it *is* his job to keep you alive. If you don't make it back from one of his ops, he'll at least have to answer for it. Which he definitely does not want to do."

"Usually, you'd be right. But as he doesn't even know I'm here…"

Gaspar's exasperation traveled with the words. "Give him an incentive to help you out, even if he doesn't want to. Just tell him you want a new partner. He'll find you another expendable schmuck now that I'm gone."

She cocked her head as if she could see him across the miles all the way to Miami. She had a plan B here. And a plan C, too. As she always did. But she wasn't ready to give up on Gaspar just yet.

"I'm not asking you to find me a new partner forever, Chico. Just for the next few days. One of our own guys. Somebody we know to be reliable. You got anybody at that fancy agency you can loan me?"

It wasn't an outrageous request. Katie Scarlett was his employer. She owned Gaspar's new agency and she had operatives. Good ones. Trained personnel. Capable in every respect. And Gaspar knew what Kim needed. He could make a solid choice.

"I don't like any of this, Kim," he said quietly. "Just go home. Let Treasury deal with their missing agent. Leave the Vigo cartel to the local FBI office. Let Finlay deal with whatever the hell it is he wants. You don't have to be there. Go home."

She shook her head slowly, as if he could see her, too. They hadn't been partners very long. Less than six months. But they'd functioned well as a team. Too well. She couldn't find another partner to do the job as well as Gaspar, and she knew it. She also knew the choice wouldn't be hers. The Boss would send her a new partner when he was damn good and ready, whether she wanted the guy or not. She'd be stuck.

Until then, she'd improvise. "What about that dude you're always raving about? What's his name? Bauxite? Onyx?"

Gaspar laughed again at her teasing. "Flint. Michael Flint. And you'd be lucky to get him."

"That's what I figured. Can you talk him into it?"

"Not likely. Flint's independent, in every sense of the word. Does what he wants. When he wants. And absolutely nothing else."

"Sounds like someone else we know," she said dryly. "Okay, then ask Scarlett to persuade him. Brothers do things for their sisters they wouldn't do for anyone else. Trust me, I know. I've got three brothers, remember?"

He sighed. "I'll see what I can do. Any chance there's some money at the end of this thing? Scarlett isn't operating a charity and Flint likes to get paid. A lot."

She smiled and said nothing. She already had him hooked. She could feel it. Her plan B could work.

If not, she'd move on to plan C, which relied on the same principle: Family First. Uncles do things for their nephews that they wouldn't do for anyone else. She didn't mention Jake Reacher because she knew Gaspar would like her plan C even less than bringing Flint into the mix.

Gaspar asked, "Do you want to hear what I found out about those names you got from Finlay? Or should I upload the stuff to your secure server and you can read it when you have a chance?"

"I can read it later. I don't have my laptop with me, but I'll figure out how to access the files. Anything I need to know right now?" she said.

"Agent Peter Ross seems like a straight shooter. Been around awhile. Knows what he's doing. Nothing special about him, but nothing hinky either," Gaspar said.

"The others?"

"O'Hare's files turned up nothing much. His paperwork says he's exactly what he seems. Pinto Vigo you already know about." He paused and said more seriously, "The brothers, Gavin and Bruce Ray, will require more digging. I'm on it."

The little hairs on the back of her neck tingled. "Why? What did you find that made you want to look further?"

"Not a whole lot. But it's weird. Two brothers from a militia family start a commune and live in peace and harmony ever after? That seem a likely story to you?" he said.

"No. But I'm a cynic by nature," she smiled.

"Yeah, well, a healthy dose of skepticism is necessary for a cop. If it ain't broke, don't fix it," Gaspar replied.

"What about the herbal products? And all the little side jobs they do?"

"They look legit on paper. They give hot air balloon rides to tourists. O'Hare does his accounting. A couple of the women run a day care in one of the homes out there on that compound."

"But?"

"But what the hell is the Vigo cartel doing involved in all of that? And you know they are involved, even if Ross hasn't locked that down yet. Otherwise, Finlay wouldn't have brought Vigo into the mix. And they wouldn't have taken Lawton." She could imagine Gaspar shaking his head and running his palm over his face. "Watch yourself, Suzy Wong. I don't like any of this."

"Yeah, I'm not thrilled, either." The hotel phone rang. "Hang on a second."

She reached over to answer. When she came back, she said, "My vehicle's here. I gotta go."

"Okay. Destroy this burner before you leave. We've used it too long already," Gaspar said. "You'll find a fresh one in the new vehicle."

"Will do. Upload the stuff to my server. Keep digging. See what you can do about Flint. Call me back as soon as you know"

Before she hung up, he said, "You do realize I don't work for the FBI anymore?"

She put a grin in her voice and said what they both knew was true. "Which means now you can do all the stuff that you wanted to do before. Neither one of us are violating orders. That's the beauty of it."

She disconnected the call and yanked the insides out of the burner. She broke the flimsy plastic with the heel of her boot and flushed everything down the toilet in three batches. Then she grabbed her gun, put her jacket on and opened the door to leave.

Which was when she saw the padded envelope on the floor.

So much for avoiding the Boss.

She bent and picked up the envelope. It could have been from Finlay, she supposed. So she opened it to look at the burner phone inside. This time, the burner was exactly like every cell phone the Boss had sent her in the past. No doubt at all.

Briefly, she considered taking his call. Instead, she dismantled the burner and flushed it, too.

She headed out, closing the door to the room behind her.

CHAPTER TWENTY-TWO

Thursday, April 14
5:30 p.m.
Albuquerque, New Mexico

MASON SAT ACROSS FROM Lawton, head in hands. He hurt
all over, from his pounding head to his swollen eye and his
tortured body. He'd never been a fighter. Never played contact
sports, either. He'd never been a threat to anyone for any reason.
He had no frame of reference for this level of pain.

But the agony was nothing compared to the unrelenting fear
that had become his constant companion. His entire body shook
with it. Even his voice sounded weak and tentative and wobbly
in his own ears.

He was a mess.

Only the certainty that Vigo would kill Cheryl and Micah, or
do something even worse, kept him going. He knew that the only
way out was to do whatever Vigo said and do it fast.

Satisfying Vigo's impossible demands was all he could

think about. He needed to learn the identity of this mole and tell Vigo and then grab Cheryl and Micah and run like hell.

If only Vigo would give him the chance.

"We need to get out of here. Which means we need a plan. Let's go over this again," Lawton commanded, swiping his palm over his face as if Mason was trying his patience. Which he surely was, but he couldn't help it. He simply didn't know what to do or how to do it.

Lawton said, "Start from the top. Exactly what is it that Vigo wants?"

Mason was exhausted. He needed sleep. He tried to take a deep breath, but the pain in his ribcage wouldn't allow it. Shallow wispy inhales were all he could manage. "He says there's a mole in his organization feeding you information. He wants to know who it is. He sent me to get the name from you. He says he'll let me go if I get the name."

"Because he couldn't make me tell him since I have no idea what he's talking about, so he brought you in to persuade me," Lawton said, exasperated. "Did he say why he thinks there is a mole in the first place?"

Mason shook his head and stopped abruptly. "No."

"Come on, Mason. Think. What did he say about the mole? Be precise. What were his exact words?"

"I don't know. He thinks someone told you he was here. He acted like that was a big problem. He doesn't want to leave. He wants to stay here until he finishes his business."

"What business?"

Mason shrugged. "That's not hard to guess. You said he's running a criminal cartel. I told you I saw young women packaging drugs. I saw a few guns. Probably doing some money laundering. Who knows what else?"

"Why does he think someone has revealed his location? Has he been served with a warrant? Has someone been arrested? What?"

"He didn't say. I don't know."

"You haven't heard any talk around Glen Haven about him or what he's doing out here at all?"

"No. We were told these people were another intentional community simply passing through. Looking for a quiet place to stay temporarily."

"If the police came to Glen Haven for any reason, you'd have known about it, wouldn't you? So whatever it is that's got Vigo worried, it must have happened somewhere else. Not here."

"I guess."

"Okay. Let's move on," Lawton said as he blew a long stream of exasperation through his lips. "Does he know you made that whistleblower complaint to the tip line?"

Mason gasped. His eyes seemed to widen of their own volition. He couldn't contain himself. Tears escaped and trickled down his doughy face. "You think he knows about that? How would he know?"

"Calm down. If he knew, you'd be dead now."

Mason's lip quivered and his heart pounded like a galloping stallion.

Lawton said quietly, "Vigo could be right. There could be a mole in his organization. Wouldn't be the first time. But I can't help him with the identity. I have no idea who these people are. You're the only one I know. You called the tip line. So if we're going to get the hell out of here and keep him from doing whatever he's threatening to do to Cheryl and Micah, you've got to hold it together and help me. Can you do that?"

Mason nodded because it was all he could manage. He swiped the back of his hand across his runny nose.

"Why would Vigo set up shop here in the first place?"

"I don't know."

"What is it about Glen Haven that would have led him to operate from here?"

"I don't know."

Lawton stood and paced the room like his last ounce of patience was evaporating fast. "Where is Glen Haven located? Exactly. Tell me about the area."

"We're about twenty minutes south of Albuquerque. Well outside of town. There's not much around here. We have a farm. You can't have a farm in the middle of town. Not around here, anyway."

Lawton nodded. "How remote is it?"

Mason shrugged.

"Describe what I'd see if I walked out the front door of the main house."

"There's a field across the road where we launch the balloons. Nothing much else. It's five miles to our closest neighbor."

"So we can assume that one reason he picked this place is because it's remote. More freedom of movement. You also have a lot of storage around here. He'd have room for his illegal inventory of all types." Lawton nodded, thinking through the angles, probably.

Mason waited for the next question.

"Okay. So Vigo's got some elbow room here. And he's also got a place he could defend, if he got raided. So far so good," Lawton said.

"Raided? Defend?" Mason squeaked as the terror squeezed his vocal chords.

Lawton ignored his fear. "Let's make a list of possible suspects. Tell me who the residents are. Precisely. You said two brothers founded the place. They're both married. They've got three kids between them, right?"

Mason nodded, unable to speak.

"There's you and Cheryl and Micah. How many others live here?"

This was a slightly safer question. Mason found his voice. "We have twenty-seven residents, total."

"Any singles?"

"Yeah. Three couples and the rest are singles, so ten singles. Mostly men."

"Ages?"

"Gavin Ray is the oldest person here. He's about forty or so. Bruce is two years younger." Mason cleared his throat. "Except for the three kids, nobody here is younger than thirty. We don't take them in unless they are self-sufficient and can pull their weight."

"Why is that?"

"Why? Are you seriously asking me that?" Mason pulled back angrily, as if Lawton was too clueless to solve anything. "To survive disaster. Everyone needs to take care of themselves."

Lawton cocked his head. "What kind of disasters are you expecting?"

"Hard to say, really. Could be anything." He shrugged and recited the list by rote. "Failure or poisoning of the water supply. Failure or sabotage of the electrical power grid. Earthquakes. Storms. Fires, accidents or arson. Attack by a foreign enemy. You name it. Gotta be ready. Plan for the worst if we want to survive and thrive."

"And who's idea was that? Gavin Ray?" Lawton paused. "Or was it Bruce?"

"What difference does that make? It's all true. We're not the only ones in the whole country who think so. There's millions of preppers like us out there," Mason said, sticking his chin out defiantly. "When the worst happens, you'd be smart to be prepared, too."

"Right. Okay." Lawton waited for Mason's annoyance to fade. "How can we get out of here? If we charge up those stairs and bust that door down, what will we find on the other side?"

"At least two guys with guns waiting to kill us," Mason said, wiping his nose with the back of his hand.

"You mean Hector and Freddie?"

Mason nodded. "Plus Vigo."

"Right. Is there another exit?"

"No."

"Then the stairs it is," Lawton said. "Once we get past the two guys with the guns, and Vigo, is there anyone else up there?"

Mason shrugged. "I didn't see anyone just now. But there are more people in the group. And I saw several in the other barracks. So it's possible."

"How many exits upstairs?"

Mason cocked his head to think. "Two doors, one at each end of the building. Several windows."

Lawton squatted on the floor. "Draw me a picture. Show me where the doors are. Show me the rest of the layout."

Mason complied without argument. When he'd finished his rudimentary drawing on the cement floor using a spit-dampened finger, he sat back on his heels and waited while Lawton studied the options.

Lawton tapped his lower lip with his index finger. The crude sketch Mason had drawn on the floor dried, leaving a barely visible salty residue outline.

"What if your plans don't work? Then what?" Mason said, chin jutting forward.

"We won't fail."

"But what if we do?"

Lawton swiped a hand through his hair and sighed. "Okay. If that happens, Vigo wants the name of the mole. So we'll give it to him."

Mason widened his eyes as his fear grew stronger. "How will we do that? I have no idea who might be doing whatever it is Vigo thinks is happening."

Lawton dusted the concrete dust off his hands. "Just pick someone. One of the men. As long as we give Vigo a name, we'll get a little breathing room. He won't kill us until he can confirm."

"But he'll kill an innocent person," Mason shook his head wildly. "It'll be like we murdered the guy ourselves. We can't do that."

"You worry too much. All you need to do is follow the plan. I'll handle the rest," Lawton said, as if he'd run out of patience. "What time is it?"

Mason shrugged. "It was still daylight when they tossed me down here. So maybe it's six now. Six thirty. Something like that."

"We've got at least two hours to wait." Lawton pushed himself up and walked over to one of the chairs. "We'll need a vehicle to get away from here. Draw Vigo toward town. And we'll need a way to communicate with the local FBI office."

"FBI? Why?" Mason's panic was barely controllable now.

"We can't save all of these people ourselves. We need backup." Lawton closed his eyes and kneaded them with one hand. "Tell me about the layout of this place again."

CHAPTER TWENTY-THREE

Thursday, April 14
6:10 p.m.
Albuquerque, New Mexico

KIM PICKED UP THE vehicle keys and directions to the
parking lot from the desk clerk and headed out. The sun was low
in the sky. Maybe another ninety minutes or so before sunset.
The wind was calm and the temperature about seventy, she
guessed. A perfect afternoon for a hot air balloon ride.

For a moment, she second-guessed her decision to destroy
the Boss's cell phone. But only a moment's hesitation. With
Gaspar's help and Finlay already involved, she didn't expect to
need anything much from the Boss. And if he had anything
constructive to offer, he'd send her another burner phone soon
enough anyway.

She walked around the building and grinned when she saw
the red Chevy Traverse waiting exactly where he'd said it
would be.

She shook her head. The Chevy was such a Gaspar thing to do.

She'd rented one exactly like it when her Reacher assignment started. The first time she'd met Gaspar at the Atlanta airport, she'd been waiting curbside, head bent to her work. He rapped on her window and startled her, which had taken about ten years off her life. Then he took the wheel over her objections and complained about the vehicle every chance he got.

Sending her this red Traverse now was Gaspar's way of saying he was with her all the way. Which made her feel a whole lot better about things, whether she should have or not.

Before she entered the SUV, where Gaspar would be monitoring her every move and Finlay would find her soon enough, she pulled the last fresh burner from her pocket and fired it up.

She sent a text to the number she'd memorized when she'd first met Jake Reacher. She needed a favor. The message was, "Ask Jack to call me ASAP." She added the phone number.

A few weeks ago, she'd discovered Jake. DNA confirmed that he was Jack Reacher's nephew. Jack's brother, Joe, was Jake's biological father. Joe was dead, but Jack was not. Kim had saved the boy's life, which Reacher duly noted. The last time Kim had heard from Reacher, he'd said, "I owe you one."

It was time to collect the debt.

Like everything else involving Reacher, collecting on his offer was like navigating a mine field.

It was risky to contact Jake.

For starters, the Boss monitored everyone known to have had contact with Reacher after he'd left the army. He also monitored anyone he suspected might have contact with Reacher now. Which most definitely included Jake.

But the Boss was working the Reacher case under the radar, too. Which meant he didn't have a team watching Jake around the clock and not in real time. He'd be reviewing the surveillance intermittently, when he had the chance to do it without being discovered.

Same way Kim did. Probably.

When the call back didn't come immediately, she figured Jake must be otherwise engaged. He had joined the army because, as he'd put it, that's what Reachers do. He was in basic training now. His time was not his own. She couldn't stand here and wait forever.

On her way to the Traverse, the phone rang. She picked up. "Hey, Jake."

"Agent Otto. Nice to hear from you. I've only got a minute. You know how it is. When you're in the army, somebody's always on your ass."

She imagined she could see his big grin. He was a good-natured kid. So much like his Uncle Jack and, at the same time, so different. When she'd been forced to describe him to the Boss, she'd said he was Reacher two point oh, newer and improved. The moniker had earned the Boss's scowl in return.

"Thanks for calling me back," she said.

"Yeah, well, I don't know what you need. And I'd be happy to volunteer. But like I said, my life is not my own at the moment."

"Right."

"I put a call in to Reacher. Haven't heard anything," he said.

"Is that unusual?"

He laughed. "Not at all. It would be downright weird if he dropped everything just to talk to me."

Kim wondered what "everything" might be in the context of Reacher. He was a vagrant. He owned nothing, he worked nowhere, and he was never required to do anything at all. But she simply replied, "Uh huh."

"So I left a message. Told him you needed him. Gave him this number. I hope that was okay."

"Yeah. That's fine. Thanks for the help."

Jake laughed again. "Such as it was. Okay, they're giving me the stink eye. Gotta go."

He hung up before she could say anything more. Maybe Reacher would call. Maybe he'd show up. And maybe he wouldn't. She needed a Plan C.

She walked to the Traverse, pushed the keyless entry to unlock the door, dropped the fob into her pocket, and slipped in behind the wheel. She put her foot on the brake pedal and used the push button to start the SUV. She adjusted the seat and the mirrors.

She noticed a gray Toyota sedan parked near the exit with the engine running. Vaguely, she recalled seeing a similar sedan when she left the hospital. Not unusual, really. Gray Toyota sedans were as common as dirt all across America these days. Probably waiting for a hotel guest, she figured.

While the SUV was warming up, she found the GPS system and entered the address for Glen Haven. The commune was about ten miles south of town. The GPS estimated her travel time at twenty minutes.

Finlay had said one of the things the commune did for cash was to offer hot air balloon rides for tourists. She'd taken a few rides in the past and sunset was a popular time for them. They might not be offering rides today, but it seemed like a perfect day for it, so she mentally crossed her fingers.

With luck, she'd find members of the commune she could interview covertly as she stood amid the guests and crew. At the very least, she'd get a firsthand look at Glen Haven.

She found the new burner from Gaspar in the glovebox of

the SUV. It was already fired up and he'd entered a number into the call log where she could reach him. She tossed the phone onto the passenger seat.

She adjusted her seat and fastened her seatbelt. Automatically, she patted her jacket pockets where she normally stashed her alligator clip. She remembered she'd left it back in her apartment. Traveling light wasn't all it was cracked up to be.

"Damn," she muttered under her breath. The seatbelt would dig into her neck and press against her sore chest every second until she found a better solution.

First order of business was to find a convenience store.

She started the GPS route guidance as she rolled the Traverse into the street. Two miles down the road, she found a store likely to have coffee and something she could use to keep the seatbelt from slicing her head off.

Kim pulled into an empty parking space in front and dashed inside. Five minutes later, she emerged with a sixteen ounce stainless steel travel mug filled with hot, black coffee, and a package of heavy plastic chip bag clips.

She glanced around. She noticed the gray Toyota sedan again as it passed the store. This was a busy street. Probably the woman behind the wheel was on her way home.

Kim made her way to the Traverse. The coffee cup fit snugly into the cup holder and one of the bag clips was sturdy enough to hold slack in the seatbelt at the retractor.

"Mission accomplished," she said, breathing easier due to reduced pressure on her lungs. She sipped the scalding coffee and turned onto the street again.

Alone in the cabin, Kim picked up the burner and hit the redial button for the number Gaspar had programmed into the phone.

"Everything satisfactory there?" he asked.

"So far, so good. You're tracking the GPS?"

"Yeah."

"Which means Finlay and the Boss can track it, too," she reminded him.

"I'm doing what I can to cloak the signal. It is what it is."

When there's only one choice... "Right," she replied.

"And what the hell do you think you're doing?" Gaspar growled.

"That's pretty obvious, isn't it?"

She checked the rear view. Traffic was light, ahead and behind. No one following her.

"Vigo's cartel is nothing to trifle with, Otto. You know that. He's gonna be pissed when he finds out you were there at the saloon. Leave Vigo to the FBI. They've got the guy on their radar. They don't need you mucking things up out there," he said.

"I am the FBI, Chico," she replied with a grin.

"You know what I mean," he growled. He was genuinely worried about her, not simply being bossy. She knew the difference.

"I take your point. I don't intend to be any kind of hero today," she soothed before she poked him again. "Besides, when your man Flint arrives, he'll want to be in on the action."

"You're killing me, here, Susy Wong," He gave a long, exasperated sigh before he said, "He's on his way. Try to stay out of trouble until he arrives."

"That's good enough for me. And I've had all the trouble I need for one day. I know you're doing your best, like you always do," she replied, even as they both recalled situations where Gaspar's best efforts fell short. Which was one reason why he'd left the FBI. His physical limitations simply made it impossible to do the job.

"Pulled the commune's address up on the satellite. Looks like Glen Haven is located at the end of a long, dusty two-track." He paused, scanning. "There's an electrical substation, a group of power lines, between the commune and the main road. Could be high voltage transmission lines."

"Sounds more than a little risky, from what I remember about the ability to steer those balloons," Kim replied. "They are dependent on wind currents and altitude. It's not like they have an accelerator and a steering wheel."

"Right. Looks like they use a field on the opposite side of the road for launching the balloon rides."

"Okay," she said, absorbing the details as she watched the traffic.

"It's a big field and it's maybe a quarter mile from the first power lines. So they must feel it's safe enough. But I agree. Not the smartest idea I've ever heard. Hang on." She heard a keyboard clacking as he looked something up. "Checking the power company's website. Says electricity can arc from those lines into the air. Says here, depending on voltage, the power can arc as high as twenty-five feet or more."

"Got it. Don't get into the balloon," Kim nodded. "You did some research on the commune's side business?"

"Yeah. For starters, turns out there's quite a few tourists who come to Albuquerque for balloon rides. There's been a festival in October that draws tens of thousands for about fifty years. Magical experience, six hundred balloons, no drones, eighteen law enforcement agencies on site, blah blah blah," Gaspar said, reading as he talked. "The balloon experience gig appeals year-round, looks like. Chamber of commerce says thousands more tourists every year come for rides even after the festival."

"The sky's clear and the wind is fairly calm. Looks like a good evening for a ride." Kim obediently turned right when the GPS prompted. "Can you see whether there's a group out there now? On the field?"

"I'm checking. The power company has cameras at the substation. From the feed, I can see them setting up. The balloon envelope is still flat on the ground. You should arrive before they get it inflated," Gaspar said.

"How many people are milling around?"

"Enough to make you somewhat inconspicuous, if you don't make a nuisance of yourself," he teased.

She took the last turn off the main road onto the two-track. "Copy that. I should be at the location within five minutes."

She saw a small cluster of people in the distance. The balloon's multi-colored envelope was inflating, rising slowly off the ground as big fans blew the hot air into the open maw.

On the other side of the two-track was the Glen Haven compound. From the road, she could only see the three McMansions in the front.

Under different circumstances, she might have simply knocked on the front door. But the crowd in the field probably came from the house, anyway, and she'd get more intel at the launch site.

Recon at the commune itself would wait until dark.

As she approached the field, she counted seven vehicles and more than a dozen tourists with their friends standing around in a loose knot near the balloon. The pilot and crew were busy preparing the balloon and the gondola for flight.

"Leave this line open with the phone in your pocket and I'll be able to hear. If you need backup, just say so," Gaspar said.

She grinned. "What if I did? It's not like you can send in a SWAT team."

"No. But I can call 911. Or, worst case, Finlay," he replied sourly, which made her laugh.

"Relax, Chico. Everything we know about Pinto Vigo's cartel says he's not much for leisurely pursuits."

"No. He runs fast and shoots faster," Gaspar deadpanned.

"Right. So I don't expect to find any of his posse in the crowd."

The balloon was about half inflated now and off the ground. Tourists were climbing into the gondola.

She pulled into the field, stopped the Traverse near the other parked vehicles, dropped Gaspar's burner into her pocket with the line still open, and hurried over to join the group of tourists watching the show.

CHAPTER TWENTY-FOUR

Thursday, April 14
6:35 p.m.
Albuquerque, New Mexico

THE BALLOON'S TRICOLOR ENVELOPE was bright against the late afternoon sky. Red, yellow, and blue primary colors arranged in a geometric pattern reminded Kim of a child's Rubik's Cube toy. Which made it starkly visible from a distance. Easy to identify, should there be other balloons or flying objects in the sky at the same time.

While the crew continued inflating the envelope by using two big fans to blow air into it, the gondola was upright and the pilot operated the burner to heat the air, making the envelope rise.

Kim had a clear view of everyone milling around. None of the men were Mason O'Hare. She hadn't really expected to find him here. But it would have been a solid break. Not that anything ever came that easily.

She approached the group as they climbed into the gondola,

one at a time. The basket itself was large enough to accommodate about twenty people, along with the propane and the burner.

Fifteen paying passengers were aboard when two women walked through the group of onlookers, asking whether anyone else wanted to join the ride. The pilot had heated the air inside the balloon enough to lift the gondola upright. The crew was holding it close to earth with big ropes, just in case another paying guest showed up.

When no adults accepted the invitation, one of the women gave a signal of some sort and three children, laughing and excited, ran over to the basket and climbed inside, clearly delighted to be allowed aboard.

One of the women stood next to Kim, smiling and waving toward them.

"Micah!" she yelled. "Put your jacket on!"

"Okay, Mom!" the boy yelled back as he slipped his arms into a bright green hoodie. The other kids had already donned their jackets.

"He seems like he's having fun," Kim said.

"He is. He loves to ride. Even when the flight will be rougher than today. When there's extra space, he jumps aboard every time." The woman smiled and nodded and spoke fondly of the boy. "It'll be cold if they go as high as a mile up. Micah knows that. But he gets excited and forgets."

Kim smiled back. "Are you involved with the ride or something?"

"I'm Cheryl. We live at Glen Haven," she replied, watching the balloon rise into the air as the big gondola lifted off. "Micah and I help when we can. You should take the ride sometime. You get a great view of Albuquerque from up there. It's a relaxing experience. Everybody loves it."

"Don't you worry about falling out?" Kim asked.

"I've fallen out before and lived to tell about it. Micah, too. It's not the most fun I've ever had, I'll admit that," she said with a grin. "Actually, we've all had extensive training for all sorts of emergencies. Hot air ballooning is one of the safest types of recreational flying you can do."

Watching the balloon float slowly up and away, Kim said, "Aren't you nervous about those power lines?"

"The pilot knows these currents out here will push him in the right direction. As long as he's got enough lift, he flies right over the lines, no problem at all. Watch," Cheryl said, pointing to the balloon.

Kim tilted her head and watched the gondola sail along, rising higher and higher until it was well above the trees. It would pass more than fifty feet above the first set of power lines. Plenty of room, just as Cheryl said.

"What about the return trip?" Kim asked, keeping her eyes on the departing balloon. "Are there good currents to bring them back?"

Cheryl turned her gaze to scan the crowd. People were returning to their vehicles. The ground crew was collecting equipment and stashing it into one of the vans.

"He won't fly back here. We'll follow along and pick up the equipment and the kids at the landing site. Want to come with?"

"Sure. I'd like to see them land. Don't you have champagne or something to celebrate?" Kim asked, her neck still craned toward the sky. The balloon was approaching the power station near the main road now, altitude still climbing.

"Technically, the bubbly is for the paying guests, but there's usually more than enough to share. And you know we can't store the stuff. So we'll just have to drink it," Cheryl smiled. "Come along. When you see how much fun it all is, you'll want to come back and try it, I'll bet."

The gondola seemed a little too low. Maybe an optical illusion. But it needed to gain more altitude before it reached the power substation.

"I won't be able to stay until you get all of the equipment stowed to come back here," Kim said, tilting her head toward the Traverse. "I've got my own wheels. Want to ride out there with me? Make sure I don't get lost?"

"Yeah. Sounds good. Come and meet everyone and I'll tell the others we'll see them out there." Cheryl started across the field, greeting the other watchers, headed toward the ground crew still packing the van.

Kim kept pace, but the balloon held her gaze. Still ascending as it traveled toward the substation. Only a few more feet to get there and get past the high voltage power lines safely.

From this distance, the gondola seemed too low. Kim's stomach tensed, but Cheryl seemed supremely unconcerned.

To calm her nervous stomach, Kim continued to make small talk. "So you live at Glen Haven? It looks like a great spot. Lots of room for kids to play out there."

"It is. Micah loves it. He had a long ride to school when we first moved out here. But we homeschool the kids now, so that makes it easier," Cheryl said.

"How many kids live there?" The gondola bounced on some sort of turbulence and fell lower in the atmosphere. The substation was directly ahead. Under her breath, Kim muttered "get up, get up."

"Just the three you saw get into the basket. All about the same age."

"They seem to really get along well," Kim said. "I grew up on a farm outside of town, myself."

Cheryl glanced at her. "Did you love it?"

"Mostly. Until I became a teenager," Kim replied with a grimace.

Cheryl laughed. "I get that."

The gondola was on course to collide with the transmission lines above the substation. She gasped and grabbed Cheryl's arm.

Cheryl looked up just as the pilot released a long blast of heat to the air inside the envelope and the balloon lifted easily clear of the danger zone. The gondola sailed past the station and the waiting crowd applauded.

"It's a stunt," Cheryl smiled. "He does it every day. To demonstrate his expertise to the nervous flyers. He's never hit those lines yet. There's an air current right at that exact spot. He lifts the balloon and the current sweeps it up and the balloon sails away. Every time. Everyone laughs and cheers."

Kim's knees felt weak. The gondola was safely on the other side of the substation. Catastrophe averted.

If she'd been a tourist considering a ride before the pilot's reckless display, she certainly would have changed her mind. But for now, she could return to normal breathing and keep walking.

They approached the vans just as a tall, dark-haired woman tossed a coil of rope into the back and closed the back doors. Another woman wearing a bright yellow fleece approached with a set of keys in her hand. "Ready to go?" she asked.

Cheryl said, "Daphne, this is Kim. She's interested in taking a ride, so she came out here to watch today. She wants to come along to the landing site."

"Welcome Kim. Sure, the more the merrier." Daphne was a couple of years older and seemed to have lost her energy along the way. "Happy to have you join us. But I'm afraid we can't offer you a ride. The passenger van is full and we've got all this equipment."

"No problem," Cheryl said, "We'll follow in Kim's SUV and I'll ride back with you in the van."

A man walked up and slipped his arm around Cheryl and squeezed her a little too tightly. Her face clouded with an expression Kim interpreted as fear.

He gave her a quick kiss on the temple before she could twist away. The port wine birthmark on his face identified him immediately from Finlay's photographs. Bruce Ray. One of Glen Haven's founding brothers. The younger son of Gavin Ray. Muscular and strong, he didn't look like he'd need Reacher's help for much of anything.

He said, "Gavin's in a hurry tonight. You about ready?"

"Bruce, this is Kim. She's observing. Trying to work up the courage to take a ride," Cheryl said in a friendly way. "We're all loaded. Tell Gavin to head out and we're right behind you."

"Hi, Kim. You should totally try it. You'd love it." Bruce nodded toward her, gave Cheryl another brief squeeze, whether she wanted him to or not. "See you at the landing site."

He turned and walked back to the second van. Gavin Ray was at the wheel. Bruce climbed into the passenger seat.

Daphne got into the first van and drove after them. By the time Kim and Cheryl made it back to the Traverse, a few of the other vehicles in the lot had followed the vans onto the dusty two-track toward the main highway.

Kim lined up at the end of the group and followed behind wondering how these friendly people could possibly defend themselves against the Vigo cartel. Given Pinto Vigo's track record, his plan likely involved killing them all.

He'd have already done that if he was ready to move on.

So what did Vigo want from the commune that was important enough to keep them alive?

CHAPTER TWENTY-FIVE

Thursday, April 14
6:45 p.m.
Albuquerque, New Mexico

VIGO PACED ONE END of the common room in the barracks, phone in hand, listening to Martin's report from the Last Chance Saloon about the FBI raid.

Martin had a good head on his shoulders and he was experienced. He'd dealt with troublesome law enforcement matters before. He knew to play it straight. Give them whatever they wanted. Above all, he knew not to draw attention to the cartel's activities.

So how did this simple two-agent visit go so horribly wrong?

Two FBI agents entered without a warrant, looking for Lawton.

Lawton wasn't there and no one in the saloon knew where he'd gone. A short conversation conveying those facts should have been the end of it. Ten minutes, tops.

"Names?"

"The man was Peter Ross. The woman didn't offer ID," Martin replied.

"You're sure she was FBI?"

"Yeah. She had the look, you know?" Martin said.

From Martin's account, the matter had been under control. A harmless exchange of questions and answers. Nothing more.

"So what happened?" Vigo asked.

"The second agent, the woman, saw Big Sela and Maria setting up in the dining room. She got past me. Approached them," Martin paused as if he didn't want to confess what went down next. "Then Maria ran. The agent ran after her. Big Sela knocked the agent down and held her down until Maria could get away."

"Then what?" Vigo asked, crushing the phone in his hand while barely holding his temper.

Martin explained precisely how Agent Ross shot and killed Big Sela when she refused to let the female agent go. Big Sela fought back. She'd done damage. But Ross recovered quickly and shot her in the head. In the end, Big Sela was dead and both agents lived.

Impotent rage flooded Vigo's body with every word Martin uttered. His sister, Maria, was right. The Asian bitch was to blame for Big Sela's death. Sela had one job only. To keep Maria from harm. She died in service of her mission. She had been a good soldier. Vigo owed her.

"What's the agent's name?" Vigo demanded between clenched teeth.

"Like I said, I didn't see her badge. Only the man. Peter Ross." Martin spoke softly, as if he was concerned about being overheard. Which he probably was.

The answer infuriated Vigo. He lashed out to kick the first

thing he saw. A flimsy metal dining chair. He kicked it so hard it fell over and skidded across the room, crashing into the wall.

Releasing a bit of rage had cleared his head slightly. Lawton would know her name. Or he could find out. Which was something else Vigo would enjoy squeezing out of him before he died.

Vigo said, "Are they gone now? The saloon is all clear?"

"No. There's two teams still here. Interviewing everyone. But none of us saw anything at all. We don't know who ran out the back door," Martin said as if it were true. He sounded convincing enough. Perhaps the FBI would believe him for a while.

"Exactly right. Keep it that way," Vigo ordered and disconnected because his sister's burner phone was vibrating in his pocket.

He pulled the phone out and looked at the screen. This time, she was calling instead of sending a coded text. A breach of security. Which meant she had something urgent to say.

Hector and Freddie and a couple of other soldiers were milling around inside the barracks. The basement door was securely locked. The soldiers were armed.

He nodded. "I'm going outside for some air," he said.

"Okay, boss," Hector replied.

Vigo closed the door behind him and walked into the gravel parking lot for privacy. There were seven vehicles parked there now. The rest of his crew was inside the second barracks preparing meals and dealing with the women.

The evening temperatures were cooling off. He glanced skyward. The Glen Haven balloon was on course, floating easily in the air currents. From this distance, he couldn't see or hear the propane blasts that heated the air and kept the balloon afloat.

He watched the balloon as he answered the phone. "Yes?"

Maria said quietly, "I found her."

Vigo knew who she meant. "How?"

"Waited for her outside the hospital. Followed her to a cheap hotel."

"She's there now?"

"No."

"Is she alone?"

"No."

Quickly, Vigo ran the problems through in his head. She was an FBI agent. Which meant he couldn't kill her until he was ready to leave town. He remembered too well what happened to his father.

A dead federal agent would bring the wrath of the government down swiftly. The hyenas in the rival cartels would immediately follow. Within forty-eight hours, his organization would be destroyed.

Or he could wait. Deal with her when he was ready. Which was a better plan.

"You found her once, we can find her again," he said.

"Or I can take care of her now and we won't need to find her again," Maria replied.

Vigo closed his eyes and shook his head, a sinking feeling in his gut. Maria had always been impulsive and uncontrollable. Big Sela would probably be alive now if Maria hadn't drawn attention to herself by running out of the saloon. What she'd done was foolish. But it didn't matter now, so he didn't say any of that.

"That's not a good idea. You'll have your chance. But not now." He imagined her listening to him. Just once. Even as he knew the likelihood was slim. Maria only listened when she felt like it. "We have other things to accomplish before we leave here."

She was quiet for a long time.

He listened closely. He could hear traffic noises in the background.

He asked, "Are you driving?"

"Yes."

"You're following her?" Vigo swallowed hard. The big shipment would arrive tomorrow. If he lost the inventory due to her recklessness, buyers would come after him like the hounds of hell. The war would rival the one he fled in Mexico. The feds would be the least of his worries.

"Of course I'm following her," she said.

"Maria, listen to me. Don't do it."

Maria didn't reply.

"If you kill her, you're on your own. Run. Now. Tonight. Get as far away as you can as fast as you can and lay low. You hear?" Vigo told her as sternly as their father would have done. If she did this reckless thing, she'd be hunted down like a dog. And he'd be hunted right along with her. "Don't come here. Don't call. I'll find you when things cool down."

Sardonically, she replied, "You're being dramatic, don't you think?"

"Not even a little bit. I know what I'm talking about. You saw what happened to our brothers. Our father. You were there with me at the battle in Mexico. I promise you'll have your revenge. But not yet," he said, pleading.

Her silence lasted a good long time. He hoped she was thinking things through and would see the situation his way.

"See you when I see you, brother," she replied before she disconnected.

He stood listening to dead air for almost a full minute before he cursed, dropped the phone into his pocket, kicked the dirt with the toe of his boots on his return to the barracks.

He strode into the big room and made eye contact with the two soldiers. "Go next door. Prepare the women and get them to town. Wait there until I call for you."

They marched quickly past him and closed the door on their way out. He waited a couple of minutes to give them time to get into the other building.

Vigo ordered gruffly, "Hector. Bring O'Hare."

Hector moved toward the basement. "What about Lawton?"

"One at a time," Vigo replied.

CHAPTER TWENTY-SIX

Thursday, April 14
7:45 p.m.
Albuquerque, New Mexico

KIM FOLLOWED THE SLOW caravan of vehicles along the dusty backroads toward the balloon's landing site. The brightly colored balloon envelope was clearly visible ahead. She guessed it was about 2,000 feet up in the air. Its flight path would have been easy to monitor even without Cheryl along for guidance.

They traveled to the main road and turned south for a couple of miles, keeping the balloon in sight. They passed a busy intersection and then ran into what seemed like nothing but desert before the lead van turned off onto the backroads.

"How far will the balloon travel before it lands?" Kim asked, steering around a deep rut in the gravel road and bouncing back onto flatter ground. The Traverse had decent suspension, but the road was far from smooth. She felt like she was riding over uneven railroad ties.

"Well, the longest hot air balloon ride was recorded at more than twenty-five thousand miles. So they can go quite a distance, depending on a lot of factors," Cheryl replied with a friendly smile. "Today? About five miles. We can run about twenty miles on our standard propane setup. In case there was some reason we couldn't land where we usually do. And sometimes we offer premium rides for ten miles or so. But the passengers are usually ready to come down after an hour."

"How fast does it travel? It seems slow from here."

Cheryl shrugged, bouncing with aplomb every time the wheels hit another hole. "Depends on the wind speed. Maximum safe speed is about ten miles an hour. Today we've got light winds, blue skies, and no rain. So it's covering about five miles an hour, so four-and-a-half knots, give or take."

Kim glanced toward her. She looked as relaxed and easygoing as she sounded. While Kim's attention was diverted, the Traverse's front wheel landed hard at the bottom of another pothole. The bounce lifted Cheryl off her seat and thumped her head on the roof.

"Ow!" Cheryl yelled. She reached for the hand grip and held on tight as the Traverse kept moving and the back wheel landed in the same deep hole. "Jeez! Watch where you're going!"

Kim nodded. "Sorry. Maybe put your seat belt on. This road is—"

"Yeah. Got it." Cheryl replied sourly as she reached for the belt and snapped the tongue into the buckle and pulled to snug the strap. She rubbed the top of her head, offering a wobbly smile. "I'm going to have a pretty solid lump there later."

"Sorry," Kim said again, slowing the Traverse to what felt like a bouncy crawl.

The balloon had begun its graceful descent, gliding down slowly, easily.

The crew van had pulled off the dirt road onto level ground and headed further off-road to meet up with the balloon's estimated landing site.

"How long will it take the crew to finish up here once the balloon lands?" Kim asked.

"It takes a while. There's a lot to do. We usually encourage the passengers to leave after about half an hour so we can finish up without interruptions," she replied.

The other vehicles followed the crew van and Kim steered the Traverse behind them to the parking place. She slipped the transmission into park, which allowed Cheryl to open the passenger door.

Cheryl pulled a business card out of her pocket and handed it to Kim. "I've got to go help with the gear. I hope you'll join us another time for a ride, now that you've seen how easy and safe it is. Set up an appointment on one of my flights. I'll be sure you have a terrific experience."

"Thanks. Will do." Kim looked at the card, which said "Glen Haven Balloons." It listed a phone number and flight times. She stepped out of the vehicle as Cheryl waved and jogged toward the gondola basket, which was only a few feet overhead now.

Kim leaned against the Traverse and watched for a bit as the gondola bounced a few times and then settled gently on the earth and the crew helped the passengers disembark. She glanced around the open area. Nothing to see much in any direction except desert sands. Scattered rocky outcroppings dotted the landscape here and there, some larger than others.

Once the gondola had landed on solid ground, the ground crew became energized into a flurry of activity. The champagne toast was set up twenty feet off to the right and the passengers' friends were encouraged to gather there to wait. Two crew members scurried to place a tarp on the ground to protect the balloon envelope while it deflated. Heavy ropes and other gear were removed from the van and placed to anchor the balloon.

Kim's body was flooded by an odd sense of déjà vu. The group standing around. Nothing but empty country for miles in every direction. Something about it made her uneasy. A wave of worry washed over her. She tried to shake it off, even as she scanned the distance for threats she could sense but not see.

One crew member placed an elevated platform on the ground while another steadied a small step ladder inside the basket. Passengers climbed out of the basket, one at a time. A white-haired man steadied himself inside the basket while another crew member assisted. He climbed the ladder's two steps, threw a leg over the basket's side, and stepped out onto the platform outside where a second crew member waited and waved him toward the champagne.

Kim watched three more passengers disembark while the crew prepared to fully deflate the envelope and collect their equipment after the toast. The whole process seemed to run smoothly, despite all the moving parts.

The last passenger was a petite woman about Kim's size with long, black hair gathered into a low ponytail at the nape of her neck by a bright yellow scrunchy. She hopped up the step ladder, put two hands on the basket's rim, and tossed herself out.

Her body twisted and landed gracefully on the platform like the gymnast she probably was. The other passengers and their friends applauded and she raised her arms in a mock "V" for victory, smiling and bowing as the others laughed.

The balloon's equipment, the crew's activities, the passengers and their friends' frivolity overwhelmed the desert's natural silence.

Which was why Kim didn't hear the first gun shot. But she saw the murderous result.

CHAPTER TWENTY-SEVEN

Thursday, April 14
8:00 p.m.
Albuquerque, New Mexico

ARMS STILL RAISED, THE gymnast collapsed on the
platform, blood exploding from her chest as if she'd been hit
with a sledgehammer hard enough to bust her tiny body open.
Her blood spattered over two of the crew members who were
standing nearby.

Kim screamed, "Get down! Get down!"

If the bullet had landed twelve inches to the right of the
gymnast, it would have hit the propane tank. The explosion would
have been spectacularly destructive. No one would have survived.

But no more shots followed the first.

She strained to hear anything remotely like a second attempt.
She drew her weapon and swiftly scanned the area for the killer.

Three rock outcroppings could have concealed the sniper's
nest. All were too far away for her pistol's range. Which meant
the shooter had used a rifle.

She saw something glint in the fading light more than a hundred yards away. A scope or field glasses, maybe. Or had she imagined the brief flash? She peered toward it, but didn't see it again.

Ignoring the panicked group lying flat on the ground, Kim crouched low and, using the vehicles for cover, ran to the fallen gymnast. When she was closer to the body, she confirmed with a glance that the woman was beyond rescue.

The colorful balloon envelope lay beside the gondola, flattening as the air escaped along with the buoyancy from passengers who had enjoyed the ride.

Kim quickly scanned for the shooter. She squinted into the distance, panning from one of the three rock formations to another and back. The sun had set before the balloon landed and most of the twilight was gone now. Darkness fell fast in the desert. Her sight distance was too short in this light.

Where was he? How did he manage to pull this off? Why did he kill that woman? Her brain kept firing questions faster than she could answer them.

The shooter couldn't have popped up from underground. There were no tunnels or underground systems out here.

He didn't drop in from the air because that would have left him no means of escape.

Which meant he'd had some sort of transportation to this precise location. And presumably, that same transportation was intended to take him away afterward.

He must have arrived and settled into his hiding place before the balloon floated past him.

Which meant two things.

Someone inside the gondola might have seen him because the balloon would have been flying low enough to allow a clear view of people and vehicles on the ground.

And he'd already known where the balloon was expected to land.

Cheryl ran up to the fallen woman. Wide-eyed, nostrils flaring, tears running down her face. "Elena!" she cried, cradling the woman in her arms.

"Who is she?" Kim asked.

Through her sobs, Cheryl managed to say, "Elena's one of our renters. She's only been here a few weeks."

"She lives at Glen Haven?"

"Yes. Elena Ochoa. She and her brother, Hector. He'll be devastated." Cheryl broke down again. Getting any more out of her was impossible.

Kim heard a helicopter in the distance headed toward the landing site. She kept her gaze on the three hiding spots, although falling darkness obscured her line of sight. She pulled Gaspar's phone from her pocket.

"The helo is your guy Flint on the way?" she asked.

"Yeah. He'll be on the ground in ten, latest. Leave the rental there. I'll get someone to pick it up," Gaspar replied. "More help on the way for the civilians."

"Good." She looked at the passengers, who were slowly finding the courage to get up and dust themselves off. Cheryl and the other crew members were making the rounds, checking each passenger. No one else seemed to be injured, but even the three children were subdued. Gone was the laughter and the horseplay now.

She heard sirens headed toward them. She asked Gaspar, "Is that your doing?"

"Indirectly. I called Finlay. He'll run interference and take care of the rest." Gaspar paused a moment before he asked, "How many casualties?"

"Only one," she said, a slight tremor in her voice. "Her name is Elena Ochoa. Her brother is Hector. Probably both members of the Vigo cartel."

"The shooter must have some kind of death wish. Vigo won't be happy." Before he disconnected, Gaspar added, "I'll look into it."

A few minutes later, the helo landed creating a dust cloud with its rotor wash. She recognized the pilot from the photo Gaspar had sent her a while back. Michael Flint. The only thing she really knew about the guy was that he was competent and Gaspar was a fan. Which was all she needed to know at the moment.

Flint pushed the passenger door open and she hopped inside.

"Hang on," he shouted over the deafening noise as she fastened her harness and slipped the headset on.

The helo was already lifting when she heard him through the earpiece. "Your shooter escaped in a gray Toyota sedan. Saw him heading out as I approached. Want to go get him?"

Kim nodded. She liked the guy already. "Hell, yes. That's exactly what I want to do."

She cinched the four-point harness tighter and peered toward the ground. From the air, the sirens she'd heard in the distance were visible atop several vehicles.

A couple of standard government black SUVs led the way. Which probably meant Ross was driving one of them since the dead woman was most likely a member of the Vigo cartel. They were followed by four standard police cruisers, first responders, and even a fire truck.

She squinted to see oncoming vehicles in the glow of their headlights. Looking for a gray vehicle in the darkness was like searching for polar bears on a glacier. Difficult, but doable.

"You didn't happen to get a license plate on that sedan, did you?" she asked Flint.

"Unfortunately, no." He turned toward her and grinned. He tapped a small screen amid many small screens on the control panel. "But it's a relatively new sedan and I located the signal for the GPS unit. We're tracking it now. Looks like its headed south."

Which made sense. Mexico. Vigo's cartel was based there. Less than three hundred miles away. Might as well have been on another planet. If the shooter reached the border, he'd be lost forever.

"Can you see inside the car?" Kim asked. Some vehicles had webcams inside. If the Toyota had one, they'd be able to identify the driver.

He shook his head. "The vehicle is too old for that tech. And we haven't had a chance to hack the camera on the phone he's using. Gaspar's working on it."

The wind speed had picked up at nightfall and buffeted the helo as if a giant tossed it from hand to hand. Flint was an expert pilot, but holding the helo steady was not easy. Progress was slower than Kim wanted, but she didn't want to fall out of the sky, either.

A couple of times, he hit bumpy air hard enough to lift and drop the helo like a child with a yoyo. Her stomach wanted to revolt, but she clamped her lips shut and forced herself to stay focused.

With the distraction of holding her queasy stomach steady, Kim lost visual contact with the sedan at busy intersections. She glanced at the screen where the GPS was still tracking the red dot as it turned west up ahead.

She peered through the helo's windshield, but there were too many vehicles on the road and the streetlights were not sufficient from this distance above the road.

She couldn't distinguish one sedan from another. Which became the least of her problems a moment later.

The GPS tracked the Toyota as it turned into a condo tower driveway and entered the multi-story parking garage.

"Got your running shoes on?" Flint said as he increased the helo's air speed and headed toward the landing pad on the roof of the garage.

Kim scowled and picked up the cell phone to call Finlay. She needed eyes and bodies on the ground. Now.

CHAPTER TWENTY-EIGHT

Thursday, April 14
10:05 p.m.
Albuquerque, New Mexico

VIGO'S PATIENCE WITH O'HARE was easily exhausted. O'Hare was useless. Even under extreme pressure, he maintained he didn't know the identity of the mole. Through his busted lip and rapidly swelling eyes, one arm hanging useless at his side after Hector snapped it like a sapling, he continued to deny all knowledge of the traitor until he passed out.

Vigo was inclined to believe him.

Which meant he was utterly expendable.

Vigo said, "Hector, carry him to the van. Put the canvas over his head. Move him out to the desert where you buried the others and kill him. Come back here."

"Yes, boss," Hector said, stooping to get a grip under O'Hare's arms and drag him to the door.

When Hector left, Vigo said, "Freddie, come with me."

They descended to the basement to deal with Lawton, Vigo leading the way.

Before he had a chance to begin the interrogation, a call came in on Vigo's business cell. He picked up and waited for the bad news. Because calls to this phone were always bad news.

"Elena's dead," one of his lieutenants said.

Vigo's belly tightened. He felt the rapid pulse pounding in his temple. Who would dare to kill Elena Ochoa? Hector and his sister were under Vigo's protection. Touching either of them was the same as harming Vigo himself.

The penalty was death. Every soldier in Vigo's army and every enemy on the planet knew that. Elena's killer was bold. Or stupid. Vigo cursed under his breath as he listened to the report.

His field lieutenant continued. "Long range rifle shot to the chest."

"Where did this happen?" Vigo said through clenched teeth.

"That's the crazy thing. She was at the landing site for one of the commune's stupid balloon rides."

Vigo frowned. "Why?"

"She was fascinated with them. She hung around the launch site whenever she had a chance and jumped into the basket when they had less than a full load. Guess she's been doing it for a few weeks now."

"Not a secret, then," Vigo mused aloud. "Who knew about this?"

"The pilots. Flight crew. Not sure who else."

Vigo stared at Lawton and lowered his voice. "Does Hector know?"

"Maybe not yet," the field lieutenant said. "Cops are there now. Someone will tell him soon. No way to keep it from him forever."

Vigo swallowed his growing anger. Before he disconnected, he said, "Keep me posted."

Vigo quickly considered his options. He'd never meant to stay here at Glen Haven indefinitely. Which was why he hadn't eliminated O'Hare before. To avoid the fallout.

Elena's death changed everything.

It meant his crew was no longer well concealed here. Cops would be nosing around about Elena. The inquiry would spread to the feds. Then his enemies would get wind of his position, if they didn't know already.

Maybe his enemies had a plan to pick off his closest confidants one by one until the crew was small enough to destroy completely.

That would be a solid plan. One Vigo would implement against his enemies, given the chance.

The last base Vigo had fled in Mexico was destroyed an hour after his crew bugged out. His enemies would attack. The trip from Mexico would take time to organize and execute, but not as much as twenty-four hours. If they had soldiers in the area already, the attack would come sooner.

Vigo had to go. The sooner the better.

His big shipment should arrive before eight o'clock in the morning. Briefly, he reconsidered his plan to wait until the product was in his hands. Should he go now?

No. The large shipment of drugs was more than he was prepared to walk away from. He'd easily turn his investment into fifty million and start over somewhere else. He'd done it before.

Waiting was risky. But life was risky. He nodded once, decisively. His plan was sound. He had much to accomplish before he left in the morning.

Near the top of his list was to destroy the mole.

He couldn't leave the mole alive. He'd lose the fear from his men and his enemies. He needed that fear to control them. Which meant he needed the mole. To make an example of him. To ensure no one else turned against him.

He'd been too lazy about pursuing the mole's identity. Perhaps Elena and Big Sela would still be alive if he'd been more diligent. That stopped now.

In the meantime, tie up loose ends. Destroy this place. Move on in the morning. It was time.

"Anything you need me to do, boss?" Freddie spoke from the shadows near the stairs where he'd been ordered to stand guard in case Lawton made any attempt to escape.

"Yeah. In a minute. We'll deal with this first," Vigo replied.

Lawton cocked his head to listen. He was handcuffed and tied to the chair. His feet were bound. He'd been in that position for hours. His muscles would be cramped and inflexible. He wasn't likely to jump up and try to escape, even if he could remove his restraints.

Vigo approached, pistol drawn. "Tell me who the informant is. This is the last time I'll ask."

"I've told you before. I don't know the answer to your question," Lawton replied.

"And you wouldn't tell me if you did know, would you?" Vigo said calmly.

Lawton's lips lifted in a sardonic grin. "Probably not."

"As you wish." Vigo nodded. He itched to shoot the bastard now. But what was the point? He'd be dead soon enough. Let him sit here and worry about it for a while. "We know where we stand. Tomorrow at dawn, we'll drive you out to the desert and shoot you. Leave your carcass for the vultures. Unless you change your mind."

Vigo turned and walked away, toward the stairs. When he reached the first step, he said, "Let's go, Freddie. We have things to do."

At the top of the stairs, Freddie dead bolted the basement door again. Hector came in from outside where he'd secured O'Hare into the van. The three sat in chairs around the fire and Vigo told them his plans.

Hector and Freddie were Vigo's oldest and closest friends. They'd grown up together in the same Mexican village. Their fathers had been members of the cartel when Vigo's father was the boss. Both were loyal to Vigo. Neither would question his orders under normal circumstances.

But these circumstances were not normal. Elena had been murdered. Hector's blood thirst for revenge was a wild card. He'd be uncontrollable if he knew his sister was dead. A luxury Vigo couldn't afford now. Hector must remain under control until they were safely away from here.

Vigo said, "There were FBI agents in the saloon today. They'll come here next. We need to move on."

"What about our shipment?" Hector asked.

"We'll wait for it. Be ready to get out as soon as it arrives. Take it with us. Use it for startup in our new location," Vigo said. "We'll leave a small crew here to clean up what we don't get done in the next few hours before the shipment arrives. They should be here before dawn. We've got seven hours or less."

Hector and Freddie nodded. It was a solid plan.

"Hector, before you head out to the desert with O'Hare, find Louis and Manny. Don't tell them anything. I'll brief them myself. The five of us can handle the inventory and get it out of here tomorrow." Vigo paused. "Everyone else can follow when we're set up."

Hector said, "Okay, boss."

"Freddie, get everyone else out of here tonight. Send them into Albuquerque. Get all the vehicles out except my truck. Tell them not to come back here, but don't tell them why. Say we'll contact them as soon as we can," Vigo said.

Freddie nodded. Hector said, "Okay, boss."

"Then come back here. We have work to do. We need to destroy this place. We don't want any forensic evidence left behind to tie anything to us. Understand?" Vigo looked them both in the eye, waited for a nod of agreement.

Freddie shook his head slowly. "There's plenty of propane on site in the barns. Because of the balloon rides and these crazy preppers. They think having their own fuel supply will sustain them when disaster strikes. They didn't consider the disasters from within."

Hector said, "Yeah, that will work. We can fill a few of the smaller tanks and put them inside the barracks. Then ignite the big storage tanks to get things started just before we leave. Safer that way. We don't want to blow ourselves up."

"Don't blow ourselves up," Freddie grinned. "Good plan."

Hector frowned. He didn't have much of a sense of humor. "Why don't we put O'Hare in the basement with Lawton? They'll both be found eventually and we won't need to make a trip to the desert tonight. Which we don't really have time for."

Vigo pretended to think about the suggestion. But he wanted Hector out of the way until the preparations were made. The longer he could keep Hector ignorant of Elena's death, the better. "We don't want anybody coming around here looking for him. We've had a couple of snoops from the commune hanging around already. Go ahead and take him out to the burial site, Hector. One less thing to deal with tomorrow."

Hector seemed like he might argue, but then he simply nodded and said, "Okay."

Vigo needed Hector to keep his head on straight. He could grieve in his own way later and Vigo would help him get revenge for the death of his sister. When the time was right. When they were out of this place.

Vigo simply said, "Meet back here at midnight."

Hector and Freddie headed toward the door. As if it were an afterthought, Vigo ordered, "And no cell phones. At all. Assume the feds are monitoring everything now. Radio silence from here on out. Understood?"

They nodded. Hector replied, "Yes, boss."

Freddie said nothing, but he wasn't the one Vigo was worried about.

When they left and closed the door, Vigo put his feet up, rested the shotgun across his lap, and stared into the fire, running through his plans in his head.

Originally, he'd intended to leave Glen Haven intact. The commune had taken them in when they'd had no other place to go after the Mexico massacre that pushed his cartel out of its home base. He'd been grateful then.

He couldn't afford to be blindsided by gratitude now.

The feds knew he was here. He felt it deep in his bones. Which made all the difference.

He knew how they worked. They'd been quietly, secretly building a case against him for their courts. After killing Big Sela at the saloon today, they'd find out she was a close associate. They would know he'd want vengeance. They'd step up their timeline.

Once they discovered the dead woman at the balloon's landing site was Hector's sister, they'd panic.

They'd be coming for Vigo and his crew. Probably tomorrow. The next day at the very latest.

Vigo had tried to intercept his big shipment with no success. Once more he came to the inescapable conclusion. He had two choices. He could wait here for the inventory to arrive in the morning. Or leave without it.

Either option was risky, but the payoff on the new inventory tipped the scales.

CHAPTER TWENTY-NINE

Thursday, April 14
10:25 p.m.
Albuquerque, New Mexico

THE SEDAN'S GPS BEEPED as the car traveled inside the garage, across to the far side, and up the ramp. Apparently the up ramps for each floor were on opposite sides of the building because the sedan crossed the second floor and headed up to the third floor. Then it did the same thing again.

Kim held her impatience and her nausea in check. The Toyota was already on the fourth floor when Flint successfully battled the cross winds and set the helicopter down on the parking garage roof.

Finlay had promised to send backup, but she couldn't wait for that.

She checked the GPS one last time. The sedan had parked in the corner farthest from the elevators on level six of the garage. It was four floors down from the roof and on the opposite side of the building from the closest roof exit.

She released her harness and jumped out of the helo as soon as the rotors slowed then hit the deck running toward the door that led to the interior of the garage. The soles of her boots landed with a loud drumbeat on every footfall.

She'd reached the door and crossed to the interior elevator banks in the center of the building long before the helo's blades stopped.

Kim glanced at the floor indicators above both elevators. The elevator cars were resting on the ground floor at the moment. Which could mean the Toyota's driver had dashed down the elevator and out of the garage already. But she hoped the driver wasn't that fast.

She didn't wait to see if either elevator car was in use before she opened the stairway door and pounded down the first flight of stairs. She was two flights down before Flint had secured the helo and followed. She heard his footsteps on the stairs above as he descended rapidly.

On the sixth floor, she left the stairwell and rushed into the parking area. An open expanse, divided by strategically placed wide support columns, spread in all directions from the center elevator bank. Vehicles of all types filled the parking slots. Trucks, SUVs, vans, cars, and even a few motorized scooters. Many of the vehicles were too high, blocking Kim's line of sight.

The helo's trace on the GPS had indicated the Toyota stopped near a corner on the sixth floor. Kim ran as silently as possible toward the location, stopping to wait and watch from behind trucks or concrete pillars.

Flint had reached the sixth floor, too. He was still behind her but coming up fast.

When she spotted the Toyota, it was parked into the slot nose first. The engine and the lights were off. Her view of the driver's position was blocked by the seat and the headrest. The driver could be inside the vehicle. Or not.

She stopped behind the closest pillar to wait for Flint.

He sprinted to another nearby pillar and signaled he was in place. They drew weapons and she waved to say she would take point. He nodded agreement.

Kim crouched low and, using parked vehicles to hide her approach, ran closer to the Toyota. She took one last look toward Flint to be sure he was ready. He made eye contact and nodded.

The driver had shot and killed a woman from a long distance using a rifle. Best to assume he would not hesitate to shoot again. Stealthily, she approached the sedan while Flint stood ready to provide cover fire if necessary.

When Kim was ten feet away, she moved to a better angle which allowed her to see into the side window.

The sedan was quiet. Too quiet. She saw no activity inside or around the car.

She raised her weapon and advanced.

When she could see inside the sedan clearly, she was sure. The driver had already abandoned the vehicle.

She signaled Flint. Together, they approached the sedan and peered inside from all angles.

Nothing.

The driver was gone.

Kim didn't try to open the doors or the trunk. The sedan might have been booby trapped to explode. But even if it wasn't, she didn't want to disturb any trace evidence that might be used against the driver.

Instead, she turned to scan the immediate parking area. No pedestrians. No cars moving through the garage. She heard no engine noise on the sixth floor and none above or below. The garage was either well insulated or well ventilated. Either way, sounds were suppressed.

She accepted what she'd seen. The driver was already gone. It was reasonable to guess that the immediate threat was gone, too. Not likely the driver was lying in wait to kill them.

It would be difficult to shoot a rifle from a distance through a full parking garage and kill a petite human. It could be done. But the chances of success were slim.

Kim signaled Flint and controlled her rapid breathing, returning to normal.

Flint walked toward her in the open parking lane and they met in the middle.

"Where did he go?" Flint asked, looking around from his taller vantage point.

"All the parking slots around the Toyota are full. Maybe they're all reserved. This is a condo building and people who own these places probably have assigned parking," Kim replied. "Which means he either knew this spot would be open or he just got lucky."

"That's a lot of luck for one guy to have today. So probably not," Flint said. "You're thinking he lives here? On the sixth floor?"

"He's familiar with the garage. But I doubt he lives here." Kim shrugged. "My guess is that a guy who was sharp enough to shoot and kill a woman with a rifle in that field wouldn't be so stupid as to drive his own car back to his own home. Would that make any sense to you?"

"Not when you put it that way…" Flint grinned.

She pulled out Gaspar's phone and snapped a photo of the license plate and the VIN number. Both the plates and the sedan were probably stolen, but they had to start somewhere. She shot the front and back of the sedan, too. Then she sent the four photos to Gaspar.

After that, she repeated the exercise with Finlay's phone.

"It'll take a while to canvas every resident and vehicle in this place. There's gotta be more than five hundred units here. Everybody probably gets allocated two parking spaces and probably on the same floor where they live," Flint said, thinking out loud.

Kim replied, "Backup is on the way. They can check it out. Do the canvas. Get witness statements. He could have friends or family living here. Or maybe he once lived here. Who knows? The locals might find him that way. Eventually."

"Meanwhile?" Flint asked, arching both eyebrows.

The gesture reminded Kim of Gaspar. But he usually only arched one eyebrow at a time. She was glad Flint was here instead. Like Gaspar had said, Flint was both skilled and reliable. Beyond that, he was physically capable of being a solid partner.

"Let's head down to the first floor of the garage. I want to see how he gained access to this place." Kim moved toward the elevator bank and Flint came along.

He said, "Since we agree he doesn't live here, what difference does it make? Whatever key card he used to get past the gate will be either a forgery or stolen, just like the car."

She punched the elevator call button and waited for the car to rise from the first floor. "So the elevator cars sit at ground level until they're called. These two haven't moved since I came in from the roof. Which means the driver didn't take the elevator down and walk out."

"No. But there's more than one staircase. He might have taken the stairs down and walked out," Flint said reasonably.

The elevator car arrived and the doors opened. They stepped inside and the doors slid closed. She punched the button for the first floor. Kim looked around. "There are surveillance cameras in here."

"There are also cameras in the parking areas," Flint said. "Can we get your FBI buddy Ross to chase those down, too? Maybe one of them has a good angle shot of the driver."

Kim nodded. "Probably. Or we can get someone else to do it."

The elevator stopped at the ground level and opened silently. They stepped out and followed the signs pointing to the exit.

Flint said, "No manned booth. Just a barrier with a key card access. After hours, it looks like a folding gate will electronically cross the entrance."

Kim nodded again. Three cars were backed up at the exit now. The barrier arm was down and didn't lift when the first driver in line waved his key card over the sensor. He tried three more times before he lost his temper and pounded on the pole, shouting for assistance.

An electronically enhanced voice came through the speaker. "The barrier arm is resetting. Please wait."

Two more cars lined up behind the three that were already waiting. After a while, a security guard waddled out from the side door nearby. He fiddled with the sensor and the arm for a couple of minutes but couldn't make the system work.

The driver of the first car was yelling about the guard's incompetence and a couple of the other vehicles honked horns to punctuate his complaints.

Finally, the security guard pulled out a set of keys, turned a lock of some sort, and raised the barrier manually to release the imprisoned vehicles.

By the time all the vehicles had been allowed to exit, the guard was already on the phone to a repair service.

Kim approached him, waiting until he finished his call and there was a lull in the exit traffic. "Mr. Potter?" she said after reading his nameplate while pulling out her badge wallet. She flashed the wallet long enough to let him see her badge and then replaced it before he could ask questions.

"Yeah," he replied hesitantly.

She pointed to a camera in the corner. "That camera aimed at the entrance and exit all the time?"

"Yeah. Why?"

"Is it recording all the time?"

"Yeah. Why?" he asked again.

"We're going to need to see the video."

"Well, I can't show it to you right now," he snapped. "I have to wait here until the repair guy comes or that jerk you saw yelling at me will have me fired."

"That's too bad," Flint said.

"Damn straight," Potter said, belligerently. "This damn thing breaks all the time. If the condo board wasn't so cheap, they could get it fixed. How is that my fault?"

"No kidding. Don't you hate that?" Kim nodded sympathetically. "I'm pretty tech savvy. I can probably figure out the video by myself. How about if I just have a look? You can keep working here. Won't take me long."

"Got a warrant?" he said, sticking his chin out, still ticked off by the unfairness of it all.

"Not yet. But I can get one. Might be a while. But we can wait here with you until it arrives. You sure I need it?" she replied.

"What are you looking for? Maybe I can help," he said, softening a little.

Flint piped in. "We're interested in a gray Toyota sedan parked up there on the sixth floor. Drove in here about half an hour ago, give or take."

Potter grimaced and frowned. "Yeah. I noticed that car come in because it was splashed with a lot of mud. Hard to get that muddy around here this time of year. Not much rain, you know? Besides, most of the roads are paved, anyway. So I wondered what the hell that pretty young woman had been doing to get her car all muddy like that?"

Flint raised his eyebrows again and shot a look toward Kim. She cocked her head. The driver of the sedan was a woman. Meaning the shooter was probably that same woman. Not a man after all.

"Do you know who owns the car?" Kim asked, taking the slim chance that he might have recognized her.

Potter shook his head. "No. That was the other thing. I don't think I've seen that car or the woman before. Can't say for sure. We have a lot of cars parked here and I don't see all of the residents since I don't work twenty-four-seven. But you get familiar with things after a while, you know?"

"Yeah. I know." Kim replied, coaxing him along. "So how about it? Can we see the video or do we need to go get that warrant?"

Potter looked from one of them to the other and finally glanced at Flint and said, "You stay here and wait for the repair guy. I'll take her back and show her the video. How's that?"

"Perfect," Kim said, nodding to Flint before he had a chance to object. She followed Potter inside.

CHAPTER THIRTY

Thursday, April 14
10:55 p.m.
Albuquerque, New Mexico

VIGO'S INNER CIRCLE SHOULD have returned to base.
None were here. Not even Louis and Manny had returned from
Albuquerque.

Freddie was busy next door sending the rest of the crew off
premises and into hiding until Vigo gave the all clear. Right
now, he didn't know how long that would be.

Maria should have returned to base by now. She had not
arrived.

Of course, Elena was also missing. Big Sela, too. He knew
what had happened to both women. But how many others in his
crew had been taken out of service today?

With the FBI nosing around the Last Chance Saloon, it was
only a matter of time before the feds rounded up his entire
Albuquerque team.

He could pull people in from other locations to help. But that took time. And he'd need a new base of operations, too.

Two hours ago, Maria had texted two ambiguous words. "Got her." Vigo knew she'd meant that she killed the female FBI agent responsible for Big Sela's death. But he had the sinking feeling that she'd killed the wrong woman.

If his fears were confirmed, Maria had irrevocably destroyed his team. Hector would never forgive her. He'd never rest until Maria was dead, too. And Vigo wouldn't allow that to happen. He loved Hector like a brother. But Maria was his actual blood.

To choose between them was at the same time impossible and inevitable.

Hector would never live without avenging Elena. Vigo knew this because Hector's values were the same as his own.

He needed Hector a while longer. But when his usefulness was done, so was he.

Vigo had waited to contact Maria until after Hector left to dispose of O'Hare and the crew had abandoned the barracks next door.

He pulled Maria's daily burner phone from his pocket and stared at it as if he could will it to vibrate with a message from his sister. Nothing happened.

Another hour before this phone expired. That was the system. At midnight, they stopped using today's burners. They switched to a fresh set in the morning.

The system assumed they'd be together between midnight and dawn. They didn't have a contingency plan because they'd never needed one before.

He'd ordered his crew to observe radio silence for solid reasons. The risk of exposure was too great to use the burner again now. But Maria wouldn't know that. She'd have contacted him if she'd meant to return after midnight. Yet she hadn't called or texted or returned.

He'd go out looking for Maria if he had a clue where to look. She'd been following the FBI agent she held responsible for killing Big Sela, which was stupid in the extreme. Had she been discovered? Was she in custody? Worse, had she been killed?

He heard a knock, two solid raps on the wood to signal he was friend and not foe, before the door opened.

Vigo glanced up. Freddie. Not Maria.

"Where the hell are you, little sister?" Vigo murmured, pressing a single character to ask the question and sending the text before he could lose his nerve.

If the feds were watching, they'd see it.

They wouldn't know what it meant.

He'd be gone before they figured it out.

Freddie came over to the fire and sat. "Everyone's gone. Sent them out in three vehicles and left the others parked outside. They'll fan out when they get to Albuquerque and wait for us to contact them with our new base location."

Vigo nodded. "Good work, Freddie."

"Hector's not back yet?"

Vigo shook his head. "It's about an hour out to the burial site. Time to do the job. Digging a grave and covering a body takes a while. Then an hour back. I don't expect him to return until an hour before dawn."

"We didn't have much product left, but I sent it out with the crew to be sold," Freddy said. "Louis and Manny put the guns and ammo into one of the trucks. Now they're out in the barns setting up the propane. Want me to go out and help?"

Vigo stood and slid his worn jeans into his boots. "Yeah. Let's both go. The work will finish faster."

CHAPTER THIRTY-ONE

Friday, April 15
12:15 a.m.
Albuquerque, New Mexico

AFTER KIM HAD COLLECTED the surveillance video on the woman driving the sedan, she sent the clip to Finlay and to Gaspar. To each, she included the same text message. "Identify this woman pronto."

When the video and the messages were delivered, she and the guard, Potter, returned to Flint, still watching the entrance gate to the parking garage.

"Any problems?" Potter asked.

"Only that your repair guy never showed up," Flint replied.

Potter grimaced as he took his post. "Yeah, that service is slow. I may be out here all night."

Flint said, "Cops are upstairs with that sedan. They'll probably tow it away later tonight. I gave them your name, in case they've got any issues."

Potter nodded. "Swell."

Kim inclined her head, said her goodbyes, and asked Flint, "There's a coffee shop across the street. How about a cup of coffee?"

"Yeah, sure. Why not." He stuffed his hands into his pockets and followed Kim out onto the sidewalk.

She watched for an opening in the traffic and jaywalked across the pavement. When they reached the coffee shop, Flint held the door open. The gesture was curious. He hadn't seemed like an old-fashioned gentleman. Made her wonder about his background.

She went inside where the cold winds had been banished by the warmth of a fireplace.

"Grab a table over there and I'll get the coffee. How do you like it?" Flint said.

"Hot and black," she replied.

He grinned. "Perfect. I like a low-maintenance woman who know what she wants."

She gave him an eye roll. "Right back atcha."

She settled into a chair near the fire. He brought the coffee a few minutes later and sat across from her. He asked, "What did you find out from the security guard about our mystery driver?"

"Not much. I interrogated him a little. I don't think Potter knew the woman. Never saw the car before, either. Just like he told us."

"That's not helpful," Flint said, sipping the steaming brew.

Kim tried to drink hers, but it was way too hot. The guy must have an asbestos tongue. "The good news is that the video was state of the art. It captured a pretty good image. I sent a copy of the video to Gaspar. We may get a hit on facial recognition."

Flint nodded. "And if not, maybe the crime scene techs will find she left prints or DNA or something in the vehicle."

"Either way, with a little luck, we'll know who she is soon," Kim replied, pulling a cell phone out of her pocket and passing the photo across the table. Flint studied the picture, committing the woman's face to memory.

"Nothing remarkable. Latina. Mid-thirties. Maybe younger. I don't recognize her," Flint said, handing the phone back. "You think she killed the woman at the balloon landing site? That was pretty straight shooting. Particularly under those conditions. Poor lighting, windy, fairly good distance. She'd have to be a solid marksman to hit the target like that."

Kim had been thinking along the same lines. Seemed like Flint had his head in the game, which she appreciated.

Instead of saying so, she shrugged. "At the moment, all we know is that she was out there. It's possible she had an accomplice. Maybe there were more people in the car, too. I didn't see anyone else on the video, but the angle wasn't that great. Hard to know, really."

Flint nodded but made no reply.

Kim said, "If we're lucky, she left the rifle in the Toyota when she dumped the car. Then we might know for sure, depending on the forensics."

"Let's say she did. Use the rifle and shoot the woman. Let's say she's that good," Flint mused. "Why did she do that? Any guesses?"

Kim shook her head. "We don't have enough intel to answer that question, either. Not yet, anyway. All we know so far is the dead woman's name and address."

"We could get more intel from those preppers at the commune," Flint said.

"She wasn't one of the Glen Haven community members. She was one of the renters," Kim replied slowly. "Intel says the renters are tied to the Vigo cartel. We think Pinto Vigo may be involved. The local FBI office thinks so, too."

Kim glanced at her watch. The locals would probably still be processing the crime scene and interviewing the witnesses at the landing site. They might not have focused on the commune yet.

Regardless, the commune and the murder and Pinto Vigo's cartel were not her mission. She'd come here to find John Lawton. And because Finlay believed Reacher was in the mix, somehow. She could leave the rest to Ross and his team in good conscience. They were capable and were well focused on the matter now.

She cocked her head and studied Flint. Gaspar said the man had skills and talent. He also said Flint was solidly reliable.

He might be the right man for hunting Reacher. In some ways, he was probably better qualified than she was. Only two problems with that so far. He wasn't FBI, which meant the Boss had zero control over him. And the second thing? Flint wasn't a guy who'd work for government wages. Not anymore, anyway.

She held the coffee cup between her palms. While she had him here, she might as well read him in and see just how good he was.

"Gaspar tells me your specialty is finding people who can't be found. That true?" she asked.

He nodded. "Pretty much. I charge exorbitant fees, too. Gaspar tell you that?"

"He might have mentioned it." She grinned. "Sounds like good work if you can get it."

"Believe it or not, I've got a waiting list," he replied, finishing off his coffee. "I'm a one man shop. I'm not looking to take on partners. But I like Gaspar. And he likes you. And I was already in the neighborhood. So here we are."

"Right."

"Who are we looking for? And does the missing person have anything at all to do with this commune and the balloon ride and the shooter and the dead woman and all the rest of it?" Flint asked, both eyebrows arched for punctuation.

Kim settled deeper into her seat. The fire was mesmerizing. Under different circumstances, she could easily fall asleep, right here.

She said, "The missing person is John Lawton. A Treasury agent. He went for a lunch meeting with a member of the commune and hasn't been seen again. Looks like he was kidnapped."

Flint nodded. "Ransom demand come in?"

"No," she replied, shaking her head. "Complete radio silence since he was abducted."

"How about the lunch partner?"

"Also missing," Kim said. "Thing is, it seems like this commune is at the center of all that's happened. But I'm not sure whether any of the rest has anything at all to do with Lawton's being missing. We don't have enough evidence that the two things are connected. Not enough for the local FBI office to get a warrant to search the premises out there."

"But now that this murder happened and the dead woman was living on the commune's premises, the FBI can get a warrant for that. A thorough search might turn up something that would help you find Lawton," Flint nodded. "So we do what? Wait for the locals to serve the warrant and go along with them? How long is that likely to take?"

She shrugged again. "I can make a call. But it's not likely to happen tonight. Tomorrow, maybe."

"Once they get out there, it'll be a circus, you know. They'll have teams of people milling around going over the place with a magnifying glass. Lawton so much as sneezed in that place and they'll find out," Flint said.

"Yeah. And Vigo will know that, too," she gave him a steady gaze. It didn't take him long to get the point.

"So you're worried Vigo will get wind that they're coming and he'll kill Lawton before they get there. If he hasn't killed him already."

She nodded. "Maybe more than just Lawton. There are twenty-seven members of the commune out there. Vigo would consider them all expendable."

"Which means we should go out there tonight and see what we can do ahead of the raid tomorrow," Flint said. "Find Lawton and rescue him, if he's out there. Deal with Pinto Vigo's defenses so the locals don't get slaughtered when they arrive."

She nodded again. She'd reached the same conclusion hours ago. She'd planned to go out to the commune and snoop around after dark. Once she'd found Lawton and figured out what the hell was going on, she'd call in Finlay and let him handle the rest.

Then the gymnast had been killed at the landing site and Kim's half-formed plan got derailed. Vigo would hear about the gymnast. He'd change his actions because he'd know the feds were coming. If he could get out before the feds arrived, he'd have no reason to keep Lawton as a hostage now. Lawton might already be dead.

Kim drew a deep breath. Time to get back on track.

Gaspar's phone buzzed in her pocket. She fished it out and answered the call.

"We got a hit on your Toyota driver. Facial recognition did it. Confirmed with fingerprints off the steering wheel. They picked up some DNA but the results aren't back yet. Likely that will be a match, too," he said.

"Okay. Who is she?" Kim asked.

"You've seen her before. In fact, she almost got you killed once today already," Gaspar said.

"You mean she was the woman who ran out the back of the Last Chance Saloon this morning?"

"Bingo. Give that girl a cigar," Gaspar said sourly.

"Who is she?" Kim asked again, like a parrot with a limited vocabulary.

"You aren't going to like it."

"So what else is new," she replied. "At this point, I can probably guess anyway."

"Not likely. But your buddy Agent Ross might have," Gaspar said. "She's Maria Vigo. Pinto Vigo's younger sister. And by all accounts, she's as cold-blooded as he is."

Kim inhaled sharply. Her stomach thrashed, churning the coffee in her belly. "Where is she now?"

"In the wind at the moment. Now that we know to look for her, someone will find her. Eventually," Gaspar replied. "One more thing. They found the rifle she used to shoot Elena Ochoa in the trunk of the Toyota. Ballistics will need to confirm, but they're pretty sure it's the murder weapon and Maria is the one who fired it."

"Why? Why did she kill someone so close to her brother? He'll be furious. Not to mention Hector Ochoa. Is she looking to start an all-out war among members of the cartel?" Kim asked.

"Not exactly. The story gets worse," Gaspar said.

"What do you mean?"

"We have been piecing her actions together. Using the Toyota's GPS, we nailed down the routes she traveled from the landing site and checked the cell phone calls along the route. Earlier today, before she killed Elena Ochoa, she talked on the phone to her brother." Gaspar paused for a deep breath before he finished. "Seems like you were the real target of her anger."

"What?"

"She was there to kill you. Elena wasn't her intended target. We're not sure whether she knows that she killed the wrong woman, even now." Gaspar cleared his throat. "She'll find out, though. And when she does, she'll try again to do the job she meant to do."

"Well, that's just great," Kim said, acid souring her stomach. "Do we know where she is now?"

"Not exactly. But we'll find her. Just stay out of sight until we do. I'll call you back." Gaspar ended the call abruptly.

Kim relayed the conversation to Flint.

He said, "So now what? Go out there to rescue Lawton or not?"

"Yeah. We can fly recon out there in your helo. Check the place out. But we can't land the helo close by. Way too noisy," she replied, pulling a different phone from her pocket to call Finlay. "We'll pick up a vehicle and drive out to Glen Haven and have a closer look around."

"Sounds like a plan." Flint nodded. "We'll need some gear, too."

"Right," she said as she made the call.

Finlay picked up and they discussed the logistics. He found a helipad where they could land and promised to deliver an SUV with four-wheel drive to the location before they arrived to collect it. He'd include all the necessary equipment in the SUV.

When she hung up, Flint said, "So we find Lawton. Spring him if we can. And do it before the feds get there. Get in, get out, nobody gets hurt."

"That's about the size of it," she replied, still thinking things through. "Except that's not where we start. We're looking for O'Hare. He disappeared with Lawton and he's likely to know where to find him."

"We don't think O'Hare is connected to Vigo?"

She shook her head. "No reason to reach that conclusion. Yet. And O'Hare should be home in bed at this hour. His room at Glen Haven has an outside entrance. Should be easy to surprise him."

"When are the locals planning to serve their warrants?" Flint asked.

"Sometime after dawn is our best guess. They're not ready and they need the time to prepare. They've got a lot of moving parts to put in place. There's only two of us. We can travel lighter," she replied.

Flint pushed to a standing position and tossed his empty coffee cup into the trash. "You ready?"

"I'm as ready as I'm going to get," she replied on her way out the door into the cold and windy darkness. She tried not to think about the hazards of flying a helo under these conditions.

When there's only one choice...

CHAPTER THIRTY-TWO

Friday, April 15
1:30 a.m.
Chihuahuan Desert, New Mexico

BOUNCING AROUND ON THE floor of the van, Mason slowly regained consciousness with an overwhelming sense of déjà vu. He'd been here before. And not that long ago. But where was he, exactly?

As the fog cleared from his mind, he realized he was in the van again and it was traveling across rough ground. Piercing pain stabbed his broken arm with every bouncing rut. Achy all over, he was barely able to see out of his swollen eye.

When he managed to force his eyelid open enough to receive a bit of light, he couldn't see anything anyway because the familiar canvas bag covered his head.

But his limited vision didn't matter. The van was dark inside and the night was black as pitch outside. He wouldn't have seen anything even if he'd had perfect vision.

He was groggy. His head was pounding. His whole body

hurt. The throbbing in his arm was bearable but certainly not pleasant. Adrenaline kept the worst of the pain at bay.

He remembered his last session with Hector and Vigo. They kept asking him to identify the mole. Over and over again, they demanded answers that he didn't have. Which they'd refused to believe.

At some point, he'd passed out from the pain and exhaustion and stress of it all. And when he came around, he was lying on the floor of the van and on his way somewhere. He had no idea where the van was headed, but he could guess the destination wouldn't be any better than the barracks at Glen Haven.

He'd made another mistake. He should have fabricated a believable story. Told Vigo what he'd wanted to hear. Giving Vigo a name for the mole, even a fake one, might have made all the difference.

Or maybe Vigo would have killed him on the spot after he thought he'd gotten what he wanted.

Not that it mattered now. Wherever Mason was being taken tonight, he figured he wouldn't be coming back.

His body was shaking. Could have been from the cold. The van wasn't insulated and the night air was colder than normal.

Or maybe the shaking was caused by shock from his injuries, or simply because he was afraid. Very afraid. And confused.

How had all of this happened to him? What about Cheryl and Micah? What about the others at Glen Haven?

The van stopped moving and Mason felt the transmission shift into park with a lurch. The dome light came on. A man gave him a rough shove with his boot before he reached down to yank the canvas bag off Mason's head.

Hector.

"Come on. You're awake. Let's go," he demanded.

The dome light was blinding in the blackness. Mason squeezed his eyes shut and opened them a few times until they adjusted and he could focus. After a couple of minutes, he could see reasonably well peering from his one good eye.

He looked through the windshield. The high beam headlights were still on, illuminating the desert in front.

Hector slid the van's door open and the cold wind rushed inside. Which was when Mason realized his hands and feet were not bound.

How had he not noticed that before?

He gave himself a mental shake. He needed to gather his wits. Maybe he could escape if Hector presented any kind of chance.

He crabbed around and struggled to a crouching position. He waved his functioning arm to find a handhold and followed Hector outside. He stood on cramped legs, walking in circles with tentative, short steps to get his circulation going.

Hector reached inside the van and pulled out two shovels. "You can walk. I'm not carrying you."

Mason's reaction times were slow. He should have jumped back in the van and sped away. The engine was still running. He might have made it before Hector had a chance to stop him.

As if he could read Mason's feeble mind, Hector said, "Don't get any stupid ideas, O'Hare. You want to breathe for a while longer, fine. I'd rather not carry your dead carcass across this damn desert tonight. But I will do it, make no mistake."

Hector continued to walk away from the van, his body illuminated by the headlight beams. Mason followed without coherent thought.

His mind was on Cheryl, Micah, and the others. What was Vigo planning to do to the only family Mason had ever known?

Whatever Vigo's plans, Mason was sure they wouldn't be good news for him. He was equally sure he couldn't run away faster than Hector could shoot him.

Dragging his feet, he followed Hector in the headlight beams, searching frantically for a means of escape in the empty desert.

Mason noticed that the van's headlights were shielded by a rocky outcropping about a hundred feet or so off the road.

Hector tossed one of his shovels down near two dirt mounds behind the rocks. With the second shovel, he began to dig in the hard earth. He lifted shovelfuls of dirt and set them aside. He didn't force Mason to help, probably because of his fractured arm.

Hector worked at a steady pace. Soon, he was standing in a shallow hole as the dirt pile grew. It was the dirt pile that galvanized Mason's fear.

He stared at the dirt pile, the hole Hector was digging, and back toward the two mounds a few feet away. Several doubletakes later Mason noticed that each mound was about the size of a human body.

Another full minute passed before he realized the mounds were graves.

His entire body began shaking uncontrollably when he understood that Hector had brought him to his own burial site.

He'd reached a decision point that could no longer be avoided.

He accepted the binary choice that faced him.

Escape or die.

The choice was easy.

The execution seemed impossible.

CHAPTER THIRTY-THREE

Friday, April 15
1:45 a.m.
Chihuahuan Desert, New Mexico

KIM HATED HELICOPTER FLIGHT, especially at night. Helo flight was always dangerous. Engines, flight controls, rotors, gears, driveshafts, and electronics required a skillful and experienced pilot. Nighttime increased the already high odds of dying in a crash. Reduced visibility meant the helicopter might hit something, which always ended badly for the helo and passengers.

Flint was an experienced and careful pilot. He surely didn't plan to die tonight, which increased Kim's comfort level only slightly. Best laid plans, and all that.

Knowing all of this, she had secured her four-point harness, popped a couple of antacids in her mouth, and climbed aboard. *Only one choice.*

Flint had vectored in a wide arc around Glen Haven to approach from the desert instead of the main road because the approaching helo's rotor noise could have been loud enough to wake the sleeping residents. Flying into the wind, he hoped to dampen the unmistakable whapping sounds and allow the strong gusts to carry the noise away in the darkness.

The plan was to get an aerial view of the Glen Haven buildings and the layout before they made a stealthier approach for a closer look later in a vehicle and on foot. All of which had to be accomplished before dawn.

There were at least two dangers to be avoided.

First, Vigo was likely to have night crew on alert. Navigating around them would be better done from the ground level.

Second, at least an hour before dawn, Glen Haven residents would begin to stir for the morning's balloon ride. Paying passengers would be arriving, parking in the field across the street.

Kim and Flint planned to deal with Vigo's crew as necessary and complete their reconnaissance before the first Glen Haven resident opened his eyes.

The journey proceeded as expected. Flying into the wind was slow going. The gusts buffeted the small helo, pushing it aside like a cat batting a yarn ball. Flint's piloting skills were tested and proved to be as solid as Gaspar had claimed. So far.

As expected, the desert was dark in the moonless night. For a time, they flew over what seemed to be a gaping hole in the earth. Kim had spent time in the desert. She knew nocturnal creatures roamed the cold sand, slithering and creepy. The thought made her shudder.

Still miles south of Glen Haven, where the desert was still cloaked in darkness, Kim noticed a beam of light in the distance.

Flint remained focused on flying the helo while Kim kept a white-knuckled grip with one hand. With the other hand, she raised the field glasses to her eyes. From this distance, everything between the helo and the light beam was as dark as standing in a closet. But in the beam's immediate surroundings, using the field glasses, Kim thought she could make out a vehicle.

Humans could see farther in the night than during the day. After all, at night, even a child could see the stars. She'd been told once that the human eye, unaided, could see a candle flame in the darkness up to thirty miles away. This light beam was way brighter and more powerful than a candle flame and she was much closer than thirty miles. She guessed ten miles, maybe, at the most.

"Flint. Look. Eleven o'clock position on your left. What is that?" she said.

Flint took a quick glance. "Dunno. Some kind of flood light. Camping lantern, maybe? Want to get a closer look?"

"Yeah. Let's do that. We're still a long distance from Glen Haven and we can't get to it without flying close to that light anyway," she replied.

"Copy that," Flint said, deftly repositioning the helo to fly directly toward the beam.

Kim continued to watch through the field glasses as the helo approached. The light source became larger, stronger, and deeper.

At first, she saw nothing but the light itself.

As her eyes adjusted, she noticed that the beam was conical, two lights emanating from a single source and joining together after a short distance to illuminate a wider swath. She guessed the beam range probably lighted a distance of 350 to 400 feet ahead.

A rocky outcropping along one side of the beam would have shielded some of the light from passing motorists on the road, had there been any. Which, up until this point, Kim hadn't seen.

Flint continued to battle the wind and the darkness while Kim watched the area around the light beam. He said, "Figure it out yet?"

"Looks like it could be a vehicle's headlights. Not a sedan. It's higher off the ground," Kim replied.

"So like a truck or a van. Something that campers might use to haul gear," Flint replied.

"Why are you so sure it's campers?" Kim asked.

"Well, I'm thinking it's not a UFO. You don't see any little green men wandering around, do you? I mean, we're not that far from Area 51..." Flint's voice trailed off as he teased.

"Point taken," she replied. "You're probably right. Not much reason to be out in the desert in the pitch black at this hour of the night. Nothing to hunt out here other than scorpions and snakes. They're certainly not birdwatchers."

He laughed. "Camping makes more sense than anything else."

"Think they can hear us approaching?" Kim asked.

"Not likely. The wind is blowing pretty strong out there. It's carrying the noise in the opposite direction," Flint replied through the headset. "And if that's a van or a truck, the engine is running to keep the lights on. That's enough to drown us out from this distance."

Still using the field glasses, the helo was close enough now for Kim to see two shadowy figures, probably men.

One was standing in some sort of pit, visible only from the waist up.

The other one was looming above and off to one side behind him, out of his field of vision.

Kim squinted through the field glasses, as if her instincts were less clear than her churning stomach insisted. "Flint, we've got to set this bird down. Right now. That man's about to die."

"Working on it," Flint replied, as he fought against the wind.

CHAPTER THIRTY-FOUR

Friday, April 15
2:05 a.m.
Chihuahuan Desert, New Mexico

HECTOR WAS ALMOST FINISHED with Mason's grave. Only a few more strokes of the shovel and Mason's chance to escape would disappear.

Shortly after that, Mason would disappear, too. Hector would kill him and bury him in the hole. He'd pile the dirt over Mason's body and return to Glen Haven, just like he'd probably done to the other two poor slobs under the dirt piles next to Mason's grave. No one would ever know what had happened to him.

For a short second, he wondered whether anyone would care until he remembered Cheryl and Micah. He knew, the way he knew his own name, that Vigo would hurt them if Mason didn't get back to Glen Haven and get them away from Vigo before he had the chance.

He could only hope he hadn't already lost that chance. He'd

been lucky enough to find Cheryl and Micah. Surely he wouldn't lose them now.

Hector was down in the grave. Mason heard Hector's cell phone ring.

"What the hell?" Hector grunted as he fished it out of his pocket. He glanced at the screen and then answered the call on speaker so he could continue digging. "I'm busy here, Elena. What is it?"

Elena, whoever she was, didn't reply. Hector kept digging Mason's grave. He was almost done now. Only a few more shovels and he'd be climbing out.

"Elena? What's going on?"

The next thing Mason heard was a female voice, barely able to get the words out between her tears. "Hector, it's not Elena. It's Cheryl."

The words, the truth of them, the voice itself, caused Mason's entire body to spasm. Cheryl. Why would Cheryl be calling this monster? Who the hell was Elena?

"Cheryl," Hector said, puzzled. "Why do you have Elena's phone?"

"Are you coming back soon?" Cheryl sniffed and stifled another sob.

"Yeah. I'm almost done here. Put Elena on," he replied.

"I c-can't. I-I'm sorry. Elena's d-dead." Cheryl broke down completely, sobs filling the grave where Hector continued to dig.

"That's not funny, Cheryl. That's crap! Put Elena on," Hector demanded gruffly.

"S-she was shot and k-killed. I-I grabbed her cell phone before the coroner took her body away," Cheryl choked out.

"Who did this?" Hector demanded angrily. "I'll kill the son-of-a-bitch!"

"I-I don't know. The police are working on that now." Cheryl's sobs mangled her words. "Come home soon, Hector. P-please."

Cheryl hung up and empty silence filled the air. Hector dropped the phone into the dirt and stomped it with a heavy boot.

With a loud grunt for extra strength or to work out his anger or something, Hector stomped on the shovel and drove it into the hard dirt. Using both hands, he lifted the soil and tossed it onto the pile. So intent was he on the job at hand that he never looked at Mason.

Maybe he thought he could simply shoot Mason if he tried to get away. Which he surely could have.

He probably figured Mason was too cowardly to run. Which, until he heard Cheryl's voice and saw the impact of her words on Hector, would have been true.

Either way, when Hector finished the grave and climbed out, Mason would be as good as dead, like Elena.

Hector bent his head to the task and, with another grunt, working faster now, stomped on the shovel again. He put his muscles into the digging and lifted the heavy weight of the soil on the blade at the end of the long handle.

Which was precisely when Mason inhaled to gather every ounce of strength he possessed, grabbed the second shovel with his one good arm, rushed forward, and slammed the sharp blade against Hector's temple putting his body weight behind the blow.

He hit Hector's head the same way he would have swung for the fences playing baseball in high school. He remembered to follow through, pushing the momentum of the blow even further.

He drew the shovel back for another swing, but he didn't need it.

For the second time in his miserable life, Mason got lucky.

The hit was solidly placed to the temple.

The blow was hard enough and the shovel heavy enough and the leverage good enough.

Hector was knocked off balance. He fell into the pit and landed on his back, stunned, slipping into unconsciousness.

Mason changed his position, settled his weight firmly on both feet, stood above him and jabbed the shovel's blade down onto Hector's throat with all the vengeance he felt in his heart.

The blade cut through Hector's skin and sliced an artery or two, Mason figured. He couldn't really see all that clearly in the dark and down in the hole, using his one good eye, but he noticed the spurting blood. Enraged and terrified, he jabbed Hector's neck again and again with the shovel until he could lift it no more.

He stood and watched a couple of minutes, breathing heavily, adrenaline pumping power and fearlessness through his body, to be sure Hector wouldn't climb up and find his gun.

Hector never moved. He lay on his back until the blood stopped spurting. His head lolled to one side, eyes open, seeing nothing.

Mason felt drained. The adrenaline rush subsided. He was as exhausted as he'd ever been. He tossed the shovel into the grave Hector had dug for himself. Mason had no strength to bury him. The vultures would arrive before dawn to pick his body clean. The circling, diving swarm would identify Hector's location precisely for the authorities. But there was nothing more Mason could do here.

He had no idea how long he stood there like that, dazed, breathing hard, courage wilting, watching Hector's body. He must have stayed awhile, though it seemed like only a few minutes at most.

An odd noise overhead jarred him back to the present. The whapping roar had probably been approaching for a while, shattering the desert quiet, but he'd been so singularly focused on Hector that he hadn't noticed.

He glanced toward the overwhelming racket, angry that help hadn't arrived before he'd killed Hector. Mason had never killed a man before and he was nauseated by the guilty knowledge. What would Cheryl think? Would she want to be married to a killer?

Which was when he recognized the unmistakable sound of a helicopter, coming closer. He watched as it hovered above him. The rotor wash, combined with the overwhelming noise, brought the full weight of the situation home.

He'd killed Hector. He would be arrested. Maybe they'd see it as self-defense. Or maybe he'd be sent to prison.

He turned and ran toward the van, which some part of his brain knew was a totally useless and stupid thing to do.

CHAPTER THIRTY-FIVE

Friday, April 15
2:15 a.m.
Chihuahuan Desert, New Mexico

KIM STARED THROUGH THE field glasses at the two men. From the helo, she could do nothing except watch as the one outside the pit attacked the other man with a shovel. He seemed to have only one functioning arm, which might have explained why he wasn't doing the digging.

"Flint, seriously. We need to land. Get us as close to those two as you can. Hurry."

"Copy that. We should be there shortly," he replied, continuing to reduce altitude while buffeted by the strong winds blowing against the helo.

The frenzied attack lasted a good, long time. Kim guessed it was long enough to kill the man in the pit. After the first blow with the shovel, he went down and never got up to defend himself. He could be unconscious. But he was probably dead.

The helo rocked and bucked against the elements, which caused her queasy stomach to revolt. She pressed her lips together and swallowed big breaths to control herself as she continued watching events on the ground.

When Flint finally landed the helo, the man had completed his attack. He was running toward the van. If he reached the van, he'd speed away. They might be able to overtake him in the helo, but it would easier to stop him now.

She quickly unbuckled her harness, pulled her gun, opened the door and hit the ground running.

He had a slight head start. His legs were longer than hers, but he wasn't in great shape. Kim was faster and her endurance hadn't been exhausted by spending the past few minutes killing a man with a shovel.

Adrenaline fueled her run, too. She wanted to catch him before he sped away in a van that resembled the one she'd seen on the CCTV footage. The one used to kidnap Lawton.

For a moment, the thought popped into her head. Lawton could be the man lying at the bottom of that pit. She didn't have enough time to follow through. Instead, she ran faster toward the killer.

He made it to the open side door and jumped inside. He was settling himself into the seat when Kim ran around to the driver's door, pulled it open, and jerked his bad left arm with all of her body weight.

He screamed in pain and leaned left, but he didn't tumble out.

Instead, he shifted the van into reverse and stomped on the accelerator.

The van jerked backward. The open door knocked Kim to the ground, causing her to release his damaged left arm.

The van reversed until it was clear of her and he'd righted himself in the seat.

He couldn't use his left arm to close the door. He shifted the transmission into drive and the van's engine screamed in protest before it jumped forward.

He was getting away.

Kim hopped to her feet.

Before the van could zoom forward and away, she raised her gun and fired three rounds straight into the moving cabin. He yowled as if she might have hit him, but he didn't stop.

Bullets had pierced the windshield and exited the van on the passenger side.

The driver's side door was still open. The gunshots might have wounded him, or his screams might have resulted from his prior injuries. It was impossible to say. He was hurting now but the pain didn't stop him.

The van came straight at her.

Kim jumped out of the way of the oncoming vehicle. She'd have fired again, but she'd lost her opportunity. No point in wasting her bullets.

She watched helplessly as the van reached the road and picked up speed.

In her periphery, she saw the helo rising. Once airborne, it circled toward the road. Flint positioned the helo to meet the van head-on.

The helo hovered in front of the van, pushing noise and raising a cloud of dust.

The van weaved erratically. Small objects inside flew out of the open side door. Twice, the van ran onto the shoulder and overcorrected as he steered across the pavement.

Kim jogged slowly toward the van, gun in hand, seeking an opportunity to shoot again.

The confrontation ended abruptly after not more than a mile when the driver must have realized escape efforts were futile.

The van simply stopped in the road. Flint hovered over the road in front of the van, but didn't land the helo. Just in case the driver decided to bolt again, she figured.

Kim jogged up closer. She didn't call out or identify herself because the helo's deafening noise would have scattered her voice to the wind.

When she reached the back of the van, she approached slowly and covered both open doors while Flint landed the helo in front.

The rotor wash pushed the air and the dirt over the strange tableau as the helo slowed to a stop. Flint stepped out, gun drawn, and signaled. They approached the van together. Flint went in from the front and Kim went in from the back.

She flattened her back against the back of the van and rounded the corner to approach the open maw of the sliding door on the passenger side. She ducked a quick look inside and drew back. The driver was slumped over the steering wheel, engine still running, transmission in park.

The rotor noise coupled with the van's engine overwhelmed all conversation. A shouted warning wouldn't penetrate. Which meant her footsteps would be cloaked and stealth could work.

Keeping her gun ready, she crouched to remain invisible in the side mirror and stepped up into the void.

She covered the steel floor of the van as quickly as she dared and reached the front seats, gun drawn, just as Flint reached the open driver's side door.

Almost at the same time, they both saw the driver, still slumped across the big steering wheel. His head was turned so that he was facing Kim.

Which was when she recognized him.

"Mason O'Hare," she said, for Flint's benefit.

The next thought came swiftly.

Had O'Hare lured Lawton to the saloon to be abducted and killed? Was O'Hare responsible for everything that had happened?

But that couldn't be true. Agent Ross had suggested the mole inside Glen Haven was a woman, hadn't he?

Flint put two fingers on the side of O'Hare's neck and checked his pulse. "Erratic, but still beating," he said.

Kim reached over and turned off the van's ignition. She grabbed the keys and dropped them into her pocket.

"See if you can wake him up and learn anything useful," she said.

"What are you going to do?" Flint replied.

"I want to check on that guy in the pit. And then I'll make a call to get us some help out here," she said.

"This will help." He handed her a big mag light.

"Thanks." She switched it on and followed the powerful beam outside. The lights from the helo were strong enough to guide her for a while.

She jogged along the road until she saw the van's tire tracks leading to the rocky outcropping and veered toward it. The mag light beam cast the rough ground in shadows along its periphery. She slowed her pace.

When she reached the last of the tire tracks, she aimed the mag light straight ahead and located the pit. She swept the beam across the area. She noticed two mounds of dirt near the pit which, she guessed, were probably recent graves.

She walked carefully across the rocky ground.

At the pit's edge, she directed the light into the dark hole. The mag light's brilliant beam showed the unmistakable grisly picture of the dead man. He was twisted at the waist and most of his body lay on its back.

His heart had long ago stopped beating, which meant the blood had stopped pumping then, too. Black, sticky pools of blood were congealing over and around him.

She needed to be sure. She held her breath and flashed the light on his face.

The man was not Lawton.

Her pent up anxiety whooshed out with the breath she'd been holding in her lungs. Her legs went wobbly and she stepped back from the pit to avoid losing her footing and ending up down there along with him.

Relief flooded her system as the truth sunk into her body.

She struggled for professional detachment from feelings for Lawton that she hadn't anticipated.

She stood aside for a minute or two to be sure she was steady on her feet. Then she moved back toward the pit and shone the mag light beam inside again. She swept the beam over the pit from top to bottom.

She pulled out her cell phone and snapped a few photos of the scene. Taking the photos with one hand while holding the heavy mag light's beam steady with the other was akin to juggling, but she managed.

She noticed what looked like a cell phone on the ground near the corpse's feet. She couldn't reach it without jumping into the pit with him.

Out of habit, she briefly considered leaving the phone for the crime scene techs to process. A moment later, she'd taken a few photos and then jumped down into the hole to pick up the phone.

When she'd climbed out again, she checked the phone's recent calls log. Surprisingly, the phone connected to a cell tower with a fairly strong signal. They must be closer to civilization out here than she'd assumed.

She scrolled through the log. The most recent was a three minute call from Elena Ochoa about an hour ago. Which was impossible. Elena Ochoa had been killed at the balloon landing site, probably shot by the woman driving the gray Toyota sedan.

Which meant this three-minute call didn't come from the dead woman. Someone else had used her phone.

Elena's phone should have been collected by the crime scene techs who processed the scene at the landing site. Who took the phone and who made this call?

Perhaps more importantly, what did the caller say to the dead man lying at the bottom of this pit?

Mason O'Hare should know the answers to these and a thousand other questions.

She glanced around again. Nothing more she could do here at the moment.

On her way back to the van, she called Finlay and brought him up to speed.

"You don't know who the dead guy is?" he asked.

"I can send you the photos. He's been severely beaten about the face and neck by the shovel. DNA or fingerprints will be needed for a positive ID," she replied. "I'll ask O'Hare for an ID when we get him awake."

A long pause ensued before Finlay said, "No sign of Reacher?"

"Not unless he's buried in one of those other two graves," she replied.

After an even longer pause, he said, "I'll take care of cleaning up the crime scene. We'll make sure your activities are excluded from the mix."

"You'll want to get them out here before daylight if you want this guy before the vultures get him," she said.

"Right," he replied, but she could tell he was distracted by something else.

"And you'll let me know if you find Reacher," she said.

He said nothing more as he disconnected the call.

CHAPTER THIRTY-SIX

Friday, April 15
3:00 a.m.
Chihuahuan Desert, New Mexico

WHEN SHE RETURNED TO the van, it was unoccupied.
O'Hare was no longer slumped over the steering wheel. And
Flint wasn't there, either.

She looked toward the helo. She couldn't see into the cabin
with its bright lights shining directly on the van, but the two of
them were probably inside.

She took a couple of minutes to flash the mag light beam
around inside the van. The cargo area was padded with heavy
blankets attached with grommets to the side walls. The floor was
uncovered. The mag light beam revealed large dark splotches
that looked like dried blood.

Canvas bags large enough to hold a human head were tossed
into a corner. Plastic cable ties were strewn about. Some were
flat, unused. Others were fastened into partial circles, as if they'd
been used to bind wrists and feet, and then cut to release their

hostages. The circles were too large for a woman's wrists.

She saw no contraband in plain sight. No guns, drugs, or anything else to suggest the van had been employed by the Vigo cartel to traffic in illegal activities. Which didn't mean much. When the forensics team finished with it, trace evidence would tell the whole story. Simply based on what she could see and what she knew, Kim figured they'd find plenty of evidence here.

She opened the passenger door and then the glove box. Inside, she found a couple of small plastic bags containing several unmarked white tablets that could have been something as harmless as aspirin or as lethal as fentanyl.

On the floor in front of the passenger seat, she noticed several large syringes, all empty.

She snapped a few photographs of the van and its contents with her phone and left everything in place for the techs to handle. The van was most likely stolen. But she captured the VIN, the license plate, and four outside views before she dropped the phone into her pocket and headed toward the helo.

When she reached the open door, she climbed inside. Flint was already sitting in the pilot seat. O'Hare was conscious and belted into the back. Flint had used two of the plastic ties from the van to bind his wrists and ankles.

She turned to O'Hare. "Who's the dead man in that grave back there?"

He cleared his throat and forced his words out. "Hector Ochoa."

"Why did you kill him?" Flint asked.

"Because he was planning to kill me and bury me in that grave he was digging," O'Hare replied.

"You know this how?" Kim asked.

"He told me so. That's why we were there."

"Why did he want to kill you?" Flint asked.

O'Hare shrugged. "Hector does what he's told."

"Who told him to kill you? Pinto Vigo?" Kim asked.

O'Hare's eyes fairly bugged out of his head. His nostrils flared and his breathing shortened like a frightened racehorse.

Flint nodded. "We'll take that as a yes."

"You have to help me. Please," O'Hare said, desperation galvanizing his entire body. "I have to get home. Right away."

"You're unclear on the situation here, O'Hare," Flint replied. "You killed a man. You're not going home tonight and maybe never again."

All the fight drained out of him. Tears sprung to his eyes and he hung his head briefly to gather his composure. He wiped his nose with his sleeve. "I have to get my girlfriend and her boy out of there. Then you can take me to jail if you want."

"You have to get them out of where?" Kim asked.

"Glen Haven. It was a sanctuary for all of us before. But now, Vigo's there. It's not safe."

"What about John Lawton?"

O'Hare's eyes widened. "How do you know about him?"

"Is he at Glen Haven now?"

O'Hare nodded. "He was there a few hours ago. Vigo's holding him in one of the barracks buildings. If you help me get my girlfriend out of there, I can show you where he is."

Kim cocked her head and studied him for a moment. "Tell you what. We'll get you some medical attention first. Then, you show us where Lawton is and help us get him out of there. After that, we'll help you with your girlfriend and her son."

"Forget the doctors. I'm fine for now." O'Hare nodded furiously. "But to the rest, absolutely yes. Quickly. We need to hurry."

"Why? What's the rush?" Flint asked.

"Vigo's waiting for a big shipment. I heard him say it will arrive early today. He's ruthless. I think after he gets whatever he's waiting for, he'll destroy Glen Haven and everyone in it." O'Hare's words tumbled over themselves rushing to get out of his mouth.

"What's your girlfriend's name?" Kim asked.

"Cheryl Ray. Her son is Micah," O'Hare said.

"I met them both today, but I didn't know their last names," Kim replied. "Cheryl Ray. Is that Gavin and Bruce Ray's sister?"

"No." O'Hare shook his head miserably. He took a deep breath for fortification. "Cheryl is Bruce's wife. Micah is his son. But Bruce is a horrible husband and father. Cheryl loves me. We're planning to marry. Just as soon as she can leave him."

"What's holding her back?" Kim cocked her head. Wives frequently threatened to leave their husbands for another man. In Kim's experience, very few actually followed through on those threats.

O'Hare shook his head as if the answer was beyond his ability to convey.

Flint looked directly at Kim and she nodded. He spooled up the helo as she settled into the copilot's seat and fastened her harness. She donned her headset.

"Good to go?" Flint asked.

"If we go out there now, Vigo will hear the helo coming a mile away. He'll bug out before we can get him. We need stealth," she said.

"Stealth? Hell, we need heavy backup and a boatload of luck if we're going to pull this off," Flint said.

"So let's pick up the SUV and then we'll head out there," she replied. "I'll make a few calls and get some back up."

"Sounds like a plan." He lifted the helo off the ground and altered course.

CHAPTER THIRTY-SEVEN

Friday, April 15
4:00 a.m.
Glen Haven, New Mexico

THEY HAD SET THE helo down at a pre-arranged private air strip and transferred to the dark SUV Finlay had provided. Kim felt the pressure of the approaching dawn, even as the moonless night sky would remain dark for another hour or so.

The SUV was well equipped. Finlay had included appropriate clothing, night vision, infrared, and flashlights as well as plenty of weapons and ammunition. He'd tossed in food and beverages for good measure.

After she'd changed her clothes, Kim found a quiet spot to call Finlay for further intel. She gave him the name of O'Hare's victim, but he already had it.

Finlay began with basic stats on Hector and Elena Ochoa. Both were wanted members of Vigo's cartel.

"You're better off now that they're gone. As long as one of them was alive, they were a threat to you," Finlay said.

That was all Kim needed to know at the moment. She'd find out more about Elena and Hector when the need arose, if it ever did.

She nodded and then realized he couldn't see her. "Right. What else?"

"Local law enforcement agencies have been busy," Finlay said. "The woman Agent Ross killed at the Last Chance Saloon was also a member of Pinto Vigo's inner circle. Her name was Sela Juarez. Called her Big Sela. She was close to Vigo's sister, Maria. Who was also, by the way, the driver of that Toyota sedan."

"What else?" Kim digested his report without comment, watching the sky as if she could actually see the time evaporate, taking her window of opportunity along with it.

"The bullet that killed Elena Ochoa has not been recovered. It passed through her body and landed somewhere out in the field," he paused. "Which means no ballistics match to the rifle in the Toyota's trunk."

All Kim needed to know was that Maria was the killer. "Okay. What else?"

"The FBI's operating assumption is that the rifle was the murder weapon and Maria Vigo was the shooter. But they are no closer to proving either assumption."

He didn't need to tell her that without the ballistics, the case against Maria Vigo was weak. But making the case wasn't Kim's problem. One of the law enforcement agencies was responsible for that.

"What about Maria Vigo?" she asked.

"No joy there, either, I'm afraid. We're still working on it. But watch your back," Finlay replied. "How about Reacher?"

"No evidence that he's anywhere around here. And that's

too bad, because I could use his help. We're seriously outnumbered," she replied sourly, again second-guessing her decision to operate here without help from the Boss. She fished a couple of antacids out of her pocket and popped them in her mouth.

When Kim hung up the call, she relayed the intel to Flint, away from O'Hare's listening ears.

Flint shook his head and swiped a hand through his hair. "Your boy Lawton has landed in a mell of a hess, as my foster mom used to say. Pinto Vigo's reputation says he's hot-headed. Likes to take his revenge first and make sure he's got the right victim later."

Kim nodded. Flint didn't need to bring her up to speed on Pinto Vigo. The FBI had been hunting Vigo for years. His methods were well known. "He's got to be feeling cornered. If he's still at Glen Haven, he's armed and ready to fight. So watch yourself."

Flint gave her a side-eye. "He's got an arsenal out there. Soldiers, too. And he's probably as mad as a hornet. I'd say now's the time to call in the cavalry."

"Long past time," Kim agreed.

She'd already called Jake Reacher, and he'd struck out with his Uncle Jack. Gaspar had sent Flint, which was all the resources he had available.

The only other call she could make was to the Boss, and she wasn't that desperate. At least, not yet.

Presumably fueled by the mole feeding them intel, Finlay had said the FBI and local law enforcement had been rounding up known members of Vigo's cartel all night. Low level operatives, mostly. Small amounts of contraband. Mostly drugs, but a few illegal guns and other weapons.

It was enough to support the FBI's request for a warrant. They had the warrant in hand and would be rolling out soon. Estimated to arrive at Glen Haven just after dawn with plenty of fire power. Local law enforcement agencies were standing by, too.

She was expecting a full scale war when the FBI team arrived. She didn't want to be caught in the middle of that. In fact, she wanted to be long gone before they approached.

Which was why she intended to get Lawton out and then get out of the way. If she'd wanted to be a soldier, she'd have joined the army.

"Let's go do this. Get in, get out," she said as they joined O'Hare in the SUV.

Flint took the driver's seat. He started the vehicle and rolled out. "O'Hare, you'll have to guide us into Glen Haven through the back way. How close can we park to the barracks where they're holding Lawton?"

"There's a parking lot right there. But Vigo and his crew will see you if you park there. Really, if you park anywhere near Glen Haven, someone is going to see you unless we get there before they wake up."

"What time does everybody rise and shine?" Flint asked.

"Well before dawn. About five in the morning, usually. Except the kids. Everyone else needs to get ready for work."

Kim asked, "How many of them will work on the morning balloon ride?"

"About the same as yesterday. It's a holiday, so the kids will be off school. They'll be out there. Cheryl's usually the pilot for the morning ride. About six in the crew all together. But they'll have prepped everything last night."

"What does that mean?"

"The gondola, the envelope, the fuel. All that will be out there, set up, ready to go. The only time they don't set up the night before is when a storm is predicted. But the weather's pretty clear this time of year," O'Hare said.

They rode awhile in silence, each gathering their own thoughts.

Flint glanced toward Kim and said, "O'Hare, what kind of shape was Lawton in last time you saw him? Better than you?"

O'Hare replied, "I guess. I mean, he and Hector got into it a few times. Vigo, too. But Lawton is bigger and stronger than Vigo. Lawton was shackled to a chair last time I saw him."

Kim cleared her throat. "How many people in the barracks where they're holding him?"

"Just Hector, Freddy, and Vigo most of the time. Sometimes Louis and Manny, I guess," O'Hare replied.

Flint asked, "How many weapons do they have?"

O'Hare's silence lasted awhile. Finally he said, "I guess I don't really know much about guns. They all had guns. I saw some lying around in both barracks. So maybe twenty? More or less?"

Kim took a breath to steady her stomach. "And how many members of Vigo's crew stay in the barracks?"

"They seemed to come and go at all hours. It was one of the things that caught my attention first. I'm sort of a night owl. I noticed they'd be driving in and out long after Glen Haven residents had bedded down for the night," O'Hare replied. "Made me suspicious, you know?"

The route they'd planned kept the SUV off the main road. They took the farming trails around the back of the property, on the other side of the fields. Those trails weren't used much until harvest season, when trucks carried the harvest out from back there.

O'Hare pointed to the tool shed on the far edge of the property, diagonally across from the barracks and behind one of the big barns. "Park there. We'll walk the rest of the way."

Flint pulled the big SUV close behind the shed into the shadows to shield it from casual observers. When the sun came up, the vehicle would be clearly visible to anyone wandering in the area. But until then, it shouldn't be discovered.

They wore black clothes, including gloves and knit caps that covered their faces. They'd fashioned a sling for O'Hare's left arm. Kim guessed the arm was excruciatingly painful, but he didn't complain.

Flint turned off the ignition and bent toward the floor. He said, "This thing has a push button start. I've left the key fob under the floormat. If you need to start it up quickly, you don't need the key."

They picked up the night vision and the infrared. Kim and Flint carried guns. They'd debated it, but in the end, decided they'd be better off if O'Hare wasn't armed. They didn't trust him with a gun and he probably couldn't shoot straight anyway.

Kim looked across the open field and the landscaped space that occupied the area between the buildings. All seemed quiet. The houses were dark, as if the occupants were still asleep. She couldn't see the parking areas or the driveways, which were on the other side of the buildings.

Lamp light shone from the windows in the barracks on the right. The last building. The one where Lawton should be. Shades covered the windows in the other barracks, the one closer to the main house. Smoke rose from both chimneys, as if a cozy fire warmed the rooms overnight.

She asked O'Hare, "Are there shades available for both barracks?"

He glanced across. "Yes. And usually they're down at night."

She took a deep breath and pulled the stocking cap down over her face. The others did the same.

When they were ready, Kim said, "I'm point. O'Hare, you follow me. Flint will take the rear. Let's go."

CHAPTER THIRTY-EIGHT

Friday, April 15
4:30 a.m.
Glen Haven, New Mexico

VIGO SENT FREDDY NEXT door to check on Lawton after they'd finished setting the propane. He planned to destroy Glen Haven as the cartel closed up shop here after the shipment arrived.

They'd strategically placed cans of Sterno and propane tanks about the property and inside the buildings. They'd placed cotton strips into the cans lest the Sterno extinguish too soon. Each can contained enough fuel to burn for two hours, but should serve the purpose far quicker. Butane lighters would ignite the Sterno just before the entire setup was covered with a big plastic bucket. Open valves on the propane would fill the buckets with the right gas-to-air mixture to do the rest.

Vigo nodded. In his experience, explosions followed by fires were fast and efficient weapons.

By the time firefighters could arrive at the scene, Glen Haven would be too far gone to save. The buildings would be destroyed and everyone inside would die. The simple act of breathing the air inside the buildings would kill them.

Any residents who had already left the commune might survive. He had a plan to deal with them, too.

Only two SUVs were still parked outside. Hector had taken the van to the desert to deal with O'Hare. The other vehicles had been moved and destroyed.

The two remaining SUVs were also stolen, but they'd been using them awhile. They were both likely to contain enough forensic evidence to bury everyone in the Albuquerque crew. From prior attempts, Vigo knew burning them would not eliminate all of the trace evidence. Which meant Louis and Manny were working on them now with bleach and other chemicals.

Also parked in the gravel space was a sedan he hadn't seen in a while.

When he pushed the door open and walked inside the darkened barracks building, his sister was waiting.

"Surprise," Maria said, as if her disappearing act had never happened.

Vigo ignored the problem of another car to deal with, swallowed his anger along with his pride, and hurried over to give her a brief, hard squeeze. "Where have you been?"

"I didn't mean to worry you," she replied. But she was grinning and satisfied with herself. "After I killed that Asian bitch, I had to get rid of the Toyota. Took me a while to find another one of our cars. Seemed like most of them were already in use. You must have a big team out there tonight. Did our shipment arrive early?"

Even though he'd already guessed that she'd ignored his

orders to leave the FBI agent alone, hearing her brag that she'd shot Elena, even if she'd made a mistake, was a gut punch.

The truth would be worse for her. She'd lost both Big Sela and Elena today, the two women closest to her in the world. Both deaths were Maria's fault. She'd be devastated.

Worse, he had no idea how he'd control Hector once he learned the truth about Elena.

Vigo wanted to avoid that conversation as long as possible. Nothing could be done to bring the dead back to life. They had more important matters to handle now. He needed to stay focused on those matters. So did Maria and Hector. The rest would have to wait.

He walked into the kitchen area for coffee and returned with two cups. He handed one to her and sat near her in front of the fire.

"The shipment should be here before daylight. When we get it, we're leaving," he said. "I sent the entire team away earlier. Louis and Manny are outside getting ready. They'll be back soon. We're taking nothing with us. We'll start over when we reach Arkansas."

She looked at him as if he'd lost his mind. "Arkansas? Do they even have running water there? Who will buy our product? Why would we move operations to such a place?"

Vigo wiped a palm across his face. "It's far enough from here to start over and the town is small enough to keep us off the FBI and DEA radar for a while. We already have a safe house set up. And it's just temporary. Six months at the longest."

"Elena and Hector are coming, too?" Maria asked, as if she couldn't wrap her head around the abrupt change.

"No. They'll stay behind," he replied. He tried not to lie to Maria and this wasn't a lie. He had plenty to deal with already.

He didn't need Maria making the already difficult situation impossible.

"I'll stay behind, too, then. With Hector and Maria. I can't live in Arkansas. I'd be bored out of my skull," she said with a grin as she sipped the hot coffee.

"My enemies will come after you. They've done it before. Keeping you safe isn't something I have the time and resources to deal with long distance right now," Vigo said with finality, barely controlling his anger. "You'll be leaving here with me."

She was his sister. His only living family. He'd promised his mother that he'd take care of her. But his patience only carried so far.

Glen Haven residents would be stirring soon.

CHAPTER THIRTY-NINE

Friday, April 15
4:40 a.m.
Glen Haven, New Mexico

WEARING THE NIGHT VISION, weapon drawn, Kim hurried across the open field opposite the main residence, toward the barracks building where Lawton was last seen. She relied upon the darkness and the Glen Haven sleep schedule to prevent discovery of her small band. Which wasn't a great plan, but it was the only option she had at the moment.

The herb crops had been planted but had not grown tall enough to shield them. The ground was uneven and overgrown with weeds. She'd tripped twice but managed not to fall.

O'Hare followed her and Flint came along behind.

They reached the outside corner of the last building in the U-shaped compound, the barracks building O'Hare had pointed out. The interior lights were on and the shades were open. With the night vision equipment to amplify the light coming from the windows, she could see almost as well as in daylight.

O'Hare had said Lawton was being held in the basement. An observer looking at the exterior of the building wouldn't know a basement existed. There were no windows, exterior steps, or other indications of any below ground structures.

The only entrance to the basement was inside the building. Kim flattened her back against the wall and advanced as quietly as possible. There were two large windows on this side of the barracks, side by side, and at least five feet off the ground. One was frosted, like a bathroom window. The other was flat plate glass. There were no lights on in those rooms.

About halfway along the exterior wall, between the two windows, she saw a squat ten-gallon propane tank resting two feet from the building. The tank was equipped with a hose attached to the connector valve. When the valve was opened, the propane would flow through the hose.

As an improvised explosive device, this one would fail. Propane tanks were notoriously stable and difficult to explode, despite what Hollywood depicted in the movies.

But the gas inside could be used for arson. And leaking gas, mixed with air, could easily explode, amplifying the fire.

She held her hand up to stop O'Hare and Flint from advancing as she completed a visual examination.

Beside the tank was a large plastic bucket and a can of Sterno with a cotton strip protruding from its center. A long-reach butane lighter lay nearby.

The tank was too heavy and awkward to carry with them easily. She glanced around the area and saw nowhere to hide it.

She checked the valve. It was already closed, but she twisted it again for good measure. Then she removed the hose and threw it into the herb garden. Without the hose, the valve should not allow the gas inside to escape. He'd need a new hose to release the propane.

She threw the Sterno and the butane lighter in opposite directions.

On its own, the plastic bucket was harmless enough, so she left it in place beside the tank.

Dismantling the setup was a huge risk. Someone had put these supplies here and they'd be back to use them. Which meant he'd discover that his plan was no longer a secret. She planned to be gone before he returned to figure that out, or to rig a new setup to start the fire.

Then she walked around the tank and gestured O'Hare and Flint to do the same. She rounded the corner of the barracks building, back flattened against the wall, and approached the front door.

She looked farther along the front wall of the building. On the other side of the entrance, about ten feet away, she saw another propane tank and Sterno setup like the one she'd dismantled.

The plan must be to set fire to the building and create a raging inferno with the propane gas when it exploded inside the bucket. The open valve would use more gas to amplify the fire. The building and everything in it would be quickly destroyed.

Flint and O'Hare caught up with her. She tapped Flint's arm and pointed to the second propane tank. "Somebody's planning a bigger fire."

Flint nodded. "There could be more of these around the grounds and inside the buildings if Vigo wants to destroy the place."

Kim said, "Yeah."

She pushed the night vision up onto her head and raised onto her toes to peer into the window beside the door. Flint glanced inside at the same time.

One man sat on a chair facing a fireplace. A shotgun rested across his lap. He was so still that he might have been sleeping. She didn't see anyone else in the cavernous room.

She pointed to him. O'Hare moved up and looked in the window.

"Freddy," he whispered. "Vigo's man."

She pushed O'Hare aside and looked through the window again. The door to the basement was across the big room from where she stood. As O'Hare had said, the deadbolt was locked. The only way to find out whether Lawton was still in the basement was to go down there and look.

From this vantage point, Kim saw two SUVs and a sedan in the parking area. She pointed in that direction.

"Vigo's crew?" she asked O'Hare.

He nodded. "Glen Haven parking is on the other side. But usually, there's more vehicles out there. Ten or so."

Only three vehicles out there now could mean that most of the crew was off-site.

Still, more of Vigo's crew could be inside the barracks buildings. There were two bedrooms and a bathroom that could be occupied in each barracks. O'Hare had said they were outfitted with double bunk beds. No way to estimate the number of people there at any given time.

According to O'Hare, this last barracks building was reserved for Vigo and his inner circle. Vigo could be inside now.

The smart thing to do was wait for backup. But how long would she need to wait?

She checked her watch. O'Hare had said the first Glen

Haven residents would awaken around five o'clock. Her window of opportunity to rescue Lawton before dawn was closing.

While O'Hare maintained that the residents were not involved with Vigo's crew, Kim didn't believe him. Not only because she was skeptical by nature. The claim was inherently unbelievable.

Mexican drug cartels had been setting up business centers across the US for the past few years. They had infiltrated small town America as well as the larger urban centers. The demand for opioids in the US population seemed insatiable and law enforcement was simply overwhelmed by the volume of crime it spawned.

All of which meant that the odds were infinitesimal that Vigo's crew had landed here in the first place without Gavin and Bruce Ray's involvement. Glen Haven wasn't that easy to find in the first place, but it was a perfect setup for Vigo's business model. The cartel had operated successfully here, coming and going at all hours, for months.

Would any of that have happened without the Ray brothers' knowledge? Kim shook her head. The thought was so unlikely as to be unbelievable.

Which meant the Ray brothers were in this thing up to their eyeballs. And if O'Hare wasn't involved in Vigo's drug business, he was probably the only Glen Haven resident who wasn't.

Before she'd found the propane, Kim and Flint had agreed. At the absolute latest, they had to get Lawton out before the ground crew began setting up for the first balloon ride at six o'clock. Otherwise, the mission had to be put off. Passengers would begin arriving by six-thirty and the early balloon ride would lift off around seven o'clock. By then, law enforcement would be here.

Simply too many eyes and ears around after six o'clock to effectively execute the rescue operation.

The propane setups changed things.

Someone planned to torch this building and probably other buildings on the compound. If Lawton didn't get out now, he'd be killed in that basement.

She hadn't come this far to leave him down there to die.

Kim readied her weapon.

Flint did the same.

As planned, O'Hare turned the handle, pushed the door open, and they went inside.

CHAPTER FORTY

Friday, April 15
5:10 a.m.
Glen Haven, New Mexico

FLINT'S LONG STRIDES COVERED the room quickly. He grabbed the shotgun off Freddie's lap before Freddie woke up and realized what was happening. He saw O'Hare standing in front of the closed front door.

"Where's Hector?" he asked nonsensically, just before Flint knocked him out cold with the butt of the shotgun.

O'Hare hurried to Freddie and, using his one good arm, struggled to bind Freddie's wrists with plastic ties while Flint and Kim checked the other rooms. When he finished, he put a piece of duct tape across Freddie's mouth to keep him quiet when he woke up.

Kim finished checking the bathroom and one bedroom. Flint checked the rooms on the other side.

"All clear," each affirmed when they returned to the main room. They'd found no one else on the first floor.

Kim said, "There's a propane tank setup like the one outside in both rooms I checked. I dismantled them. The fuses in the Sterno are meant to burn awhile before the propane from the tanks explodes to further fuel the fires."

"I found a setup in each room, too. No buckets, though. It seems like the gas was set to fill the entire rooms," Flint replied. "Someone will be coming back to ignite them and probably soon."

Kim nodded. "Vigo's not planning a simple arson. He wants to destroy this entire place, level it in one big attack, like Hiroshima."

"And we want to be out of here before he starts." Flint gave O'Hare the shotgun. "You know how to use this?"

"Yes," O'Hare replied, pulling his knit cap off and taking a few deep breaths as if he'd been suffocating.

"Anybody comes through that door, shoot first and ask questions later. Got that?" Flint asked.

Kim said, "And that means anybody, O'Hare. Even someone you know."

O'Hare's eyes widened and he nodded. "Okay," he managed to croak out.

Kim wasn't confident that he'd follow orders, but she had no time to persuade him. She followed Flint across the room to the basement door.

He slid the deadbolt open and drew the door back on its hinges. Kim flipped on the basement lights. Gun drawn, she headed down the stairs while Flint removed the hinges, lifted the door and set it aside.

"Lawton," she called out as she hurried down the steps. "Are you down here? Lawton?"

No response.

She reached the bottom step and landed on the concrete.

The basement was set up with double bunk beds, a table, chairs, and a television. In the middle of the room, she saw an empty chair.

Restraints had been tossed beside it. What looked like blood had dried in several places close by.

Lawton had probably occupied the chair at one time, but he wasn't there now.

She adjusted her stance and fanned her gaze around the room. Flint had finished with the door and followed her down. He'd covered the steps in half the time.

"Where is he?" Flint asked, quickly sizing up the situation as quickly as Kim had.

The open area was divided only by furniture. Bunk beds, a table with chairs, a television with viewing chairs were grouped together.

Lawton could have been hiding under one of the beds, but that would have been a tactical rookie mistake. From that position, all he could do was hide. He'd have little chance of fighting back or escaping from a prone position under a bed.

There was only one other room back in the far corner. Probably a bathroom. The door was closed. Kim pointed in that direction. Flint nodded and headed toward it.

Near the bunk beds, several areas were cast in shadow by the harsh overhead lights. Lawton could be waiting there to ambush his captors. Kim pulled her flashlight and aimed the beam as she advanced.

"Lawton? John, it's Kim Otto. Are you back there? Come on out." She rounded the bunk beds. The flashlight illuminated the entire shadowy corner. No Lawton.

She heard a noise behind her and turned swiftly to face it, ready to shoot.

Lawton had emerged from the shadows behind another set of beds and stood ten feet away, hands in the air. Weakly, he joked, "I know I should have called, but…"

"I told you never to stand me up or you'd pay the consequences," Kim quipped in response, surprised by the flood of relief that almost swamped her. She pulled her knit cap off so he could see her face and confirm she was who she claimed to be.

She rushed toward him, scanning his body for injuries. He gave her a weak hug. She hugged him, too, and planted a quick kiss on his mouth.

When she stepped back for a wider view, he looked like a prisoner of war after a long stint in a cage. His clothes were tattered and dirty. His skin was cold and clammy, and his eyes were sunken. His pulse was rapid and breathing shallow. He was probably in shock or dehydrated. Or both.

"Can you walk? We have to get you out of here and I certainly can't carry you up those stairs," she said.

"I'm a little weak," Lawton replied. "They haven't fed me much."

Flint came up behind her, his knit cap still on his head but rolled off his face. "I'll help him upstairs."

Kim moved away from Lawton to let Flint take over. He grabbed Lawton's torso under the arms. Lawton threw one arm over Flint's shoulder.

Lawton was wobbly on his feet at first, but as Flint moved him toward the stairs, his stride improved.

Kim dashed up the steps. Flint and Lawton labored up behind her.

When she reached the top, she moved through the open doorway into the main room, gun still drawn. O'Hare stood near Freddy with the shotgun pointed at the front door as if he hadn't moved an inch.

No one else had come inside.

Freddy remained unconscious.

With little effort from Lawton, Flint had managed to lift and drag him from the basement up into the main room of the barracks.

Kim said, "O'Hare. I'll take the shotgun. You help Flint with Lawton. We've got to hurry." She grabbed the shotgun from him and shoved him in the right direction.

With Flint on one side and O'Hare on the other so he could use his good arm, they managed to get Lawton across the barracks and near the front door. His brow was damp with sweat. The effort had already taken its toll. She doubted he could make it all the way across the field to the SUV they'd left behind.

"Let him rest for a minute," she said to Flint, gesturing toward one of the sofas. They maneuvered Lawton over and he plopped down as if he'd just climbed Mount Everest.

"Get him some water and something to eat," she said to O'Hare, simply to get him out of earshot.

"On my way," O'Hare said, moving toward the refrigerator.

She lowered her voice, speaking only to Flint and Lawton. "We need to put some distance between us and Glen Haven. I saw another propane setup out there before we came inside. My guess is that they've got them everywhere around the compound. We don't have time to dismantle them all, even if we could find them soon enough."

Flint raised his eyebrows. To bring Lawton up to speed, he said, "We think Vigo is planning to torch the place."

Lawton said, "He is. I overheard him talking about it to his henchmen, Freddy and Hector. They're waiting for some big shipment and then they plan to burn this place down and bug out. Most of his crew are already gone."

Kim nodded. "How many cartel soldiers are still here?"

"I don't know. At least Vigo and Freddy. They were waiting for Hector to get back after he killed O'Hare," Lawton said, his voice so raspy and weak that Kim leaned in to hear. "Vigo mentioned a couple of other names. Louis and Manny, I think. And he's waiting for his sister to show up. Maria."

Flint said, "So he's gathering his closest allies and then they'll destroy Glen Haven and leave town. Just ahead of the raid by the feds. Which means he definitely knows the feds are coming."

Kim met his gaze. "Yeah. Sounds like it."

Flint said, "How much time do we have?"

Lawton shook his head. "Another hour, maybe? Not long."

O'Hare came back with the water and a couple of energy bars he'd scrounged in the kitchen. He'd overheard the last of the conversation. He was breathing hard, panicked.

O'Hare said, "Vigo's planning to burn Glen Haven down? We have to get our people out of here. We can't let them die in their beds."

"There's two SUVs out there. We could steal one," Flint said, turning to Lawton. "Where is Vigo now?"

Lawton shook his head. "These two barracks buildings are his command post. You steal his vehicles and he'll know about it."

O'Hare said, "His people have been using both buildings. He could be next door. It makes sense if they're working on an evacuation plan."

Flint said, "I'll get our SUV. Bring it across the field as quietly as I can. If I go alone, it'll take me less than ten minutes. Pick the rest of you up here and go back the same way we came in. We can be far enough away from the compound to avoid the worst of what Vigo's planning."

Kim thought about it a couple of moments. A dozen objections formed in her head and she squelched them all.

The only other realistic option she could fathom would be to leave Lawton behind. She definitely wasn't willing to do that.

Which meant there was only one choice. So she simply nodded and said, "Okay."

Flint was already on his way to the door.

"No way," O'Hare objected, his whole body shaking violently. "I can't leave here without Cheryl and Micah. We have to take them with us. I'll get them out myself. I won't let Vigo burn them to death. Don't ask me to do that."

His words broke with the last sentence and tears formed in his eyes.

Flint had paused, one hand on the doorknob, waiting for Kim to decide. This was her operation. He was number two. Number one called the shots. Simple as that.

She glanced at her watch. She couldn't force O'Hare to come with them. And she couldn't let him leave this building alone, either. He'd be discovered before he made it halfway across the compound. With his broken arm, he was in no shape to fight Vigo alone, even if he was stupid enough to try.

Kim's gaze met Lawton's. They were the two trained agents in the room. Because she knew him, knew his training, his capacities, she knew he was weak, but not helpless.

"Don't worry about me," Lawton said as if he was reading her mind. "Freddie and I will be just fine here until you get back."

She nodded and clapped him on the shoulder. She handed him the shotgun and said to Flint, "We'll meet you back here in fifteen minutes. If we don't make it back, don't wait for us. We'll find another way."

Flint tossed her a mock salute and said, "You're the boss."

She grinned. "And don't you forget it."

Then she turned to O'Hare. "Quickly. We need to find Cheryl and Micah and get them back here."

O'Hare sniffled and wiped his nose with the back of his hand. "Thank you. You won't be sorry."

But he was wrong. She was already sorry.

She pulled her black cap out and replaced it on her head. O'Hare did the same.

"Lead the way," she said, as she followed Flint through the door and into the night, adjusting her night vision, with O'Hare right behind her.

CHAPTER FORTY-ONE

Friday, April 15
5:40 a.m.
Glen Haven, New Mexico

MASON'S HEART WAS RACING, beating so hard he thought his chest might explode. Vigo was planning to burn Glen Haven to the ground. His home and everyone he cared about in the world would be destroyed. He had to get Cheryl and Micah out of there. Now.

He followed Agent Otto out of the barracks building. They had both pulled their black caps over their faces and wore the night vision, which made it possible to avoid tripping.

She kept flat against the wall as she crept forward at a brisk pace. She was stealthy and he was as clumsy as any oaf he'd ever met. But they made it to the back of the barracks building unscathed.

If anyone saw them, nothing horrible happened because of it. He exhaled a long, pent-up breath as he caught up to her.

"Can we cross from here to your room without being seen?" she said quietly.

"I've done it before. Want me to lead the way?"

She paused and he knew it was because she really didn't want him to lead anything. He couldn't blame her. He'd screwed up royally already. There was no reason why she should trust him.

She must have concluded his offer wasn't a viable option. "Just point me in the general direction. I'll go first."

He did as she asked. She set off again, stealthily but quickly, and he followed close behind.

Along the way, he saw at least four more propane tanks around the center of the compound close to the commune's living quarters. He supposed it made sense to have extra firepower outside the bigger buildings. He'd never tried to burn a building to the ground, so he didn't know.

These tanks had been set up to ignite with Sterno like the others, but they'd also been dismantled.

He wondered who had dismantled them, since it wasn't Otto or Flint. And it certainly wasn't Lawton. He could barely walk. He wasn't capable of any sort of clandestine activity now.

Otto stopped to look at the setups and glance around the open space before she moved on.

She must have realized they didn't have time to do anything more than stay on mission. She couldn't go looking for the anonymous benefactor now.

When they reached the door to Mason's room, Otto checked her watch. Flint should have been about halfway to the SUV.

Mason never locked the patio door and it wasn't locked now. She shoved it aside and stepped into the room.

She glanced around to be sure the room was unoccupied.

Once she'd satisfied herself, she removed her night vision and flipped the overhead lights on, still wearing her knit cap.

Mason had removed his night vision a fraction of a second too late. The bright light blinded him for a minute. He closed his eyes and opened them again, trying to focus.

"Where is Cheryl's room?" Otto asked.

He cleared his throat. He knew the answer. Problem was, once they got there, they were likely to find Cheryl in bed with Bruce Ray. Which would be embarrassing in the extreme. But he couldn't worry about that now.

"This way," he said, as he pulled off his cap, opened the interior door and slipped into the corridor.

He walked quietly on the carpeted floor. Down the hallway, around the corner, and up one flight of stairs. The mansion had two master suites, one at each end of the oversized house.

Gavin Ray and his wife, Daphne, occupied the three room suite on the north end. Their two children had rooms next to their parents.

Bruce Ray shared the second master suite with his wife, Cheryl. Their son, Micah, slept next door.

Mason had never been in this area of the mansion before. Cheryl always came to his room. Or they met somewhere else. The Rays' private rooms were off limits to the other Glen Haven residents.

When they came up the staircase, the magnitude of what he was about to do suddenly landed with its full weight upon Mason's shoulders. He slumped against the wall.

Otto said quietly, "Which room?"

He pointed to the suite on the south end of the hallway. "We can't go in there."

"Kind of impossible to rescue Cheryl and Micah if we don't," Otto replied, pulling her cap from her head and stuffing it into a pocket. "And we're running out of time. Do you want to do this or not?"

Before he had a chance to answer, the door to Gavin Ray's suite opened and Daphne walked out, fully dressed and carrying a sweater. She'd taken a few steps before she saw them. Her eyes widened and she cocked her head.

He must have looked alarming, to say the least, with his battered face and his swollen eye and his broken arm in a sling. His clothes were dirty and torn. He probably didn't smell all that great, either.

He should have said something, but he couldn't think of a single socially acceptable thing to say.

Otto stepped into the awkward moment. "Daphne, you remember me. Kim Otto. We met yesterday at the balloon launch."

Daphne stood staring at them both as if she had no words she could speak. Her mind had gone blank.

Otto said, "Daphne, we need to get you out of here. Now."

"What? I'm on my way to the launch site. I came back for my fleece. Don't worry. I won't be late," Daphne said holding up the yellow fleece, as if launching the balloon on time was the issue.

"That's great. Where's Cheryl?" Otto asked.

"She already left. She's piloting this morning. There was a lot of setup to do after all that happened yesterday. We wanted to be sure, you know?" Daphne said.

Mason wondered whether Cheryl's excuse was true or if she knew more about Vigo's plans than she'd told her sister-in-law. Bruce Ray was prone to pillow talk, Mason knew. He had never interrogated Cheryl about what she learned from her husband. He should have.

Daphne said, "The kids are having breakfast now. They'll head out in a few minutes, too."

Mason was so relieved to hear that Cheryl and Micah were out of the house that he almost collapsed. He leaned against the wall to keep himself upright.

"What about your husbands?" Otto asked.

"Oh, they had some kind of business with the renters. They got called a while ago. Over to the barracks, I think," Daphne said, buttoning the cuffs of her shirt and pulling the warm fleece over her head.

The more she talked, the more normally she began to behave. Perhaps she wasn't as horrified by Mason's appearance anymore. He didn't know.

"There's nobody left up here?" Otto asked.

"Nobody except me. And if I keep talking to you, I'll be late," Daphne replied. "Can we finish this discussion, whatever it's about, on our way?"

Mason said, "Yes, of course."

She linked her arm through Mason's good arm and walked along with them. "What happened to you? You didn't get into a fight, did you? That's not like you Mason. And how do you know Kim?"

Daphne continued talking all the way down the stairs to the first floor. They walked past the kitchen. The kids had left empty cereal bowls and juice glasses on the table, but they were already gone.

A few other residents had wandered into the kitchen. They were making coffee, moving about quietly as they woke to begin another normal, productive day. Mason had been focused on

Cheryl and Micah. Now that they were safely out of the house, he could get the others out, too.

Daphne said, "I've really got to get out to the launch site. Aren't you supposed to be on the ground crew this morning, Mason?"

"I'm afraid I won't be able to help much." He nodded and patted his sling. "You go ahead. I'll get a shower and join you out there."

She waved and headed toward the door.

When Daphne was out of hearing range, Mason turned to Otto. Urgently, he said, "Gavin and Bruce Ray went over to the barracks building. You have to go get them."

Otto didn't move.

He urged her. "Vigo will kill them. I know it's more than you agreed to do, but we can't abandon Gavin and Bruce like that. They've done so much for me and the others. Please. I'll get these people out and then I'll go out to the launch site where Cheryl and Micah are."

Otto seemed like she might argue, but Mason said, "We don't have time to debate this, do we?"

He could tell that she wanted to do the right thing here, even if it wasn't her job. One last time, he pleaded, "Please."

Probably because it was expedient to simply agree with him, she said, "Make it fast. You don't know how many of these people are involved with Vigo's cartel. So watch yourself."

"What?" Mason rounded his eyes as his heart pumped faster and roared in his ears. "None of the Glen Haven residents have anything to do with Vigo's business. We're not monsters."

Otto gave him a withering look, as if he was the stupidest human on the planet. At this point, he realized the odds were slim, but he wanted to believe he was right about these people.

"Just get as many out of here as you can and then run," Otto warned. "When those propane tanks are ignited, this whole place will go up fast. You won't survive it if you're still anywhere near the compound."

"See you at the launch site." Mason gave her a little shove and she let him push her in the direction she already knew she needed to go.

He took a deep breath and moved into the kitchen. Once he herded these people out, he'd search the buildings. He'd seen Otto disarm the Sterno and propane setups. He knew what to do. Glen Haven and everyone who lived here could still be saved.

He glanced at the clock on the wall. But Agent Otto was right. He'd need to hurry.

CHAPTER FORTY-TWO

Friday, April 15
5:50 a.m.
Glen Haven, New Mexico

VIGO SAT AT THE table with his coffee, thumping his fingers along the surface absently while he quickly reviewed the logistics.

The FBI had a warrant to search the premises and seize both evidence and contraband. Vigo's informants said the feds planned to show up for the raid in full SWAT gear with plenty of manpower. All of which took some time to coordinate. They planned to attack at nine o'clock. Of course, they didn't call it an assault, but that's precisely what it was.

Vigo's options were to stay and fight or retreat before the FBI arrived. He understood the pitfalls. He'd employed both options in the past. From experience, he knew that leaving was the better choice. Too much collateral damage with any of the alternatives.

He had sent Maria into the bedroom to get some sleep. He'd wake her up when he had the new inventory in hand.

The driver's estimated time of arrival was five minutes past six. Fifteen minutes away.

The inventory was both more valuable and more lethal than the size of the packages suggested. Twenty kilograms of fentanyl weighed about forty-four pounds. The whole shipment would fit in a plastic storage container, twenty inches wide by thirty inches long by twelve inches deep.

As soon as the driver pulled up, Louis and Manny would move the product into one of the SUVs. They'd finished setting up the propane accelerators. Then they had moved the heroin, methamphetamine, firearms, and cash inventory from the barracks into the same SUV for transport.

Vigo, Maria, and Freddie were set to leave immediately.

Louis and Manny would ignite the propane. The resulting fires would take care of Lawton and most of the evidence remaining at Glen Haven. Anything left behind would take weeks to process through the ashes.

Vigo's crew would be long gone before then.

He ran the logistics through his head twice more.

"Acceptable," he murmured to himself.

He still had to deal with the mole. His continued leadership of the cartel depended on dealing swiftly with informants. The punishment was death. There were no other options.

The mole had caused several members of his crew to be arrested or killed. Not to mention thousands of dollars lost to seizures by local cops. The mole deserved the death sentence. No one would disagree.

Early on, he'd realized the mole was one of the Glen Haven residents. But which one?

A process of elimination, focused on opportunity and timing, had narrowed the potential names down to four solid suspects.

All four had the opportunity to learn the information they'd passed on to the FBI and had done so within reasonable time frames.

That was as far as the process of elimination had taken him.

Neither Lawton nor O'Hare were the mole and both had proved to be ignorant of the mole's true identity.

Despite his best efforts, he hadn't identified the specific informant.

Which was why he planned to kill all four suspects, Lawton, O'Hare, and the rest of the residents with the fire. To be sure he destroyed the mole.

And to be sure every member of his cartel as well as his enemies couldn't possibly believe he'd let the mole live.

As a solid deterrent for anyone else stupid enough to think they could do the same and live through the experience.

Two hard raps on the front door was the code for friendly visitors. Vigo's hand went to the shotgun across his lap.

With luck, the visitor would prove to be the man he'd been seeking.

"Come in," he called, shotgun ready to fire beneath the table toward the doorway.

The brothers, Gavin and Bruce Ray, stepped inside and closed the door behind them.

Vigo relaxed slightly but kept his hand on the shotgun.

"We're sorry we didn't get here sooner, Vigo. We came to pay our condolences to Hector," Gavin said solemnly, hat in hand. "Elena was such a delightful woman. All of our Glen Haven family will miss her. Hector must be beside himself with grief."

Vigo gave both brothers a steely-eyed stare and said nothing. Bruce Ray lowered his gaze, as if he had something to feel guilty about. Which he probably did.

They both should feel guilty.

One of them was likely the mole. But even if they weren't, they had housed and nurtured the mole. The mole was responsible for Big Sela's murder and Elena's murder as well.

The brothers and everyone who lived at Glen Haven deserved what was coming to them. If he'd had the time, he'd have tortured them in front of his crew before he killed them, simply to sharpen the lesson.

Gavin advanced into the barracks and approached Vigo at the table. "Got any coffee?"

Vigo nodded. "Help yourself."

Gavin sat and Bruce filled two cups and joined him at the table. If they noticed the shotgun, they gave no indication.

"The police were at Glen Haven yesterday, interviewing the ground crew after they finished with the other witnesses at the landing site where Elena died. They said they'd be back today to finish up," Gavin said. "They may want to talk to Hector at some point, if they haven't already."

Vigo nodded again. "They tell you who shot Elena?"

Bruce shook his head. The port wine stain on his face seemed like a dark shadow in the lamplight. "They said they didn't know yet. They didn't find the spent bullet. They didn't find the shooter. But they will, Vigo. Hector will have justice."

Gavin frowned and added, "Not that justice will make up for losing Elena."

Vigo nodded. Hector had no need for justice. He'd have vengeance, which was as it should be. Vigo would make certain of it.

The three were silent for a few moments before Gavin cleared his throat and said, "That's why we came, Vigo. To ask you to let the authorities deal with this. We can't have any trouble here at Glen Haven. We're sorry for Elena and for Hector, and for all of you. But Glen Haven isn't the place for Hector to find justice. Elena's death had nothing to do with us."

Vigo could feel his temperature rising along with his anger. Bruce jumped in. "We'll help however we can. Tell us what to do, and we'll do it."

"That's right," Gavin continued, nodding like a bobblehead doll. "But we don't want any trouble here."

Vigo's stare was the kind that had sent stronger men sniveling in terror. Gavin Ray might have been too stupid to understand it. Bruce was not. Sweat broke out on his brow and he wiped it away with his sleeve.

"Hector will have his vengeance," Vigo said quietly, watching Bruce sweat. "Nothing anyone can do about that. Not even me."

"Come on, Bruce." Gavin said quietly as he pushed his chair back and stood. "We'll go next door and talk to Hector. We should convey our condolences in person."

"Now is as good a time as any," Vigo replied.

It would have been simple enough to shoot them in the back as they departed. But the deafening gunshot would have ignited chaos before he was ready. Their time was coming. After his inventory was safely stowed in the SUV.

He waited a bit until Gavin and Bruce were well outside before following them to the other barracks building with the shotgun.

CHAPTER FORTY-THREE

Friday, April 15
5:50 a.m.
Glen Haven, New Mexico

KIM HAD BEEN GONE too long. Flint and Lawton would be waiting. O'Hare said he could take care of himself. Which she didn't believe for a moment, but she couldn't force him to come with her, either.

She retraced her steps, hurried through the main house, and back to O'Hare's room, where she slipped outside through the sliding glass door.

She let her eyes adjust to the darkness as she pulled the ski cap down over her face and replaced her night vision. The last thing she needed was to trip and fall out here.

Briefly, she considered searching for more propane setups to dismantle and rejected the thought. No time. She kept moving.

O'Hare was evacuating the residents and the FBI would arrive soon enough to deal with Vigo and his crew.

Kim's mission was to get Lawton and Flint out alive. No more, no less. Finlay could coordinate the rest.

On her way across the open space, she noticed that two more of the propane setups she'd passed on the way into O'Hare's room had been dismantled in the ten minutes since she'd seen them earlier.

The Sterno cans were missing. So were the propane tanks themselves. Someone had taken the fuel from the setups.

She might have been mistaken about the location of those two tanks, so she stopped to check. There were the depressions in the soil where each tank had been. There were no tracks suggesting a cart of any kind had been used to move them.

Each tank probably weighed close to forty pounds. Maybe more. Carrying two tanks around on the uneven ground in the dark meant whoever had taken them was probably a strong man.

Briefly, she wondered if Reacher had done it.

"Get a grip, Otto," she murmured to herself. Then she shook her head and kept moving.

Reacher had done similar things before, and last time, he'd said he owed her for saving his nephew. Which he did.

But she'd seen no evidence that he was around at all this time. He was too big to hide, even if he'd wanted to. Which he usually didn't. He met physical challenges head-on and never lost a fight as far as she knew.

Mrs. Otto's daughter Kim lacked Reacher's giant-like assets.

She'd often wondered how her life might have been different if she'd been as physically imposing as Reacher. Now was not the time to think about it.

Question was, what had happened to those propane tanks?

She made it to the back of the barracks building where Lawton waited. The lights were still on inside. She rounded the far corner.

Flint had moved the SUV. It was waiting in the shadows along the west side of the building, but he wasn't there. He must have gone into the building for Lawton.

Briefly, she wondered if Flint had been the one who moved those propane tanks. Had she been gone long enough for him to accomplish the task? No. He'd been busy with other things.

As she was nearing the southwest corner, she heard footsteps on the gravel parking area approaching the building next door. She flattened her back against the building and extended her neck to see around the corner.

Two men walked side-by-side toward the door. From this distance and wearing the night vision, Kim could not identify them. They didn't appear to be carrying weapons. Nor did they carry themselves like cops.

At first she thought they were probably the two guys Lawton had said were members of Vigo's crew. Louis and Manny.

But then, the taller one knocked on the door. Which suggested these two were visitors.

After a moment, the man turned the knob and pushed the door open. Light spilled out of the open doorway for a moment before they went inside and closed it again.

Kim waited to be sure they weren't coming out again, and then she hurried to the door of Lawton's barracks building. She put her ear against the door, listening for trouble. She didn't hear any.

She removed her night vision, turned the knob, ducked inside, and closed the door behind her. Lawton and Flint were waiting for her. Like her, Flint was still wearing his knit cap that covered his face.

Freddy was on the floor near the fireplace where Flint had dropped him, but his eyes were open. Which meant he could probably hear them talking.

"There's activity next door," she said. "The building seems dark from outside, but people are moving around. Two guys just arrived. I couldn't see their faces. If we're going to get out of here, we need to go now."

Flint said, "What about Freddy, here? Take him with us?"

Kim definitely didn't want to do that. When the FBI arrived, they could pick him up. She didn't need to be accused of abducting one of Vigo's gang. How the hell would she explain that one to the Boss?

Lawton said, "Toss him in the basement and lock the door. If anyone comes in, they'll think I'm still down there."

Kim said, "Okay. Let's do that."

Lawton pointed the shotgun toward Freddie. "Don't think I won't shoot you."

Flint yanked Freddie up off the floor and patted him down while Lawton held the shotgun aimed toward Freddie's head.

From Freddie's pockets, Flint removed a handgun, a wallet, a cell phone, and some cash. He tossed the cell phone to Kim. He dropped everything else on the floor and kicked it under the sofa.

Flint said, "You can walk, or I can throw you down the stairs. Your choice."

Freddy nodded and grunted something behind the duct tape before he shuffled toward the basement. He walked through the opening and down the stairs while Flint replaced the door on its hinges. Flint closed the door and threw the dead bolt.

Kim had fired up Freddie's disposable cell phone and scrolled through the call log. Nothing but a list of numbers came up. The last call had come through half an hour ago. It lasted two minutes.

In a nanosecond, she thought of five good reasons to leave the cell phone here and a dozen good reasons to take it. She dropped it into her pocket.

When Flint finished stashing Freddie in the basement, he strode back toward the door.

"Ready?" Kim asked Lawton. "We go outside. Turn right. The SUV is around the corner. You'll have to walk fifteen feet. No more. Can you do it?"

He nodded, but she knew the gesture was pure bravado.

Flint helped him off the sofa and he tossed his arm over Flint's shoulders again. Kim went first, headed toward the door. The two men followed.

She flipped off the light. She and Flint adjusted their night vision. Then she opened the door and ducked her head outside for a quick look first.

Just as she did, the door from the other barracks opened. Light illuminated the same two men she'd seen entering earlier. When they turned to walk toward her, she saw their faces.

She ducked back into the room and closed the door. "Gavin and Bruce Ray are headed this way."

Lawton said, "The founders of Glen Haven? What the hell are they doing over there with Vigo?"

Flint replied, "They're probably not having a friendly game of poker."

There was no back exit to the barracks building. No means of escape.

Two hard raps on the door and Gavin's voice said, "Hector? Can we come in?"

Kim pulled her gun. Flint did the same.

"Are they armed?" Lawton asked as he leaned against the wall and hefted the shotgun.

She heard three voices outside talking and then a firm pounding on the door. Another man must have joined the Ray brothers. "Freddie. It's Vigo. Open up."

Then she heard a fourth voice call out, "Vigo!"

She couldn't make out the muffled conversation between Vigo and the newcomer, which seemed to have moved away from the door toward the gravel driveway.

Gavin rapped on the door a couple more times, pausing between rounds. "Freddie! Wake up! It's Gavin Ray!"

Kim heard a vehicle engine coming up the driveway. It sounded like an old diesel pickup truck.

Then Vigo came back to the door. "Step aside, Gavin. I've got a key."

Lawton and Flint positioned a chair in front of the door. Lawton sat in the chair. Flint and Kim stood behind the door in the shadows.

Vigo inserted the key into the lock and turned it. Kim heard the deadbolt slide open.

"Freddie, where are you?" Vigo said as he pushed the door open, stepped inside, reached over, and flipped the lights on.

Gavin and Bruce Ray followed Vigo inside leaving the door open behind them.

"Hands up. You're under arrest," Lawton said when all three men were inside. Gavin and Bruce complied. "Drop the shotgun, Vigo, and kick it aside."

Vigo didn't move. Lawton said, "I can't possibly miss you from this distance. Want to test me?"

CHAPTER FORTY-FOUR

Friday, April 15
6:30 a.m.
Glen Haven, New Mexico

"YOU COULD SHOOT ME in cold blood, Lawton. But we both know you won't. Because you'd go to prison for it." Vigo continued to stand his ground inside the barracks, staring at Lawton.

"Not likely." Lawton shook his head and grinned. "Right after you rushed in here, waving your weapon around, you attacked me and I shot you first. Self-defense, plain and simple. You're dead. I walk. Hell, they might even give me a medal."

Vigo didn't believe a word of it. Too many witnesses in the room with a contrary story, for one thing. But Lawton was sitting there with a shotgun. So he stalled.

Never breaking eye contact, Vigo lowered his shotgun's butt and eased it to the floor. He pushed it along the hard wood with his foot, out of reach.

"What's going on?" Gavin Ray said from Vigo's right, as if

he had no clue. He was a better actor than Vigo would have guessed. He knew damn well who Vigo was and why hundreds of people might want to kill him.

Gavin probably also knew Lawton was a federal agent, since Gavin was one of the four prime suspects Vigo believed could be the mole.

In Vigo's periphery, Bruce Ray stood in stony silence with his hands in the air like an idiot. He was another of the four suspects. And a more likely one. Bruce knew Lawton was in the basement and he'd known why.

Lawton wasn't as strong as he had been before Vigo's interrogations. Even so, he could make good on his threat if he shot directly at Vigo from point blank range right now.

What he needed was a momentary distraction.

Louis and Manny must have finished unloading the inventory. He heard the diesel truck's engine as it revved up in the gravel driveway and turned around to head back toward the main road.

Hector had not returned, which worried Vigo. But he couldn't wait any longer. He'd see Hector in Arkansas.

It was time to waken Maria and hit the road, leaving Louis and Manny to ignite the propane they'd placed.

Starting on the northwest end of the horseshoe shaped compound, working their way around and back here to the southwest end.

By the time they returned, Vigo would be long gone. Louis and Manny would meet him in Arkansas.

Gavin couldn't seem to keep quiet. He said, "Who are you exactly?"

Lawton replied. "You say that like you don't already know me, Gavin."

"What?" Gavin said, plainly astonished. "I *don't* know you. Why would I?"

Pounding came from the basement door. It sounded like someone kicking the door with hard-toed work boots. Lawton ignored the noise, holding the shotgun steady and pointed at Vigo.

Vigo cocked his head. "Have you put Freddie in the basement? Bruce, go let him out."

"Don't move, Bruce. Leave Freddie where he is," a man's voice said from behind them.

Vigo turned his head to see a guy wearing a knit cap and face mask standing in the shadows.

Bruce whirled his body around and drew his gun and fired. He missed when the shot went wide. Bruce was a lot of things, but a marksman wasn't one of them.

Before he had a chance to shoot again, the man stepped forward. With his momentum and weight fully behind the punch, he hit Bruce's jaw with his right fist. Bruce went down.

The man kicked Bruce's gun aside and gave him a hard kick to the kidneys. Bruce doubled over, grabbing his stomach and yelping in pain.

"Stay down there," the man said. "Next time, I won't go so easy on you."

Vigo should have taken the chance to rush Lawton. But he'd been surprised and missed his opportunity.

Freddie continued kicking the basement door.

A woman's voice behind Vigo's right approached Bruce on the floor and demanded, "Hands behind your back!"

Which was the exact moment the first propane setup exploded in the big barn across the open space in the middle of the compound. Precisely as Vigo had planned.

Gavin seemed totally bewildered by the chaos around him and the explosion. "What the hell?"

No one else in the room so much as flinched. They'd all expected the blast.

The petite woman hurriedly approached Bruce and slipped plastic ties around his wrists. She didn't bind his ankles. Probably because he'd need to run from the fires.

Although she wore a black cap covering her face, too, Vigo realized the woman must have been the one who got Big Sela killed at the Last Chance Saloon. Which meant she was FBI.

Lawton held his shotgun steady and pointed at Vigo, center mass.

The first explosion across the compound was followed by a second. And a third.

Vigo couldn't see outside, but the inferno had to be spreading fast. The fire must have caught and burned in the buildings across the open space, gaining strength as it gulped the night air and consumed the fuel in the barns.

If Glen Haven was equipped with fire suppression equipment, it was already overwhelmed.

Vigo needed to deal with the mole and then go while he still could.

The fire department was miles away, but they would get the alarms soon enough. All the way to the main road, the two-track would be clogged with passengers for the balloon ride and first responders for the fire, rescue, and evacuees.

A fourth explosion and then a fifth sounded. Both were closer. The propane was making its way around the U-shaped compound buildings at ever increasing speed.

He wanted to get Freddie and Maria first and then go.

But until Lawton's shotgun was out of the way, he stood rooted to the spot.

When she finished with Bruce, the woman approached Gavin and bound his hands next. He barely squeaked in protest. He was so overwhelmed by these events that Vigo silently crossed Gavin off his list. Which made him expendable.

And now there were only three suspects.

CHAPTER FORTY-FIVE

Friday, April 15
6:40 a.m.
Glen Haven, New Mexico

ANOTHER EXPLOSION BLASTED FROM the other side of the compound. Definitely closer. The fires would reach them soon.

Kim finished with Bruce Ray and then snugged a set of plastic ties around Gavin's wrists. She looked at Lawton. "You got this?"

"Yeah, I'm good," he replied, keeping his steady gaze on Vigo.

She turned to Flint. "Get these two outside. I'll get Freddie."

"Let's go." Flint grabbed Bruce and yanked him to his feet. Then he took both brothers by the arms and shoved them through the exit. They stumbled and landed hard on the gravel outside.

Kim hurried to the basement door. Freddie was still kicking the door with his boots. When she slid the deadbolt back and yanked the door open, he fell forward and tumbled onto the floor, banging his head, busting his nose, and splashing blood all over his face.

She bent and grabbed the edge of the duct tape and pulled it off his mouth so he could breathe, now that he'd ruined his nose.

Another explosion. Followed by another. These blasts must have exploded inside the main house. She heard breaking glass and a loud whump, as if the explosion had sucked all the oxygen from the atmosphere.

She hoped O'Hare had evacuated all of the residents. There was no saving those buildings or anyone remaining inside them now.

Kim reached down and yanked on Freddie's arm. "Let's go. Unless you want to die here. The fire is coming this way faster than you can run."

Freddie must have heard the explosions, too. He didn't bother to argue. He stood, swiped his bloody nose across his sleeve, and headed toward the door.

He paused briefly when he saw Lawton holding Vigo at gunpoint.

Kim pushed him in the back with her weapon and he kept moving. She followed him as far as the door and shoved him toward Flint, who was still dealing with the Ray brothers.

Two more explosions blasted through the already noisy night. Sirens approached in the distance. Screaming came from across the two-track where the passengers and their guests had gathered for the balloon ride. The cacophony was already deafening and new explosions were coming every few minutes.

When the fire reached the larger propane tanks stored in the big barns closer to the barracks, it would also ignite the fertilizers used in the herbal products farming. Every inch of Glen Haven and everything in it would be burned to the ground.

Two SUVs and one sedan were still parked in front of the barracks.

She hurried across the parking lot, pushing Freddie forward, until she reached Flint and the Ray brothers.

The situation had always been dangerous. Now it had become cumbersome.

She had no means of securing the suspects until the FBI arrived.

They needed to get out of the path of flying debris and the conflagration that had been the compound.

She had no means of transport for the prisoners, either. And even if she called a wagon, it would never make it through the crowded two-track now.

The only way out of here was by air, and they had left the helo twenty miles away.

More explosions blasted the main living quarters and the two smaller residences. Even though she knew the blasts were coming, she flinched every time.

Vehicles were parked along the two-track and in the field across the street. The screaming sirens were approaching from several directions now, but none were close enough. By the time the firefighters arrived, the compound would be well on its way to a pile of ashes.

"Any bright ideas?" Flint yelled over the noise. "I can put them in one of those SUVs and lock the doors. We'll have to drive them somewhere. When the fire reaches this point, they won't survive if we leave them here."

"Okay. Do that," Kim shouted back. "I'm going in for Vigo and Lawton. Watch for Louis and Manny. They should be back here any minute. Don't let them catch you unaware."

She turned toward the barracks. She'd taken a few long strides toward the entrance. She saw Lawton and Vigo inside.

Lawton glanced at her briefly, as if to warn her, before another woman stepped forward.

"Stop right there. Raise your arms and turn around or I'll shoot you in the back," the woman said.

Kim did as she was told. When she turned to face the woman, she recognized her instantly from the Last Chance Saloon and the video feed at the garage in Albuquerque. Maria Vigo.

The distraction was enough to give Vigo the chance to attack Lawton. Kim kept her gaze trained on Maria. Behind her, Vigo and Lawton scuffled inside the building.

A moment later, Lawton's shotgun fired.

She heard a shout followed by loud groans from one of the men. But which one?

Kim blocked Maria's view of the confrontation as well.

Conflicting emotions warred on her face. "Vigo!" she called out to her brother. "Vigo, answer me!"

Kim used Maria's momentary lapse against her.

She rushed forward and knocked Maria to the ground. The gun flew out of her hand and skidded along the gravel, out of reach.

The element of surprise followed by overwhelming force might have been enough to subdue some women. But not Maria.

Screaming her brother's name with greater and greater urgency, Maria fought like a hellcat. She pulled the knit cap from Kim's head. When she saw Kim's face, she yelled with rage.

Blood from a cut on her forehead blinded Kim for a moment. She wiped her eyes on her sleeve. In that moment, Maria escaped and scrambled to retrieve her pistol.

Kim got enough leverage to land a solid blow to Maria's stomach. A loud whoosh escaped her lips followed by a cry of violent uncontrolled anger.

Lying on the floor, Maria leaned to her left and raised the gun to fire.

At the last second before Maria pulled the trigger, Kim rolled out of range.

The momentary break was long enough for Kim to retrieve her weapon and fire back.

Kim's aim was true.

Maria took the bullet in her chest.

She flopped onto the ground, dead eyes staring at the sky.

Kim glanced up to see Vigo still standing inside, shotgun in hand.

CHAPTER FORTY-SIX

Friday, April 15
6:55 a.m.
Glen Haven, New Mexico

THE RAGING INFERNO, REGULAR explosions, and Maria's attack had given Vigo the distraction he needed.

He had seized his chance to knock Lawton off the chair. He grabbed the shotgun. Lawton struggled, but Vigo was simply stronger than Lawton and had better leverage.

He heard Maria fighting with the woman they had called Otto.

A brief grin crossed his face. Maria was fierce and fearless. He wasn't worried. He had scars from fighting with Maria left from childhood battles. Otto didn't stand a chance.

Vigo grabbed the gun from Lawton's hands and pulled the trigger. His aim was off, but as he'd said, it's hard to miss with a shotgun at that range.

Lawton yelled with pain when the shell hit him in the abdomen. He covered the wound with both hands, but blood gushed around his fingers and rapidly spread, draining his remaining strength.

Vigo considered shooting him again, just to be sure. But he only had one shell left and Lawton would die anyway. He'd never seen a man survive a gut shot at close range.

A moment later, Maria's pistol shot rang out. Vigo whipped around to see both women entangled on the ground and blood everywhere.

"Maria!" he shouted to be heard above the constantly increasing roar of the fires.

When Otto rolled off Maria, covered in blood, Vigo saw his sister's dead eyes.

"What have you done?" he yelled as he rushed to Maria and shoved Otto aside with a vicious kick.

Two more propane explosions blasted though the overwhelming noise. They must have been close. Vigo looked around, eyes wild. Soon, the propane tanks exploding close to the barracks would make leaving here impossible.

There was nothing he could do for Maria now. He bent to hug his dead sister one last time.

Briefly, his gaze swept the barracks, searching for Otto, but she had somehow disappeared. He saw smoke billowing around the gravel drive.

The fires were close now and coming closer every minute. Another explosion, even closer, hammered his body as if he'd been shot himself.

It was time to go. He could waste no more energy here.

He held the shotgun and ran through the open door to the gravel parking area. The sedan Maria had arrived in was still parked outside. Whatever trace evidence it might contain after it burned was of no consequence now that Maria was dead.

One of the SUVs was gone. Louis and Manny must have taken it already. But they'd taken the wrong one. The inventory had been packed inside the black one. They'd left the green one here.

Briefly, he wondered if Louis and Manny had suddenly turned against him. Joined another cartel. Stolen what was rightfully his.

He shook his head. No time to deal with that now. At least his inventory was already on the road. He'd find them soon enough once he got away from here.

He glanced toward the southbound two-track. It looked like a parking lot. Vehicles were backed up along it for at least a mile. He couldn't possibly drive through to the main road with his product in the remaining SUV.

Across the two-track was the open field launch site for the morning's balloon ride. Passengers, guests, and Glen Haven residents were milling around, staring at the constantly building fire at Glen Haven. The balloon was inflated and the crew held the gondola tethered to the ground.

Sirens in the near distance were headed toward him. Some were first responders for the fires, no doubt. But the others were likely law enforcement from various agencies and departments.

There was no way to get past the gridlock in the green SUV.

He might escape on foot. But he wouldn't get far enough fast enough.

The only option was to rise above the chaos in the balloon. He headed toward the gondola. It would be a ridiculous slow speed getaway, but at least he could go somewhere. He'd put the balloon down in a parking lot where he could steel another vehicle. From there, he'd drive to Arkansas to find Louis and Manny and his inventory.

He'd find Hector, too. They had something in common now. Both had lost beloved sisters.

From Arkansas, he could start over.

Vigo started to jog toward the gondola. As he ran past the barracks building, another explosion went off inside the barn next door on the east side. There were at least three propane tank setups inside. More explosions would follow. And then the two barracks buildings would catch fire and explode.

Lawton, Maria, and the FBI agent would be cremated. It should take a good long while for their remains to be identified by the FBI and the other agencies. He'd be long gone by then.

Vigo folded his arm over his mouth and nose and jogged faster through the smoke and across the road, leaving the fires behind.

When he reached the field, the breezes provided fresh air. He could breathe again.

He jogged up to the gondola. The passengers were milling around, not sure whether they should get into the basket or stay on the ground. There seemed to be an equal number of gawkers, watching the fires with gaping mouths, and thrill seekers wanting an aerial view of the fires.

The pilot was Bruce Ray's wife, Cheryl. Vigo knew her better than some of the others. She had a solid head on her shoulders. She wasn't likely to panic.

Gavin Ray's wife, Daphne, was close by. He grinned. Perfect. His last two suspects were already here. He could eliminate them both at the landing site before he left for Arkansas.

He saw Cheryl's kid, Micah, standing inside the basket with her. Too bad about the kid. He shrugged. Kids died every day.

While the passengers continued to mill around, Vigo approached Daphne. He jabbed a pistol in her ribs. "Get in. We're going for a ride."

The look of pure astonishment on her face mirrored her husband's earlier. Maybe she wasn't the mole. And if not, that left Cheryl Ray. Which made a lot more sense anyway.

He should have guessed it was Cheryl long ago. She was always questioning Bruce about Vigo's business.

Bruce had been a member of the cartel, but not a solid performer. Cheryl could only have known enough to reveal low level dealers to the feds.

Vigo smirked. This was perfect. He'd kill them both. Then he could start again in Arkansas without looking over his shoulder for the feds.

Daphne dropped the rope and climbed into the basket. Vigo followed. When she released the anchor, the gondola began to rise off the ground. With only the four of them inside, the gondola might travel faster and higher, too.

"Let's go, Cheryl," Vigo said, brandishing the gun.

"What? We can't fly out of here now," she replied. The sirens were closer. They'd turned off the main road and ran through the line of traffic like the prow of a slow ship parting the water.

"We can fly out of here and we will. Do it," he said, grabbing Micah by the shoulders. "Micah here wants to fly today, don't you?"

Micah seemed unsure, but he nodded.

"Let's go," Vigo said. "Unless you'd like me to shoot all three of you and fly this thing myself. It's not that hard to do."

Cheryl's eyes widened and she swallowed hard. With a shaky hand, she gave the air another burst of heat from the propane burner.

The gondola rose quickly above the heads of the spectators and drifted with the currents away from Glen Haven.

CHAPTER FORTY-SEVEN

Friday, April 15
7:05 a.m.
Glen Haven, New Mexico

AFTER VIGO LEFT, KIM crawled around the sofa and found Lawton slumped in the chair. He was clammy and in shock, but he opened his eyes and gave her a weak grin.

"Sorry," he whispered.

His belly wound was still pulsing blood. She pulled her sweatshirt over her head, balled it up, and pushed it against his wound. She placed his palm on the sweatshirt.

"Keep as much pressure there as you can. I'll get you out of here before this place goes up in flames." She pleaded with him when she saw his face relaxing, "Hang on. Don't give up."

She'd seen adrenaline give victims superhuman strength in the past and later, she figured that's what must have happened to them both.

Somehow, she managed to get Lawton to his feet. Supporting him around his torso, with one of his arms thrown over her shoulder, he staggered and she dragged until they made it to the door and down the front steps.

She whipped her head around in all directions. She saw one SUV gone and Vigo jogging toward the road. Flint was nowhere. He might have put the Ray brothers and Freddie into Vigo's black SUV and driven them off-site, but she didn't know.

She and Lawton made it to the gravel parking area before he fainted. She couldn't carry his dead weight, so she placed him on the grass as far from the burning buildings as possible.

To be heard above the roaring fire, she leaned in toward his ear and said, "Please don't die, John. Hang on until I get someone here. Can you do that?"

He might have grunted in response. She wasn't sure.

She turned toward Finlay's SUV that Flint had parked on the far west side of the barracks. When she got there, it was unoccupied. Wherever he went, he wasn't here to help now.

She looked into the open space. Vigo's black SUV was parked in the middle of the garden. Quickly, she ran toward it and opened one of the back doors.

A quick glance inside was all she needed. She saw two dead bodies. Louis and Manny. The cargo section was piled with drugs and guns. On the front passenger seat, she saw a propane tank with a hose and the valve open. A can of Sterno with its cotton strip already burning rested on the floor.

Briefly, she thought Flint was responsible for this. But he hadn't had enough time.

As soon as the propane filled the cabin, the whole SUV would go up in a bigger blast than any of the others. Both bodies, the drugs, and the weapons would be destroyed. There was nothing she could do but get out of the way.

She turned and ran full out toward Finlay's SUV and hopped inside.

Kim closed the door and pressed the pushbutton start. When the SUV's engine fired up, she drove around to the spot where she'd left Lawton.

The continuing explosions had moved closer to the last barracks. The fire was raging out of control. The only thing keeping the fire from the gravel driveway and parking area were the winds flowing softly from the east.

First responders were streaming in from the main road, plowing through the traffic like a slow motion parade.

She made a quick assessment of the traffic and concluded the same thing Vigo must have determined. The only means of escape was due east. Toward the launch site.

Smoke filled the air and covered the awakening sunlight. She put the headlights on and left the SUV running when she jumped out to get Lawton.

He was out of his head with pain, shock, and blood loss, but she managed to get him up off the ground. Together, they staggered the few feet of distance to the SUV's back seat. Kim tumbled him into the seat and closed the door solidly.

She ran around to the driver's side just before the first of the propane tanks exploded in the barracks building next door. The window glass blew out onto the gravel drive.

Kim felt the percussion of the massive blast from Vigo's black SUV in the courtyard as she steered past the buildings and kept driving.

She drove the SUV across the two-track and into the field in a desperate attempt to reach the balloon before Vigo escaped.

She was too late.

The balloon was already lifting into the air.

She pulled the SUV as close to the balloon's rising basket as she could get. Then she jumped out and ran to the crew.

The balloon was already more than twenty feet into the air, and still rising.

From somewhere, O'Hare had run up to the launch site just ahead of her. He was standing there, head titled back, gaping at the floating gondola.

"Cheryl! Micah!" he yelled over and over. As if they could hear him over the noise of the propane blasting heat into the envelope. Or that they could do anything at all if they had heard.

Kim grabbed O'Hare's arm and shook him.

She broke his concentration and he looked at her. "Cheryl and Micah are in the basket. Daphne, too. Vigo forced them to take off."

"Do you know where they're going?" Kim yelled above the thundering noise of the fires, the sirens, the bystanders, and the flame that heated the balloon's air for lift.

"There's only so many places they can land," he shouted back. "But there's no way to get them down safely until they're ready."

"How far can they travel before they run out of fuel?"

"Depends on weather, wind currents, and stuff. Also which setup they've got today. Some of the propane tanks will last about three hundred miles," O'Hare said.

Kim watched the balloon rise higher as it neared the first set of power lines. Cheryl had told her that the pilots knew the air currents well. They chose the correct currents by raising and lowering the balloon's altitude. The first set of powerlines were about forty feet off the ground. She needed to raise the balloon twenty-five feet above them to cross safely.

The balloon seemed to be having trouble. It lifted easily, but then it dropped down, as if it had failed to catch the current.

It approached the first set of power lines without sufficient altitude.

"What the hell is she doing?" O'Hare said. "She needs to raise the gondola at least another fifty feet in the air. There's a current there that will carry them up to the next level. Otherwise, she won't clear the substation."

The spectators on the ground were watching the fires and the balloon, heads turning side to side, as if they were watching a tennis match. A few had realized that the balloon was flying too low to clear the power lines. Others seemed simply overwhelmed with the entire situation.

A few of the first responders had arrived at Glen Haven. Fire trucks were beginning to fight the blaze, but it seemed like a losing battle. All they could hope to do now was to keep the fire from spreading along the dry landscape.

"Come on." Kim said to O'Hare before she turned to jog back to the SUV. "I think the balloon is going to hit those power lines. Which either means Cheryl is in trouble or she's not piloting the balloon. Either way, they'll need help."

She reached the SUV half a second before O'Hare. They jumped into the front seat and snugged up their seat belts. Kim engaged the four-wheel drive and headed across the field toward the power lines.

The SUV bounced over the rough terrain. Lawton groaned every time the springs rose and sagged.

"Keep your eye on the balloon," she said to O'Hare. "I've got to navigate around the holes and obstacles in this field."

Up ahead, the balloon continued to travel at low altitude. From this vantage point, it seemed there was no way Cheryl could miss the power lines. But Kim didn't trust her own eyes. Perspective was important here. Cheryl simply had a more accurate view. Maybe she saw a path that Kim couldn't see.

If Cheryl hit the lines with the balloon's envelope, they might survive. If the gondola hit the lines, the electricity would probably arc and ignite the propane and explode the whole thing.

Either way, the passengers would fall almost three stories to the ground. They could survive a fall like that. Maybe. But the shorter the distance, the better.

CHAPTER FORTY-EIGHT

Friday, April 15
7:35 a.m.
Glen Haven, New Mexico

VIGO LOOKED OVER THE edge of the gondola. The balloon was floating lower than it should have. They were only about fifty feet off the ground.

The first set of power lines were coming up fast. If they didn't get more altitude, the balloon would hit the wires.

"Cheryl," he yelled pointing his thumb upward. "Don't mess with me. Get this thing up. Now!"

Cheryl nodded and added a short blast of heat and the balloon barely lifted. She was an experienced pilot. She knew these wind currents better than she knew the roads around Glen Haven. She was deliberately sabotaging his escape.

Vigo didn't trust her. Why should he? She'd been feeding information to the feds for weeks. He felt sure she was the mole now.

He grabbed Daphne by the hair and pointed the pistol to her head as he yanked her toward the sidewall of the gondola. The stable gondola rocked as he moved passenger weight to one side.

Daphne screamed.

Vigo shouted to be heard above the roar of the propane. "You don't believe me?"

He lifted Daphne off the ground by her hair. She screamed and kicked and punched to break free, but Vigo was too strong for her. He lifted her and pushed her over the gondola's edge.

Cheryl's hands flew to her mouth and her eyes widened to the size of pie plates as she screamed. Micah yelled, "Aunt Daphne!" and ran to the edge to watch as she plummeted toward the ground.

Daphne's screams diminished on the way down while Micah's sobs filled the air.

Whether she'd survived was irrelevant to him. He'd have killed her later anyway. This way, she had a chance. Which was more than Elena and Big Sela had.

His sister was dead. Why should these three live when Maria did not?

Vigo had a bigger problem. Before he threw Daphne out, he'd had three hostages and now he only had two. He couldn't kill another one too soon.

When Cheryl screamed, she inadvertently released the handle on the propane valve, and the balloon had drifted a little lower, gliding quietly.

The silence inside the gondola was punctuated only by Micah's sobs and continued shouts to his aunt who was already gone.

Vigo pointed the pistol toward the kid. "Shut up."

Micah's tears continued to flow but he closed his mouth and stopped yelling, which helped.

Then Vigo pointed the gun toward Cheryl. "Get this thing up and over those power lines now. Otherwise, the kid goes out next."

Cheryl opened the valve and blasted the air inside the balloon for several continuous seconds. The balloon rose gracefully as it floated toward the power lines, increasing altitude at a faster pace than before.

Which simply proved Vigo had done the right thing. Cheryl could pilot the balloon safely over the power lines. All she'd needed was motivation.

Vigo had heard enough stories from Bruce and Gavin Ray to know balloon crashes were rare. Fatal balloon crashes were even rarer.

The envelope could sustain significant damage before the gondola crashed.

The problem was the propane, which was actually a liquid. An intact tank itself was unlikely to explode under almost any conditions. But the propane became a gas when it was released and then ignited by the burner. Which was how fires and explosions could kill if the basket hit the wires.

None of that should happen in good weather like this with a pilot as experienced as Cheryl. Vigo wasn't worried. But he didn't have any intention of committing suicide, either.

Cheryl blasted the air again. The basket lifted as the envelope caught another level of air current and picked up speed.

Elevation and wind speed pushed the balloon higher and faster. When they reached the power lines, the gondola glided thirty feet above the power lines, easily passing the danger zone.

Vigo nodded. So far, so good.

The next hurdle was the substation. After that, he could fly this thing himself.

Vigo watched the substation seem to grow larger and more menacing as the balloon approached.

A dozen times over the past few months, he'd seen the pilots perform the trick to entertain the tourists. The balloon would dip before the substation and then rise immediately afterward, high enough to clear the towers like a feather floating on the air.

From the launching site view back at Glen Haven, Bruce Ray had explained, it appeared to the guests that the gondola was within a few feet of the substation when the big dip occurred. But inside the gondola, passengers could see the distance was actually well within the safety zone.

If Cheryl did her job, everything would be fine. They'd pass the substation. Then he'd find a parking lot where he could steal another vehicle and get away.

Albuquerque was a relatively small city with limited resources. The metro area was estimated at under a million people. The city didn't have an infinite number of first responders and other agencies. Most of them would be focused on the disaster at Glen Haven. Long enough for him to flee, anyway.

If Cheryl did her job.

Vigo wasn't alarmed when the balloon dipped lower as long as the speed kept them moving at a good clip away from Glen Haven.

The FBI would arrive soon to serve their warrants, if they weren't already there. At some point they'd figure out he was in the gondola and come after him.

The further he was from Glen Haven when that happened, the greater his chances of escape.

He kept looking ahead. A stand of trees filled the open space between the balloon and the substation.

Cheryl had used the currents to steer the balloon directly toward the trees.

Then she decreased the gas feeding the burner.

The gondola dipped too low.

It would brush the tops of the trees. She made no move to heat the air and lift the gondola.

What the hell was she doing?

Vigo grabbed the boy and pointed the gun toward his head. "Cheryl. I'll kill him. Don't push me. You know I've done worse."

"I know," the stupid woman replied. It was the last thing he'd ever hear her say.

CHAPTER FORTY-NINE

Friday, April 15
7:40 a.m.
Glen Haven, New Mexico

KIM DROVE AS FAST as she could across the open field,
dodging ruts and holes and rocks and bushes and trees along the
way, always keeping the balloon in sight. The SUV bucked like
an angry stallion. Holding it on course required intense
concentration.

O'Hare had cinched his seatbelt tighter and grabbed the
handholds to stay upright. He peered out of the windshield,
providing a running commentary on the path of the balloon like
an annoying sports commentator. She did her best to ignore him.

The first set of powerlines was coming up fast.

O'Hare said quietly, coaching from the sidelines, "Come on,
Cheryl. Lift up. You're too low. Give it some gas."

Kim flashed a quick glance in the rearview mirror. Lawton
wasn't moving. She thought briefly about stopping the SUV to
check on him, but then she rejected the idea.

Vigo was in that gondola with Cheryl and Micah. She could still capture him alive. Or at least, keep him in sight until backup arrived.

When she twisted her gaze back to the path ahead, she saw a pair of trees and a few bushes clustered around them. She turned the steering wheel to the right to avoid the obstruction just as the gondola tilted dangerously.

She saw Vigo's torso above the gondola's side as he lifted a passenger over and pushed the person out. From this vantage point, Kim couldn't see well enough to determine the passenger's identity.

O'Hare sucked in his breath. "Daphne! He threw Daphne over the side!"

"How do you know it's her?" Kim asked.

"She's wearing that bright yellow fleece. The crew wears different colors so we can distinguish between them from our vantage point on the ground," he replied.

Then he pointed toward the trees.

"Looks like she might be okay if she landed in those bushes. She knows what to do. She's got to stay flexible. Try not to land on her head," O'Hare said, as if he was coaching her now.

"I'll pull up. You get out and help her. Call 911," Kim said.

O'Hare shook his head. His nostrils had flared and his eyes were wide with shock. "I have to get Cheryl and Micah."

"I'll go after them." Kim said. "Vigo's armed and dangerous. I'm better equipped to deal with him than you are."

"Cheryl will try to bail out of the balloon. She'll find a place to jump. Like another stand of trees," O'Hare said.

"Okay. Got it," Kim replied, giving him a push. "Help Daphne. Go!"

Kim pulled the SUV to a rolling stop near the bushes and O'Hare scrambled out. He closed the door and Kim accelerated again to follow the balloon.

She'd lost ground while slowing and dropping O'Hare off. The balloon was farther ahead now. She accelerated as much as she could to try to make up for it.

Vigo's demonstration of cruelty must have been enough to persuade Cheryl not to try running into the first set of power lines. The balloon lifted higher, hit an air current and kept going toward the substation.

Kim followed behind in the SUV, watching the balloon and scanning the field. If O'Hare was right, Cheryl would be looking for a good spot to bail out. She might have taken a bigger chance. But with Micah in the gondola, too, she'd be more cautious.

After Cheryl and Micah jumped out, Vigo would be alone in the gondola with the propane and the burner. He'd be armed.

She continued scanning the area for Cheryl's most likely jumping spot. She wouldn't try to land the balloon. Vigo would kill her and Micah, too, before he let that happen.

So Cheryl would be looking to fly as low as she could and then bail out. The stand of trees closest to the substation was the spot most likely to break their falls and leave them both alive.

Kim thought O'Hare was right. But she also needed a plan B, just in case he wasn't. And whether Cheryl and Micah were still in the gondola or not, the substation was the best place to take Vigo down.

He wouldn't fly into the substation deliberately. He was more likely to try evasive maneuvers. If Kim could take the balloon down before he reached the substation, she could capture Vigo alive.

Maybe she could help Cheryl get the balloon's altitude down low enough to improve the odds of survival.

Although Kim was a good marksman, the shorter the distance between her and the balloon, the better. Too many variables between the bullet and the target could alter the shot in ways she didn't want. She saw two rocky outcroppings near the substation. One was nearer than the other.

Kim accelerated the SUV and headed for her nest between the stand of trees and the substation. She parked the SUV behind the rocks and hurried around to open the back of the vehicle.

She found the best long distance weapons Finlay had packed. She pulled out two rifles and ammunition and rushed to set up.

She looked through the scope preparing to take her shot.

The balloon was a ridiculously easy target. It sailed along in a predictable path and at a steady speed. Even adjusting for the wind, it would be almost as easy as shooting on a range at a stationary paper silhouette.

She shot into the top of the envelope near the flap pilots called the parachute. It was used to release hot air to help with the rate of descent on a normal landing.

If Kim could open the parachute, and hot air escaped through the top, the envelope couldn't achieve higher altitudes. Cheryl and Micah would have a better chance to survive the jump.

Hitting the spot was fairly simple.

Kim shot three times, ripping the parachute and opening the area around it wider. The balloon descended, just as Kim had hoped.

She was counting on Cheryl to bail out with Micah.

She watched the balloon approach the stand of trees. The gondola's base swiped the treetops.

"Come on, Cheryl. You've got this," she whispered, staring at the target through the rifle scope, waiting for her chance to take the balloon down, and bring Vigo to justice to pay for his crimes.

CHAPTER FIFTY

Friday, April 15
7:50 a.m.
Glen Haven, New Mexico

VIGO WAS IN THAT place where the action was fast but it felt slow. Like watching slow motion in a movie.

Cheryl released the handle on the propane valve. She bent to embrace the heavy tank and lifted it in one easy motion.

The gondola rocked like a small boat on a choppy ocean.

Then she used her entire body to pitch the tank toward Vigo.

He stumbled on his feet as he moved aside and ducked to avoid a direct hit.

The tank hit his legs and coupled with the shaking gondola, knocked him off his feet.

He lost his grip on Micah.

The tank landed with a heavy thud on the floor.

The tank's valve was still open. He could hear the hissing gas as it escaped.

The balloon drifted slowly downward.

The descending gondola's base bumped against the treetops.

Cheryl rushed toward Micah and grabbed him.

She lifted the boy and tossed him over the side and into the trees.

Micah screamed.

Then his mother jumped after him.

Vigo had landed on his butt on the gondola's floor.

He scrambled to stand as the gondola righted itself.

He'd lost his gun in the scuffle.

A moment's indecision.

Should he shoot Cheryl and Micah or save himself?

He ignored the gun.

He scrambled to upright the tank and return it to position.

He opened the valve all the way.

The gas burner flamed, sending hot air into the envelope.

He kept the valve wide open and the balloon began to rise as it floated along with the air current.

The balloon continued bobbing toward the substation, as the constant flame heated the air and pushed its altitude higher and higher.

Vigo grinned. He was going to make it over the substation. From there, he'd find a place to land and escape.

He kept the valve open, heating the air in the envelope and lifting the gondola higher.

But before he reached the substation, an odd noise caught his attention.

Had he heard it earlier, too? Just before Cheryl and Micah jumped?

The rushing noise of the gas burner was interrupted by whizzing sounds firing past Vigo and through the flame into the colorful envelope.

Vigo had been shot at before. Many times. He recognized the sound of bullets when he heard them.

"What the hell?!" Vigo yelled.

He twisted his head to look around beneath the balloon for the shooter.

He saw two rock outcroppings large enough to shelter a shooter with a rifle and a scope. He couldn't pinpoint which of the two the shooter had chosen.

His pistol rested solidly in a corner of the gondola.

He couldn't reach it unless he let go of the valve and stopped heating the air.

If he stopped heating the air, the balloon would lose altitude and might lose the current keeping him above the substation completely.

The bullets kept coming, zinging through the flame, making big exit holes in the envelope.

He couldn't tell for sure, but now it seemed like there were two shooters, one behind each rock outcropping, both shooting at the balloon.

The exit holes in the envelope led to rips and big tears and the volume of hot air escaped too fast.

Vigo kept the valve open, feeding propane to the burner and heating as much air as possible.

The hot air escaped from the top too fast. He was losing the battle.

The propane wouldn't last forever. But he couldn't back off on the feed. The substation was too close now.

The balloon dropped lower, losing the air current that had been lifting it.

The next bullet severed a cord that held the balloon above the gondola.

A lucky shot.

The gondola bumped and tipped, eliminating its level base.

Vigo lost his footing and stumbled onto the basket's floor just as a bullet whizzed past the empty air where his head had been.

The bullets kept coming.

The balloon descended.

The gondola tilted unsteadily as it drifted forward in slow motion, heading squarely toward the powerlines at the substation.

CHAPTER FIFTY-ONE

Friday, April 15
8:00 a.m.
Glen Haven, New Mexico

AFTER CHERYL AND MICAH bailed out of the gondola, Kim had continued shooting the envelope. She heard rifle shots coming from the second rock outcropping.

Maybe Flint had made his way out here to help. Or maybe it was Agent Ross, finally. Whoever it was, shooting into the area below the envelope was much more dangerous. Bullets could pierce the propane tank and, coupled with the mix of propane and oxygen already in the path of the burner, cause an explosion.

Which was one of the reasons she hadn't tried to shoot Vigo. She wanted him alive.

The second shooter had no such concerns. He had aimed directly at Vigo, and he went down. From her vantage point, Kim couldn't tell whether the shooter had hit his target or if Vigo had simply fallen again.

She couldn't waste time figuring any of that out now. At the moment, her attention was concentrated on bringing the gondola down in one piece before it hit the substation.

She aimed and fired at the envelope again, half expecting Vigo to shoot back. He didn't.

The gondola continued its slow forward momentum, traveling at a downward angle and ever closer to the substation.

She adjusted her aim and split one of the ropes that connected the envelope to the gondola. The basket tipped. She aimed at another rope and fired again.

The gondola floated toward the substation. Her efforts had slowed the balloon, but hadn't stopped it.

She fired again and again, hitting the ropes or the envelope every time, but the balloon kept gliding.

Until one of the other shooter's bullets made the final hit, piercing the tank, just as the gondola slammed into the electric power grid at the substation.

A split second later, a deafening explosion filled the air.

The gondola fell into the power station and burned with Vigo still inside.

Kim lowered her weapon, mouth agape, as the explosion rocked the ground beneath her feet and the SUV bounced on its tires.

She raised up above the rocks to see the fireball spread from one power line to another, arcing electricity into an overwhelming inferno.

The only thing she could do was stare.

She stood there for a good long time, mesmerized by the fire, wondering whether her bullets had brought the balloon down or if the second shooter had made it happen.

She couldn't sort out the immediate cause, but it didn't matter.

Vigo was dead. His sister, too. The cartel's reign of terror that began with Vigo's father was over. At least for a while. Until someone else moved in to take Vigo's place.

Then she returned to the SUV to check on Lawton. He was unconscious, but still alive. She drove back to rescue Cheryl and Micah from the trees.

CHAPTER FIFTY-TWO

Friday, April 15
8:30 p.m.
Albuquerque, New Mexico

KIM SPENT THE NEXT hours assisting with the aftermath of all that had gone before. What the locals needed was another pair of capable hands, so she offered hers. The chaos was so overwhelming that no one thought to ask for her credentials. Nor did she volunteer them.

Flint was there to help, too.

She was glad not to be a part of the official team. The work at the Glen Haven compound alone would last for days and then the techs would pore over the evidence for months. The paperwork would be a total nightmare for the agents in charge. *Thanks but no thanks.*

One of the best things about her Reacher assignment was that she never had to deal with the bureaucratic baloney that came with her normal job. The freedom to do as she pleased these past few days, not even subject to the maddening whims of her Boss, had felt more liberating than she'd expected.

Which was why she'd destroyed his cell phone back at the hotel. She wasn't his puppet anymore. He should have known she wouldn't take orders from him forever.

He'd delivered another phone a few hours ago. She opened the envelope and dropped the phone into her pocket, but she was too busy to answer when he called. He'd be pissed when she finally talked to him. Too bad. She shrugged and stayed on task.

There would be enough time to deal with the Boss and Finlay later.

After she'd brought down the balloon, Lawton, Daphne, Cheryl, Micah, and O'Hare had been transported to local hospitals. Early reports were that all five would survive after aggressive treatment and lengthy recoveries.

Lawton's injuries were the worst. But he would live, which was all that mattered right now.

After dark, Kim met up with Flint back at the helo. They shared a coffee as he prepared to leave. She told him what happened with Vigo.

"There was a second shooter out there this morning. Helped me bring the balloon down. Was it you?" she asked.

He cocked both eyebrows and shook his head, puzzled. "Not me. I was in town. I delivered Gavin Ray and his brother Bruce, along with Vigo's man Freddie, to the FBI, courtesy of Agent John Lawton, US Treasury, IRS Enforcement."

Kim had liked Flint from the moment she'd met him. Gaspar had said he was a straight shooter with skills and talent. There was a sizeable reward available for tips leading to the arrest of members of the Vigo cartel. He could have claimed it. She liked that he hadn't.

"Nice. Why'd you do that?"

"There's something poetic about tax man Lawton making a big arrest on tax day. Great irony, don't you think?" Flint said with a grin.

Kim nodded but she couldn't bring herself to smile. The cost to Lawton had been too great. Word was that he'd come through the initial surgery okay, but he was in for a long hospital stay and a longer stint in rehab afterward. She hadn't had the time to sort out her feelings about all of that yet, and neither had he.

More seriously, Flint said, "Since Lawton isn't likely to return to work soon, or maybe at all, at least he'll go out on a high note."

"Right." Kim cleared her throat and changed the subject. "Another odd thing. Before all the explosions started, I found Louis and Manny both dead in Vigo's SUV full of drugs and guns in the center of the Glen Haven compound."

Flint cocked his head and frowned. "Not me, either, I'm afraid. Although I'd have done that if I'd had the chance. So your instincts about me aren't wrong. Was there an undercover agent on the compound giving us a hand?"

"Maybe," Kim replied, as if the possibility was remote. Which it was.

Anybody with an official status would have had too many eyes watching their actions. Too many penalties for doing something like that. They'd most likely have gone for the professional rewards from arresting those two and confiscating the drugs and guns for evidence.

Flint had climbed under the helo to check a few things. When he finished, Kim said, "I heard the Rays and Freddie refused to talk without lawyers, which was the smartest thing they could have done."

Flint nodded. "They'll be facing enough charges to keep them in prison for decades. What about the wives?"

"Too early to say. But it's likely Cheryl and Daphne will be offered the chance to testify against them. Both are smart enough to take the deal," Kim replied.

Flint nodded again as he continued his preflight check on the helo.

Kim said, "They've got kids they want to raise. They'll all probably end up in witness protection, too."

"Makes sense." Flint replied. When he finished his preflight, he dusted his hands and drained the coffee cup. "So do you need a lift?"

"Where are you going?"

"Back home to Houston for now. Take a couple of weeks off. You?"

She kicked the dirt with the toe of her boot. "Debriefing first. Then back to Detroit, probably. Unlike you, my life is not my own to manage."

"Right. Well, it was a pleasure working with you. Scarlett wanted to bill you, but I talked her out of it. The FBI couldn't afford my rates, anyway. This one's on the house, but we won't make a habit of it," Flint said, like a guy who'd come to dinner at her parents' house might say on his way out.

They shook hands and he climbed into the helo.

"You've got my number now. Don't be a stranger," he said as he closed the door and fastened his harness. He slipped his headset on and spooled up the engine.

Kim moved out of the rotor wash and stood aside as he lifted off. She turned toward the small terminal. She'd walked half a dozen steps when one of the phones in her pocket vibrated with a new text.

She read it quickly. Reacher. His text said, "Everything turn out okay?"

She texted back. "Yes, but you still owe me one."

She waited a bit for a return text, but nothing came through.

Before she made it to the terminal, the Boss's phone rang. She wasn't ready to talk to him yet, so she ignored it again. She'd need to deal with him soon. Right now, she felt like she had the upper hand because he needed her more than she needed him.

And she still had to deal with Finlay.

At the terminal, Russell waited for her in another rental. She was glad to see him. She'd been wondering how she'd get home. She climbed into the front seat.

"Seems like you've had plenty of excitement," Russell said with a grin. He set the GPS to meet Finlay at the same location where they'd dropped her off what seemed like a lifetime ago.

"What have you been doing while I was busy?" she asked, simply making conversation. She liked Russell, but she didn't expect him to share any important intel. He was loyal to Finlay. Simple as that.

"Handling the fallout from your adventures, mostly." Russell replied with a sideways glance that seemed like an attempt to convey more than his words. "We had a couple of visitors. The woman you met back in Bloomfield Hills, Holly Johnson. And a big guy. Scruffy. Cheap clothes. They left a couple of hours ago."

So Holly Johnson had lied. She found a way to contact Reacher after all. And if Holly Johnson could find him, then Kim could find Reacher, too.

Not that she'd ever doubted her skills. Probably. "They left together?"

"Separately." Russell shook his head.

The sinking feeling in her gut filled in the blanks. Finlay had wanted to connect with Reacher. Seemed like he'd achieved his objective. "What did they want? Johnson and the big guy?"

"Beats me. You know they don't tell me anything." He shrugged. An all-purpose gesture that could mean anything or nothing at all.

What she suspected was exactly the opposite. Russell was way more aware of Finlay's activities than she was. Not that *he'd* tell *her* anything. So there was no point in badgering him about it.

"How long did he stay?"

"Long enough, I guess." Russell pulled the SUV to a stop near the stairs leading up from the tarmac to Finlay's private jet. "You go on up. Finlay's waiting. I'll be there in a minute."

"Okay." She climbed out of the vehicle and closed the door. She still had nothing to carry except the stuff in her pockets. Traveling light had its disadvantages, but it certainly made coming and going easier.

She approached the jet stairs just as Jake Reacher's phone rang.

She pulled it out and paused on the tarmac to talk. "Good to hear from you, Jake. What's up?"

"Wanted to let you know that I got a message from Reacher a couple of hours ago. I was out in the field. Just now had a chance to pick up the message and call you," Jake said as if he'd been exhausted by his field maneuvers.

She understood the feeling. "No worries. So what's up?"

"He said sorry for the delay, but he'd been busy." Jake replied. "Anyway, the message was a little garbled. Sounded like he said he was doing some hot air ballooning or something."

Kim had to laugh. Not only was Reacher a good partner when he wanted to be, he had a sense of humor, too. Who knew?

The other big news is Diane Capri—a friend of mine—wrote a book revisiting the events of KILLING FLOOR in Margrave, Georgia. She imagines an FBI team tasked to trace Reacher's current-day whereabouts. They begin by interviewing people who knew him—starting out with Roscoe and Finlay. Check out this review: "Oh heck yes! I am in love with this book. I'm a huge Jack Reacher fan. If you don't know Jack (pun intended!) then get thee to the bookstore/wherever you buy your fix and pick up one of the many Jack Reacher books by Lee Child. Heck, pick up all of them. In particular, read Killing Floor. Then come back and read Don't Know Jack. This story picks up the other from the point of view of Kim and Gaspar, FBI agents assigned to build a file on Jack Reacher. The problem is, as anyone who knows Reacher can attest, he lives completely off the grid. No cell phone, no house, no car…he's not tied down. A pretty daunting task, then, wouldn't you say?

First lines: "Just the facts. And not many of them, either. Jack Reacher's file was too stale and too thin to be credible. No human could be as invisible as Reacher appeared to be, whether he was currently above the ground or under it. Either the file had been sanitized, or Reacher was the most off-the-grid paranoid Kim Otto had ever heard of." Right away, I'm sensing who Kim Otto is and I'm delighted that I know something she doesn't. You see, I DO know Jack. And I know he's not paranoid. Not really. I know why he lives as he does, and I know what kind of man he is. I loved having that over Kim and Gaspar. If you haven't read any Reacher novels, then this will feel like a good, solid story in its own right. If you have…oh if you have, then you, too, will feel like you have a one-up on the FBI. It's a fun feeling!

"Kim and Gaspar are sent to Margrave by a mysterious boss who reminds me of Charlie, in Charlie's Angels. You never see him…you hear him. He never gives them all the facts. So they are left with a big pile of nothing. They end up embroiled in a murder case that seems connected to Reacher somehow, but they can't see how. Suffice to say the efforts to find the murderer and Reacher, and not lose their own heads in the process, makes for an entertaining read.

"I love the way the author handled the entire story. The pacing is dead on (ok another pun intended), the story is full of twists and turns like a Reacher novel would be, but it's another viewpoint of a Reacher story. It's an outside-in approach to Reacher.

"You might be asking, do they find him? Do they finally meet the infamous Jack Reacher?

"Go…read…now…find out!"

Sounds great, right? Check out "Don't Know Jack," and let me know what you think.

So that's it for now…again, thanks for reading THE AFFAIR, and I hope you'll like A WANTED MAN just as much in September.

Lee Child

ABOUT THE AUTHOR

Diane Capri is an award-winning *New York Times, USA Today,* and worldwide bestselling author. She's a recovering lawyer and snowbird who divides her time between Florida and Michigan. An active member of Mystery Writers of America, Author's Guild, International Thriller Writers, Alliance of Independent Authors, and Sisters in Crime, she loves to hear from readers and is hard at work on her next novel.

Please connect with her online:

http://www.DianeCapri.com

Twitter: http://twitter.com/@DianeCapri

Facebook: http://www.facebook.com/Diane.Capri1

http://www.facebook.com/DianeCapriBooks